In the

NEIGHBORHOOD

of

TRUE

Also by SUSAN KAPLAN CARLTON

Lobsterland

Love & Haight

In the

NEIGHBORHOOD

of

TRUE

Susan Kaplan Carlton

Algonquin   2019

For Annie and Jane

Published by Algonquin Young Readers
an imprint of Algonquin Books of Chapel Hill
Post Office Box 2225
Chapel Hill, North Carolina 27515-2225

a division of Workman Publishing
225 Varick Street
New York, New York 10014

Library of Congress Cataloging-in-Publication Data

Names: Carlton, Susan Kaplan, author.
Title: In the neighborhood of true / Susan Kaplan Carlton.
Description: First edition. | Chapel Hill, North Carolina : Algonquin, 2019.
Summary: In the very white, very Christian world of
Atlanta society in 1958, New York transplant Ruth decides not to tell
her new high school friends and boyfriend that she is Jewish, but when
a violent act rocks the city, Ruth must figure out where her loyalties lie.
Identifiers: LCCN 2018028820 | ISBN 9781616208608 (hardcover : alk. paper)
Subjects: | CYAC: Jews—United States—Fiction. | Antisemitism—Fiction. |
Hate crimes—Fiction. | Atlanta (Ga.)—History—20th century—Fiction.
Classification: LCC PZ7.1.C412 In 2019 | DDC [Fic]—dc23
LC record available at https://lccn.loc.gov/2018028820

10 9 8 7 6 5 4 3 2 1
First Edition

It is an old, old story. It is one repeated over and over again in history. When the wolves of hate are loosed on one people, then no one is safe.

—Ralph McGill, editor and publisher of the *Atlanta Constitution*
(from front-page column, October 13, 1958)

1

The Whole Truth

1959

The navy dress was just where I'd left it, hanging hollow as a compliment behind the gown I'd worn to the Magnolia Ball the night everything went to hell in a handbasket.

I thought of Davis and his single dimple and how his hand had hovered at the small of my back, making me feel its phantom weight even when he wasn't touching me. I thought of a different day and a different dress, this one with sunburst pleats—how he'd unzipped it and fanned it out on the grass that night at the club, how the air was sweet as taffy, and how when we rejoined his family I'd wondered if every pleat was back in place.

"Ruth!" Mother's voice burst into the closet. "Not the morning to dillydally."

"Coming," I said, but I did the opposite of not-dallying. I put the navy dress on over my slip and sat, right there on the closet floor, not giving a fig about wrinkles. It was as if my nerves had pitched the world ten degrees to the left and I had to plunk down to find my balance.

It was cool at the back of the closet—in what I'd come to think of as my New York section, the land of navies and blacks and grays—where the floor was concrete, smooth and solid beneath me.

When we'd first arrived here at the end of an airless summer, Mother, who'd changed from Mom to Mother when we crossed the Mason-Dixon Line, told her parents, whom we'd always called Fontaine and Mr. Hank, that Nattie and I needed wall-to-wall carpet to cushion our landing. Maybe we needed cushioning after the shock of our father's death, or maybe we needed cushioning after moving from our apartment in New York to our grandparents' guesthouse behind the dogwoods. Either way, the next afternoon, two men turned up with a roll of white carpet and stapled it over every square inch of the place, save for the closets.

Just like that, we were blanketed in an ironic, improbable snowstorm.

"*Now*, Ruthie," Mother said, on the other side of the door.

I stood up and pulled in, feeling the dread in my chest prickle from the inside out.

The dress reminded me of Leslie Caron in *An American in Paris*, except I was an American in Atlanta, and in the six months I'd been here, my taste and I had gone from simple to posh to simple again. If the girls in the pastel posse were in the courtroom today, I bet they'd be in shades of sherbet, rays of sunshine against the February sky.

Today, I didn't want to be sunny.

Today, I wanted to be Plain Ruth, teller of truth.

On the drive downtown, Mother said, "You be yourself up there, Ruthie. It doesn't have to get ugly." Her short bangs curled down her forehead like a question mark.

Here, nothing was supposed to get ugly.

As we passed the putting greens on Northside, I watched the trees sway, thinking that winter was different—prettier— in a place where the trees cared enough about their leaves to hold on to them year-round. And also thinking that prettiness had to be planned, that the sprinklers had to work hard to keep the perfect green lawn from turning back to plain red clay.

I cranked down the window, needing to feel the air.

We were twelve minutes late. Mother was often late, a leftover New York affectation, but today my dallying about dresses had held us up. For a half second, I paused in front of the large door with FULTON COUNTY SUPERIOR COURT etched in gold, then inhaled and turned the knob gently, hoping to avoid a clang.

Clang.

A hundred or more heads swiveled in my direction.

Mother dropped her smile, but then she touched her pearls and reassembled herself. I followed her lead, hand to my throat, where my own string of pearls—along with my stomach and other major organs—had taken up residence.

The courtroom was impressive, with a soaring ceiling and sunlight flooding in from impossibly tall windows. It looked not unlike the temple at the center of the trouble.

The pastel posse was here after all. I tried to catch Gracie's eye, but she was busy tugging her apricot twinset into place. Mother and I walked past Rabbi Selwick and his wife, both turned out in tweed, and I thought of him at our house with his daughter and her gift of peach preserves. Behind them were women in fur and men in pinstripes. The couples— probably from the Club—looked like they were waiting for a tray of martinis to glide by.

Mother stepped into the third row, and I slid next to her. Davis was five feet away, at the defendant's table. The collar of his white oxford shirt, crisp and starched, poked out above his blazer. I couldn't tell a single thing Davis was thinking, from looking at the back of his very handsome head.

The attorney nodded to me and twisted his mouth. "You're late." To the judge he said, "We apologize for the delay, Your Honor. We call Ruth Robb to the stand."

My pumps *click-click*ed on the marble floor. A woman with coral lipstick motioned for me to sit in the witness chair, like on *Perry Mason*. Goose bumps inched up my arms. I wished I'd thought to bring a cardigan.

She turned to me and said, "Raise your right hand and repeat after me."

I raised my hand and noticed a sunburst carved into the paneling over the door I'd just walked through, a little moment of brightness.

"Other right," she said.

"I'm sorry." I raised my other hand. "I'm terrible with left and right. I always—"

"Miss—" the judge said, looking down at a note card. "Miss Robb. No need to talk now." He had gray hair and half-glasses, and he gave a half smile.

And I thought: But that's why I'm here. Because I couldn't keep my mouth shut.

The woman picked up a Bible, and I placed my free hand over its worn leather cover. I knew there were two Bibles—

one for whites and one for Negroes. I knew because Rabbi Selwick was on a mission to have Negro witnesses use the same Bible as the rest of Atlanta. I thought about asking for the Negro Bible, even though every single person in the court-room was white, but as the judge himself had said: "No need to talk now."

"Do you swear on this Bible the testimony you are about to give is the truth, the whole truth, and nothing but the truth, so help you God?" the woman asked.

In the distance, I heard a sprinkler turn on. *Tsk, tsk, tsk.*

I glanced at the Bible, the King James version, and it occurred to me I was swearing on the sacred text of another religion, that there wasn't a Tanakh for Jews to pledge their truthfulness upon.

I wanted Davis to look up. I wanted to see if his tie was straight. I wanted to see if he'd nicked himself shaving. I wanted to see the constellation of freckles across his eyelids. I wanted to see how he looked when he looked at me.

And then he did—his true-blue eyes locked right on mine. I felt the heat slide up my cheeks. Davis, who taught me about the *Un*civil War, and blowing perfecto smoke rings, and real honest-to-God French-kissing. Davis, who said he wanted us to get married the second we turned twenty-one.

I swallowed. "I do."

2

Dishing Up Elvis

SIX MONTHS EARLIER

Lipstick melted fast down here. Last night, I'd left my Fire & Ice on the windowsill, and by morning it was fondue-y. I dabbed a bit on my lips anyway. I put on pedal pushers and a sleeveless blouse, and then, with a wad of TP, tried to squish the lipstick back into an approximation of a bullet.

Nattie was foraging for cereal when I got to the kitchen. The guesthouse was tiny. According to my little sister, who was precise about such things, it was eighty-seven steps from the bedroom, which we shared, through the living room, where Mother slept on the daybed, to the foyer, where the telephone sat on the table, to the kitchen.

"Don't even ask," I said, standing the lipstick up in an ice-cube tray and hoping for the best. The freezer was full of

Pyrex dishes, the neighbors' pity casseroles piled like a lopsided wedding cake—turkey tetrazzini, tuna noodle, chicken divan, and something labeled "Momma's Surprise."

"About what?" Nattie shoveled cornflakes into her mouth. She didn't care if she faced the day without a lick of makeup on, which was the advantage of being eleven. It wasn't like I troweled on the stuff or anything, but there was power in the perfect red lipstick. According to *Mademoiselle* magazine, red draws attention to both your mouth and your words.

I made coffee, because I lived for coffee—for coffee and two stirs of cream and an avalanche of sugar.

Before I finished my second cup, the doorbell rang the first few lines of "Dixie," an old southern song Fontaine said was the anthem of the Confederacy, even though it was written by a New Yorker. Since we'd moved in, "Dixie" had been announcing the arrival of southern hospitality in the form of casseroles and such.

On the other side of the door stood a woman in white gloves, no casserole in view. "Well, hello, *hello*," she said. "I'm Mrs. Eleet."

Frooshka, our enormous poodle, jingled over for a look-see.

"Elite?" I said. It was a name begging for wordplay. I was what my father had called a words girl. He'd always been on the lookout for a good line. "We're crossing into Georgia," he'd said when we'd made the annual drive to visit Mother's family. "Set your watch back thirty years." But then he died 127 days ago on Forty-Ninth and Park—a heart attack after a business lunch—and the rest of us set our watches back permanently and moved down here, poodle and all.

"We're all 'e's. E-l-double-e-t," the woman said. Her dress was a shade of piercing pink not found in nature.

"I'm Ruth." I held my hand out for a shake.

"I'm Natalie." My sister slid in on her skinny legs wearing a no-nonsense navy-blue bathing suit. That was one good thing about Fontaine and Mr. Hank's place: They had a beauty of a pool. The main house was a beauty, too. Fontaine had grown up inside its brick walls.

With the tips of her gloved fingers, Mrs. Eleet touched my hand. To Nattie, she smiled and said, "Pleased to see you."

"Say hey, I'm Gracie." A girl around my age—sixteen or maybe seventeen—leaned against the doorframe.

"Hay is for horses," Mrs. Eleet said.

"Neigh," the girl said back. Her blond hair flipped up at the ends like the hook of an umbrella. A baking dish gift-wrapped in foil was balanced in her hands. There was Pyrex after all.

Frooshka trotted over to her, aligning herself with the more glamorous of us.

"I'm so sorry to hear about your daddy," Mrs. Eleet said. "Is your momma here? I'd love to offer our sincerest condolence." She took a step forward, her pointy pump an arrow on the white carpet. "We're acquainted from way back."

I dug my bare feet into the pile. "My mother is . . . out."

"She's at work," Nattie piped up. "Her first day at the newspaper."

"Of course," Mrs. Eleet said after a slight hesitation. "Poor dear. Of course."

"Here's chicken à la king," the blond girl said with the kind of sky-wide smile you don't see much of in Manhattan. "I'm sure there's nothing in this world you've been craving more than chicken à la king."

I laughed as I accepted the casserole. "Who is this king, though? The king à la chicken?"

"Elvis, maybe," she said. Her flowered skirt had the perfect pouf.

"Good," I said. "Elvis is someone we don't have in the freezer."

"And I—*we*—also want to give this to you." Mrs. Eleet placed a whisper-pink booklet on top of the foil: *Belles of the Ball: A Pre-Debutante Guide.* "Ruth, do join us for Tea and Etiquette tomorrow," she said. "Or T and E, as we like to call it."

"Ruthie," Nattie beckoned in a low voice.

"Shh," I replied.

"Bless her." Mrs. Eleet waved in Nattie's direction. To me she said, "You know, Gracie is a third-year over at Covenant. She loves it! Don't you love it, Gracie?"

"Oh, yes. I do love it," Gracie answered in a voice I recognized, a voice that said, I'm embarrassed by my mother.

"I'll be a third-year at Covenant, too—a junior, right?" I fluffed Frooshka's poufed-up poodle head. "And Natalie will be in sixth grade."

"We know!" Mrs. Eleet clapped her gloved hands together. They made no noise. "Girls from your year will be over for T and E. We're on Arden. Fontaine knows the place. We've got the little front porch!"

Gracie tapped her front tooth with a manicured nail.

"*Ruthie*," Nattie whisper-shouted.

"Excuse me," I said to Mrs. Eleet, and I took a half step to Nattie. *"What?"*

"You've got lipstick on your teeth," Nattie said, which explained Gracie's tapping.

"Drat." I worried my tongue over my teeth.

"You smeared it," Nattie said.

"So, tomorrow—at three!" Mrs. Eleet said over my shoulder.

Gracie poked her head into our lipstick tête-à-tête. "It'll actually be fun," she said, and I noticed a cluster of tiny

11

pimples along the bridge of her nose. I can't tell you how happy it made me, seeing those pimples.

"All right!" I said. And because perhaps that wasn't clear, I added, "Great." And then, "Thank you." Whatever it was that happened at a T&E, it would surely beat sitting here wishing every single thing about life—and death—were different.

"It's not fancy. Just wear a tea dress," Gracie said.

"A tea dress?" I asked.

"A tea dress or the like," she clarified, except not really, before turning on her heel and following her mother out the door.

While I stuck Elvis in the freezer, below the lipstick and the tuna noodles, Nattie disappeared from view. Frooshka and I found her poolside, nose in the pink booklet. She shaded her eyes and said, "I quoteth page nine: 'Never show one's bosom before evening.'"

I unbuttoned my shirt an extra button. "Oops! Bosom in the morning."

"I quoteth again. Page twenty-seven: 'A lady never walks while holding a cigarette. Indeed, a lady should avoid smoking in public, as the habit borders on the unattractive.'"

"Knock-knock," said a voice, followed by no actual knock, since we were all outside. Fontaine tipped her straw hat toward us. Her butterscotch hair, colored by Frederic every third Thursday, was pulled back in a low bun. She wore a triple loop of pearls—faux for everyday—and a gardening apron, even though she had two gardeners. "Birdie thought y'all could use something green," she said, presenting a platter of deviled eggs.

"Eggs are yellow," Nattie said.

"These've got pickles," Fontaine said. "Was that Mrs. Eleet I saw? She and your mother go back to the days of the Magnolia Ball. Your mother was queen, of course."

"Were you a Magnolia Princess?" I said. Clearly the answer would be yes.

"Oh, no," Fontaine said. "Queen. I was queen two years in a row—unprecedented."

"She dropped off this." Nattie stuck the pink booklet between her teeth like a bone.

"Don't be a child," Fontaine said, taking the booklet from Nattie and smoothing out the bite marks. "I know you're modern in the North and unimpressed by our ways, Ruthie. But, believe me, you will praise the day you got this." She flipped the brim of her hat back. "It's a gift, knowing what to do."

I popped an egg into my mouth. The pickle added something, I had to admit. A snap.

"Take the egg in two bites next time," Fontaine said. "North end, then southern end."

"What does that mean—north end?" I pictured the egg with a compass.

She waved the question away. "If you want to know the truth, I asked Millie to drop by. She's handling membership and recruitment. I told her about your daddy—not everything about him, not more than she needs to know." Fontaine paused. "What I told her was your daddy passed on and now here you are, Alice's daughters, back where you belong."

"Thank you," I said. Already, I'd learned to say thank you first and ask questions later.

"As a for-instance"—Fontaine's voice hitched up the tiniest bit—"I didn't mention your mother had married a Jewish man." She mouthed "Jewish" like it was a curse word. I tugged at my neck, where my Jewish star would be nestled if I ever wore that necklace, which I did not.

"How come?" asked Nattie. My question exactly.

"Firstly, it didn't come up," Fontaine said, readjusting her brim. "People weren't all that curious, frankly. Secondly, I want you girls to have the full debutante experience— Ruthie, you will adore the dresses. This is something I can give you that New York cannot. Not that New York doesn't have a deb situation; it does, of course, but more geared to countesses and college girls. We do things earlier in the South. So better not to mention certain subjects, especially since the religious business did not come up."

Maybe I should have been surprised that Fontaine, the chitchat champion, just ignored Dad and his Jewishness. But I felt a whoosh of something else. I decided it was something like awe. Awe for a woman who could bend the world exactly to her liking.

"Thirdly," Fontaine went on. "Aside from your hair, which you certainly picked up from your father, you don't look—"

"Don't look what? Jewish? Is that a compliment?" I'd heard many such compliments—"I didn't realize you were Jewish"—from plenty of friends, many of them Jewish, my whole life. As if all Jewish girls had madman hair, which I did, and a nose the shape of New Hampshire, which I did not. As if being Jewish was somehow shorthand for not being pretty, which was ridiculous and awful, though Fontaine likely hadn't meant it that way.

"Yes, it *is* a compliment that you look beautifully exotic," Fontaine said, her gaze not exactly on me. "And you must learn not to dodge these niceties when they come your way. Simply say 'Thank you.' Now . . ." She straightened her back as if pulled by an invisible string. "Birdie'll be pouring up some Co-Cola floats. She'll have them out at lunchtime for my Magnolia Queens in training."

"Will you jump in the pool with me?" Nattie asked, tapping Fontaine's elbow, seemingly oblivious to the compliment conversation. "Just the shallow end?" Nattie had unsuccessfully tried to lure Fontaine and Mr. Hank and even Birdie into the twenty-two thousand gallons of water sloshing around our grandparents' quite grand pool. Nattie had asked the gardener about the capacity—it was the kind of information she liked to collect and write in minuscule print on index cards.

"Would love to, buttercup. But Mr. Hank and I are off to the Club for lunch," Fontaine said.

Honestly, I didn't want to dive in either. It would take me hours to redo my hair—hair that revealed its Jewishness, hair that had a habit of poufing up and out into a cumulus cloud. Instead, I gave Nattie half of what she wanted. I changed into a bathing suit—black with a big daisy—and kept her company while she splashed. I brought out Dad's lousy transistor radio, which I'd tucked into my suitcase, for whatever reason, before we left the Upper West Side.

I settled into a chaise and sunned my legs. From here, up the curving brick path lined with dahlias (so I learned from the gardener), I could see the back porch and kitchen door of the main house. Nattie had counted the steps here, too. Two hundred and ninety-three, almost a football field, separated the main place from our guesthouse.

Birdie and her noiseless shoes delivered Coke floats—four for the two of us—on a silver tray. "Here you go. This is your grandmother's favorite summer chiller," she said.

"Thank you, Birdie," I said quietly. "Nattie, say, 'Thank you, Birdie.'"

"Thank you, Birdie," Nattie repeated.

Birdie had worked for our grandparents for fortyish years, but accepting something on a silver platter from her, from anyone, was still new to me, so I tried to always be quick with the thanks.

When we all first arrived a few weeks ago, it seemed entirely weird to have a housekeeper make our meals and fold our gunders. Of course, I knew people in New York who had maids—mainly Negro or, in Miriam's case, a white Polish lady by way of Akron, Ohio. But Mother was opposed on principle, and so Nattie was in charge of cleaning the bathroom and I was in charge of ironing and chasing dust balls around the floor. Already, I was in love with the idea of never picking up an iron or a broom, which I realized was a shallow way to think about housekeeping, but shallow was my middle name. Actually, Tarbell was my middle name, for the journalist Ida Tarbell, but I knew my way around the shallows pretty damn well.

In the actual shallow end, Nattie was practicing her dead-girl float. "Count. And see. How long. I can hold. My breath," she said, spitting out fountains of chlorine.

"Ready, steady, go," I called, thinking a Coke float was the perfect summer drink—cold and creamy and bubbling with happiness. It gave me hope I could survive one-hundred-degree days and being secretly Jewish and all the rest.

Frooshka dozed under my chair, and I half sang along to "Great Balls of Fire," wondering if I'd find anyone in Atlanta to shake my nerves and rattle my brain, when Mother appeared in her shirtdress, casting a shadow over me.

"How was the paper?" I moved over to make room for her on my chaise. Last week, I'd seen the gardener take out a ruler to measure the distance between the lounges.

"It *was*. Where's Nattie?" Mother looked washed out—shortish brown hair, simple dress, sensible-heeled pumps. If Fontaine was Kodachrome, Mother was black and white.

Oh, right. Nattie.

Just then, she shot up for air. "How long was that?" Nattie gasped.

"Fifty-seven seconds," I said. It could have been five minutes for all I'd been paying attention.

Mother sighed. She'd begun sighing—a barely audible form of complaining—before we'd even packed up in New York. "Mr. Hank must've told them to give me the easiest assignment. Garden club. Pest control, starting with slugs."

That was the other reason we were here: Fontaine and Mr. Hank and the rest of the Landry family owned the newspaper, had owned it for seventy-odd years, and Mother was guaranteed a job. Before Mother had moved to New York to study poetry at Sarah Lawrence—*and* met Dad *and* decided to stay *and* converted to Judaism—the plan was always that she'd be part of things here.

"You have a black thumb."

"So ironic."

I handed her my not-touched second Coke float, even though it was now flatter than flat. Mother downed it anyway.

"Momma, change and come in," Nattie yelled. *"Come."*

On the word "come," Frooshka roused from her nap. She shook her ears, stretched her neck, and jumped into the pool with an impressive splash. The poodle paddled over to the steps and sat, half in, half out. The first time she'd plopped in, we all flipped. But Froo knew what she was doing, and now the sight of her black fur bobbing around in the blue was positively ordinary.

Amazing what you could get used to in a few weeks.

Mother shimmied her dress up high enough to unhook her stockings from her garter belt. "How about toes, Nattie?" she said.

I felt like a finker for not going in earlier. Hair be damned, I got off the chaise and dove in now, letting all twenty-two thousand gallons of water slip over me. The water was warm and forgiving, enveloping. I pushed off from the side, my arms out in front, pale against the pool-blue light, then submerged. Beneath the surface, everything was shimmery and quiet. Nattie and I somersaulted, forward, back, back, forward, until there was no telling which way was up.

Later, when I hoisted myself out, I saw that one of us—human or canine—had splashed Mother with water in the shape of continents, darkening the gray of her shirtdress. And I had to give her credit: She hadn't said a word.

Mother's generosity of spirit sloshed over to dinner. She turned on the ceiling fans, changed into a white top and checkered culottes, and poured herself a glass of sherry.

I opened the freezer, deciding which slab to slide into the oven. Obviously, the chicken à la Elvis. "We have something new in the casserole department, and it arrived with an invitation to Tea and Etiquette," I said. "The woman says she knows you: Mrs. Eleet."

Nattie stuck her head in the freezer. "Your lipstick's still crooked."

Mother spritzed a tablecloth with water and draped it over the window to chill the air on its way in, an ad hoc air conditioner. The guesthouse was sans air-conditioning. Mother said the human body was surprisingly adaptable and we must cope with the air we have. The spritzy-tablecloth trick helped.

"Eleet? Millie?" Mother paused. "Ruth, I know you

need friends here, but please, *please*, do not slip right into that pre-debutante piffle. Make some excuse and skip it."

"I already said yes. She has a daughter my age. And Fontaine asked her to invite me."

"Ha!" Mother said. I waited for her to expand on her "ha," but she didn't. Instead, she took a long sip of sherry.

At that moment, I missed my older sister, Sara, even though she was going through a bouffed-up phase and liked to refer to herself as Sara-without-an-h, who was a junior at Sarah-with-an-h Lawrence. I last saw h-less Sara the day Mr. Hank arrived to pack us up; she arrived with her guy, Jerome, who'd driven her to the city in a brand-new Thunderbird. Saying goodbye to her had left a jumbo lump in my throat.

"Fontaine said you were a Magnolia Princess," I added after a minute.

"Queen," Nattie said.

"There were many opportunities to be a queen," Mother said, again with the sigh. "Chrysanthemum. Magnolia. Maid of Cotton. Reverie. Holley with a superfluous 'e.' Don't be too impressed."

But I was impressed. "School doesn't start for two more weeks," I said, trying to keep the gloom out of my voice. "I need a friend who isn't forty years old. Or eleven." Mother shot me a look. "And it's all sanctioned by Fontaine."

"Of course it's sanctioned by Fontaine," she said.

I dished up Elvis. We slid into our usual spots, Mother at the foot of the table, me in the middle, and Nattie across from me, in Dad's chair. Mother had wedged a single chair with a squishy red vinyl seat into Mr. Hank's cavernous trunk so one thing would be the same when we gathered together. Most nights, Nattie claimed it as her own.

Elvis wasn't quite warm. The cream and mushrooms were a little congealed.

Mother pushed a pimento around her plate in a figure eight. "I'm sorry, Ruthie. You'll have to send regrets," she said. "Believe me, Mrs. Eleet will not be fond of the fact I am raising you and your sisters Jewish. As a rule, the people and places that celebrate the pre-debutante are those at which Jewish girls are summarily not included—or invited, wanted, desired. Choose your verb."

"Fontaine says it didn't come up," I said, warming up to her omission strategy. (Or maybe the warming was the lack of air-conditioning.) What hadn't come up would let me make friends with girls with umbrella-flipped hair.

"But I bet—" Mother straightened her collar for dramatic effect. "I bet Millie Eleet said something like: 'Say hey! I'd be *honnnorred* if *y'all'd* come over to my little old house for a little *elitist* tea.'"

"No, she didn't," I said. "She said, 'Hay is for horses.'"

"Gracie did," Nattie said. "She definitely said, 'Say hey.'"

"What's the harm in a little tea?" I asked, thinking if Mother threw one of her independent-minded fits I would go mad. "Whoever died from a little Lipton's?"

The ceiling fan's blades beat at the air. I could feel my hair lift and sway, wider and wilder with each revolution.

And then Mother laughed her great laugh. "All right. But forget Mr. Lipton. It'll be sweet tea or lemonade." The tablecloth fluttered from the window, and it was like Mother herself was waving the white flag of surrender.

3

Southern Discomfort

"Are you thinking *this* is a tea dress?" Nattie pulled my gingham fit-and-flare from our closet.

I sat cross-legged on the bed. "I haven't the foggiest."

"Maybe white is better?" Nattie shoved the gingham back in and held up the eyelet sheath I wore to Sara's graduation at least one size ago, before my breasts came in. I was still five feet flat, but my chest had landed in true-bosom territory. Nattie balanced the hook of the hanger on the top of the closet door. The dress swung to and fro to the rhythm of the ceiling fan.

Yesterday it had seemed a swell idea to have tea, certainly sweller than sweltering in the guesthouse with only a little sister and giant poodle for company. (Mother was off covering the record pecan crop.) But today it seemed less swell because I didn't know what to wear. And I liked to think I always knew what to wear.

I read *Mademoiselle* every month. Cover-to-cover read it. In New York, I'd buy a copy on the newsstand under the clock near Grand Central Station, right across the street from the magazine's offices, because that particular newsstand had *Mademoiselle* two days before any other place in the city. The round woman behind the counter would bark "This is not a lending library" if you weren't fast enough with your money, but I'd fist my change before she even saw me.

Mother thought my dalliance (her word) with fashion was shallow, but fashion was about art and creation and self-expression. If that counted as shallow, count me in.

Now I tried to picture how *Mademoiselle* would photograph a tea party. I remembered a story about London with flowered frocks and heathered sweaters. I closed my eyes to conjure up the details, but instead of teacups, I saw Dad's favorite white coffee cup, the one he stole ("borrowed") from the best diner on 110th. Some people closed their eyes and the world dropped away, but when I closed my eyes, Dad came alive.

Nattie threw a strappy Mary Jane at me. "Wake up! You can't be more than ten minutes late. It isn't *fashionable*."

"According to?"

"I read it in the pink book. Page fourteen."

"You've memorized the rules?" I threw the shoe back, and it sailed past her braids.

"Not all of them."

In that second, I missed Nattie's old room with her too-many stuffed animals. I missed so, so much. I missed Dad and his quips—"The only change you can count on is from a vending machine." I missed our revved-up sidewalk talk, missed slices of standup pizza on upper Broadway. I even missed the ripe smell of garbage on summer days. Well, that one less, but here everything was so green and pretty. How could it be a city? And how could it be a city where only three of us lived?

"If you're going to throw shoes at me, I'll leave," Nattie said.

"Shoe, singular. Stay."

She crawled under my coverlet and didn't look like she was going anywhere.

I put the eyelet away and took out a black shift—sleeveless, citified. A look-alike style was in the window at Saks Fifth Avenue last May, but my version cost six dollars at a place on Amsterdam where girls from Barnard College liked to shop. Classic black was always sophisticated, according to *Mademoiselle*, because you could both blend in and stand out.

"Does it look tight?" I asked Nattie from her perch on my bed. In the dressing table mirror, I saw only a slice of myself.

"In a good way," Nattie said, but I had to consider the source: an eleven-year-old who hadn't mastered the art of braiding her own hair.

Earlier this summer, not even three weeks after the funeral, Danny Rosen told me I had curves like a Corvette. I didn't like Danny. He had a habit of standing on one leg like a stork. But, oddly, that didn't stop me from necking madly with him and guiding his hands up and down those curves he couldn't get enough of. Sara said the grief had turned me around, but it had turned her around, too. She and Jerome were all over each other, all the time.

Now, on this T&E afternoon, I put on stockings, lining up the back seams as best I could, a squirrelly task since the nylon stuck to my clammy calves. I secured the tops into the hooks of the garter belt. I folded the girdle in half and stepped into it, rocking it back and forth until it came up over my hip bone. "Heat is misery," I said.

"You're supposed to wear proper foundation garments, even if it's hot," Nattie said.

We walked to the kitchen, and I swiped on a little from-the-freezer lipstick. "Don't tell me the pink booklet has rules about what kind of gunders to wear."

"Okay, I won't."

One problem with girding yourself for change—the change of, say, making a friend or two in a southern climate—

27

was the girdle itself. It sliced off circulation to your waist and possibly your brain. Pink booklet be damned, I went to the bathroom and peeled the girdle and stockings right off.

It took only ten minutes and a bucket of perspiration to walk the five blocks to the Eleets' place, a white-columned house at the foot of a long U-shaped driveway. I was clearly late, though at least I didn't smell—I did a quick sniff test to be sure.

I smiled my way through a small circle of girls in frosted-sugar dresses on the lawn. Every one of them had on stockings with straight seams. There was the scent of something velvety in the air. Maybe it was gardenias, but maybe it wasn't. I really had no idea what gardenias smelled like.

Gracie was nowhere in sight. At the edge of the not-small-after-all porch, I struck what I hoped was a nonchalant pose, ballet flats turned out, a passable first position. I practiced pulling my stomach in, along with something else, my otherness.

A very tall girl in a blue dress so pale and icy it looked almost silver held court near the front door. "I *haaaate* Davis E. Jefferson." She swiveled around to the others, and her hair—white blond with knife-edge bangs—swung after her.

"Davis Jefferson?" I said. I didn't add: Wasn't the real person Jefferson Davis?

She ignored me. "I *haaaate* him, even though he's divine."

"You hate him as much as I hate éclairs, which is not one single bit," a girl in a dress the color of pistachio ice cream said. Her pocketbook had a fabric flap on the front that matched her dress exactly.

"Oh, hey! Here you are," Gracie said, coming out the door in what must have been a proper tea dress, soft pink with an impossibly swingy skirt.

"Me?" I fanned my forehead. The heat pressed in, ironing itself against my skin. My formfitting, hopefully slimming, straight black linen sheath seemed spectacularly ill-advised.

"Silly!" Gracie put her hand on my elbow and turned me toward the girls by the door. She was sunshine, Gracie was. Wherever her gaze went, a shaft of light seemed to follow. "Y'all, this is Ruth. Thurston-Ann, say hey. And the tall one, that's Claudia."

The girls looked at me. Thurston-Ann, the girl in pistachio, trilled her fingers.

"I'm Ruth. Ruth Robb." I was aware of being very one-syllable.

"Now that Ruth Robb is *finally* here, let's get this show on the road," Claudia said, swishing her icy-blue skirt around.

Gracie picked up a crystal bell from the porch railing and ding-a-linged it. "Y'all!" she said to the seven or nine girls I'd walked past out on the lawn. "Everyone, Ruth. Ruth, everyone." She delivered it like a line from a movie, with cool confidence. "Ruth will be a third-year with us at Covenant."

I gave an inane wave.

Gracie opened the screen door and called: "Norma! Whenever you're ready!"

A slight Negro woman with a bubble of shellacked hair slid through the door, balancing a silver pitcher and tray of glasses. She set the tray down and disappeared, only to reappear with a second tray, artfully piled with lemon squares.

"Thank—" I said. Norma had turned away before I could say "you."

"Hey, Ruth. Let's indulge!" Thurston-Ann put a lemon square on a glass plate and passed it my way.

The lawn girls drifted up to the porch and took perches on the wicker chairs.

Gracie waited for the group to go semi-silent, then bowed her head. "Gracie always says grace," Thurston-Ann said, a little powdered sugar on her nose, adding to her freckles. "Because of her name."

"Come, Lord Jesus, be our guest. And let these gifts to us be blessed," Gracie recited. Fontaine and Mr. Hank never said grace when we visited with Dad, but lately they'd been saying prayers before every meal, and I was getting used to it.

"Amen," the girls said in unison. "Ah-mein," I added, a second too late, and in the Yiddish-y way Dad said it, even though Fontaine had been quick to say her amens over me, trying to nip this particular habit of mine in the bud.

"Oh, your accent! It's fabulous," Thurston-Ann said. "And you know what else is fabulous? Your hair. It's come-hither, is what it is. And your eyes?" Thurston-Ann leaned in. She and her freckles were nose-to-nose with me. "Are they black? So exotic! Is your momma Natalie Wood and you're here hiding from Hollywood?"

I blinked. "They're brown."

"Her momma is a Landry!" Gracie said. To me, she added, by way of explanation, "T-Ann is a majorette. Always enthusiastic." She paused. "Want mint with your sweet tea?"

"Sure. We call it iced tea," I said, thinking of the sugar party I liked in my coffee. I might love sweet tea.

"Oh, no, no. Sweet tea is not iced tea." Thurston-Ann shook her head, and her blond curls bounced about. "Norma pours the right amount of sugar in when the tea is hot—not too much, not too sweet—and it *mellllts* into heaven."

I took a sip. The tea was divine.

"Tell us, where are you from *exactly*?" Claudia held her tea the way my mother held a martini, elegantly and a little detached.

"Near Columbia."

"*Columbia*? Well, not so far then. Just South Carolina," she said.

I bit back a smile. "Columbia the university, in Manhattan."

"Oh, why didn't you say so?" Claudia put her glass down with a hard knock. "I've been up north to see the Rockettes."

"You could be one, Claud," Thurston-Ann said. "Your darling long legs. Don't you think so, Ruth?"

"She's tall enough." It wasn't my most darling response, but I was feeling rather black-sheep-ish (or black-eye-ish) in this sea of sherbet.

"Oh, are we going to go around the porch and state the obvious?" Claudia asked. "You're short, Ruth Robb. Does that mean you're something like a jockey?"

"Ruth, pay her no mind," Gracie said. "Claudia's tongue is sharp as a razor."

"It's all right. I do ride," I lied for some reason, taking another sip of tea. "In Central Park." I conjured up the time I'd watched snooty Sylvia Wexler, a velvet helmet perched on her head, canter her dappled pony around in circles. I could be a champion equestrian. Why not? I could be any number of people in front of these girls who had no idea who I was or had been.

"You? Ride?" Claudia said.

"You'll have to come out to the barn," Gracie said. "We have a few show hunters at Chastain. Do you ride English?"

I had no idea what I rode, since I rode not at all.

"You know what I remember about New York?" Claudia

asked, saving me from having to answer. "It was dirty. Cigarettes flung willy-nilly."

There was no dirt here, that was for sure. My mind got stuck on a picture of Norma wiping dust from the porch, chasing nearly invisible specks with a cloth in hand, but I blinked it away because maybe she didn't dust one bit. Maybe I didn't know what I was talking about.

Thurston-Ann scooted her rocker closer. "What the heck, you live in New York?" Up close, I saw her pistachio dress was freckled, too—a print with a million dots.

"Lived." There—one true thing.

"Still! *Still*," Thurston-Ann said. "Daddy says I can't go until I'm married. He says New York is full of communists. Commies and Jews," she said. "True?"

"Hell, no," I blurted, even though almost everyone I knew in New York was Jewish and my father's father, long dead, had called himself a socialist. I fanned myself sort of frantically on the spotless porch, hoping it wasn't the worst thing in the world to leave out the part of your life, the part of yourself, that was inconvenient in the southern sun.

"Whoa-etta! With your colorful mouth you really are from up north," Thurston-Ann said, holding her glass out for a clink. "Cheers!"

I picked up my glass and ran my fingers over the etched leaves, so delicate they might shatter on sight.

"Cheers! Cheers!" echoed the circle of voices around the porch.

Was I cheering a lack of commies and Jews? *Be strong when everything is going wrong.* I'd read that in *Mademoiselle.* I straightened my shoulders and threw out a "Cheers!"

"So your momma's from here." Claudia poked around in her pocketbook and extracted a pack of Pall Malls. "What about your daddy? My daddy's on the board of Covenant, so you know." She shook out a ciggie, lit up, and exhaled in a long twirl. I thought of the pink booklet's admonishment about smoking in public and wondered if a porch was considered public or private.

"*My* dad?" I played with the sprig of mint.

"Yes, what about your daddy, Ruth?" she repeated.

"Ruth's father passed on." Gracie shot Claudia a look. "As I told you."

"He died," I said. After the funeral, Sara and I'd made a list of rotten metaphors for death. Dad wouldn't have wanted to pass on, shuffle off the mortal coil, get a one-way ticket, or cross the divide. He would've wanted to die. Well, he would've wanted to live.

"That explains the shroud." Claudia tipped her head toward my dress. "Remember when Hillary Jane wore a black sack to Annie Lewis's afternoon birthday. Black by day? Scandalous. Tell us—what'll be your church, Ruth Robb? Because you'll need to repent for that fashion faux pas." She smiled the smile of someone who was never off an invitation list. "Just joshing."

"Oh, please, Claud. Ruth'll be at Wesley Methodist, right?" Gracie answered for me. "Her momma and my momma won the three-legged picnic race many years in a row." She turned my way and added, "But now our home church is Northside Prez because Daddy's family's worshiped there since time eternal."

"Wesley Methodist," I said. "I've been there lots on Christmas Eve." That much was true; we'd all gone, Dad included. But I still let out an exhale of relief that Gracie was at a different church and I wouldn't have to make excuses for why I wasn't Bible studying by her side.

"Oh, terrif," Thurston-Ann said. "I'm secretary of the youth group there—at Wesley Methodist."

"Oh, terrif." I gave my glass a spin and watched as the ice rearranged itself.

Thurston-Ann put her hand on my hand, in religious solidarity, I guessed. Two seconds later, she let go. "Wouldn't you say it's time for some So Co?"

"Always." Claudia ground out her cig, though she'd barely smoked an inch, and pulled a silver flask from her handbag. She had all sorts of vices in there, apparently.

"What's So Co?" I asked.

"Southern Comfort," Thurston-Ann said. "A southern

tradition. It's like whiskey, vanilla bean, lemon, and cherry all got together."

"Everyone has a first So Co story," Gracie said. "And it often ends with a blackout or someone's hair being cut against her will."

I held on to my hair without really meaning to. "I had gin gimlets in the Village all the time," I said. Once, actually. But I was all for a sip of something that would go over with this crowd and their Fontaine-sanctioned crowns and gowns.

"By all means, let's give Ruth a double swig before we go inside for decorum," Claudia said, ribboning the liquor, quickly and definitively, into one glass, then another.

The first gulp was sort of fantastic, but then the aftertaste banged in.

Gracie leaned over. "They say it's like a tail stuck halfway down your throat."

The tail of *what*, I wondered, as I took another sip that sailed right down.

Spiked sweet-tea glasses in hand, we walked into the Eleets' living room, where everything was both cooler and also spectacularly in bloom: a gold rug with large lilies, green sofas with garlands, and billowy curtains with roses climbing up, like they were looking for a way out.

"Thank God for Mr. Carrier!" Thurston-Ann said, fanning herself with her napkin. "Inventor of the air chiller."

Praise be to Mr. Carrier.

Gracie patted the sofa, and I took a seat next to her. As we waited for Mrs. Eleet, Claudia topped off my tea. Up close, I saw a monogram on the flask—a C encircled with a wreath. Even liquor was an occasion for decoration.

Beads of sweat were making friends on my top lip. My hair felt like a giant pouf, like Frooshka ungroomed. No matter how long I'd spent on my hair in the weeks since we'd arrived—showering, then sitting under the dryer hood, then smoothing with the curling wand, then Spray Netting—I always came undone in the afternoon.

"This is the perfect time to join us," Thurston-Ann said, and I was a little in love with her freckles. "The first mixer is girls-ask-boys. In two Saturdays."

"Aren't you asked to a bance by a doy? I mean, boy?" My head felt curiously heavy.

"Boys, doys, potato, pa-tah-toh," Gracie said. "I'll ask Buck, of course."

"Because you like to see Buck buck naked," Claudia said. Her ice-blue dress looked cool enough to dive into. "Buck is a specimen, but he's no Davis Jefferson."

"Who is Davis Jefferson, and why is his name backwards?" I knew it was the wrong tone—too New-York-y

37

and not enough pastel-y. As Fontaine had told me, my voice was a strong spice and I had to use it sparingly.

Claudia straightened up. "Our mommas have been fixing us up since we splashed around the club pool in nappies. Long before you had any idea about doys or boys." Even her laughter was sharp, as if it were shot through with shrapnel.

"At least some of that is not true," Gracie pointed out.

"Isn't it warm in here? Even with Mr. Carrier?" I asked.

"Next time, put your girdle in the freezer first—makes a difference," T-Ann said.

I smoothed my ungirdled lap, imagining freezer shelves lined with gunders and crooked tubes of lipsticks, just as Mrs. Eleet joined us. She wore a shift dress with embroidered sailboats, pressed into shipshape.

"I trust you've all made the acquaintance of Ruth." Mrs. Eleet motioned to me.

I stood, feeling everything about me—too much hair, not enough girdle—was wayward.

"Ruth, dear, tell us the most important thing about yourself." Mrs. Eleet nodded, which I took as permission to plunk back down.

"I'm . . ." I'm a Yankee, a brunette, an Adlai Stevenson Democrat, an aspiring journalist, a grieving daughter. And Jewish. "I'm happy to be here."

"You're missing a word," Thurston-Ann stage whispered.

"I'm *super delighted* to be here." My tongue felt thick, and I worried I'd said "thuper."

"Nope," Claudia said, shaking her pin-straight bangs.

"I'm sure, dear," Mrs. Eleet said with the suggestion of a smile. "Thurston-Ann is correct in that you're missing the honorific, the 'ma'am.' But that isn't what I mean. The most important thing about you is this: You're the daughter of a Magnolia Queen, which I'm sure your momma told you gives you a certain pre-debutante status."

She obviously did not know my mother very well.

Thurston-Ann elbowed me. "A Magnolia Queen? Whoa-etta!"

"My mother and my grandmother," I said. The room tilted to the right. It seemed I shouldn't move, if I could help it. It was so heavy, my head.

"Time for a pink-booklet review," Mrs. Eleet was saying. "What letter should a lady's legs make?"

I didn't think she was asking me, but as the legacy queen in the room, I wanted to be a good pink student. "An A?" I'd go from A to Z—that's how much I liked knowing the answer. If there were to be pink quizzes, I'd wrest the booklet from Nattie and study up.

"It's S," Thurston-Ann whispered, her breath so close I could smell the lemon zest. "As in 'secretary'!" I was a sudden fan of Thurston-Ann and her pistachio kindness.

"Thurston-Ann is correct," Mrs. Eleet said from above my head. "If a young lady curves her legs into an elegant S shape, a young gentleman will see the length of her limbs, but nothing he has no earthly right to see."

"A young gentleman like Jefferson Davis—or Davis Jefferson?" I asked before letting out a small burp.

"Mercy!" Claudia snapped.

"It's all right." Gracie walked her fingers along the sofa to give my arm a squeeze.

"Mrs. Eleet, I'm wondering if it's possible Miss Ruth is under the weather," Claudia said. "Or the effects of liquor," she added under her breath. Across the room, one or two or three girls stifled a giggle.

I gazed at Mrs. Eleet's knees. Knees were funny when you looked at them too long.

"To think, I was wondering if you were under the same cloud, Claudia"—Mrs. Eleet paused for a breath—"but since everyone seems to be feeling fine, let's get to it. The social season is nearly underway."

I burped, louder this time. *"Excusez-moi."*

Mrs. Eleet reached down and took my hand. I liked her more here, without her white gloves. "Ruth, as the daughter of a queen, you must—"

"I must!" I stood up, fast. The Southern Comfort wasn't all that comfortable in my stomach, even though the other girls seemed to hold their liquor well. My mouth filled with spit, and I feared I might throw up right there on the carpet of lilies. "I must . . . I must go and walk the poodle."

"I'll see you out." Gracie steered me to the door by my elbow.

I waved to Mrs. Eleet. "Ma'am, thank you for the tea, ma'am."

"Well, she learned one thing today," Claudia said.

Gracie cracked the front door. "Don't worry about Momma. She's seen one or more of us bombed before."

I wanted to nod, but I didn't want to move my head.

"You may want to wear red next week—on the first day, I mean," Gracie added. "We like to start the year with school spirit. Red and white."

"Cheerio!" I said, idiotically, as I went out the front door, playing the opening scene in reverse, leaving the girls in their pastel circle, Claudia towering over Gracie's shoulder, wearing the smile of the smug.

I lost my cookies—well, my lemon squares—before I even made it up the drive, leaving my otherness and a little heap of Southern Comfort as my calling card in a bunch of pretty pink flowers I didn't know the name of.

4

The War of
Northern Aggression

In the week following the vomit vignette, life at the guest-house settled into our new southern routine. I unpacked the last of the book boxes, even though we had no room for books. (Mother's novels were stacked under her daybed, and Dad's biographies were lined up, Leaning Tower of Pisa–style, on either side of the front door.) Mother reported on slugs and bugs. And Nattie held her breath, over and under the water.

By the time the first day of school rolled around, Mr. Hank was the only one of us who could get even half a smile out of Nattie, and so he'd told Mother he'd happily drive us to Covenant in the Savoy.

At least I had the fashion figured out. I went with a cherry-print dress and a red bolero jacket. Olé. Thankfully, the temperature had dropped to a semi-civilized seventy-nine, so I didn't worry about sweating myself silly.

"You look neato," Mr. Hank said as I got in the car. One of his ornately carved canes sat between us on the front seat.

A fashion compliment from Mr. Hank was not a hopeful sign. He may've had a hundred canes, but he had just one suit, rumpled, and three ties, red, red, and red striped.

Covenant's cross was not a hopeful sign either. It couldn't be seen from the road, but once we turned into the school's driveway, there it was—big and brass, rising straight up from a steeple. Covenant was new, and it was the best private school in Atlanta, according to Fontaine. Cross or no cross, Mother, who valued education over almost anything, agreed to send us, particularly with Mr. Hank writing the checks. So Fontaine pulled a string to get us in. "She pulled not just a string, but a whole ball of twine," Mr. Hank had said, but he said it with one of his wry smiles.

That morning, in the circle drive in front of the upper-school building, Mr. Hank tapped my knee, short and sharp. "It's the first day for everyone," he said. "Show 'em who you are."

Whoever that was.

"See you later, Nattie-gator." I reached over the seat and tickled her before getting out and hugging my blue linen binder to my chest, hoping to seem confident and not like the girl who'd recently heave-hoed in a bush. I swung the car door closed with my hip.

This was what I heard as I approached the girls by the picnic tables:

"Have you seen her hair? It's *black*."

"Like a communist."

"I hear her father dropped dead right on the streets of New York."

"Her mother was a Magnolia."

"She somehow already went to Columbia—the university."

"She's a Landry."

"She's a champion equestrian."

True, false, true, true, false, true, false.

"Oooh, you went really red." Gracie stood in the center of a group of girls in a dress the color of a Creamsicle. She was the eye of the flower, the pistil amid her pastel-petaled friends, and I wondered if she'd white-lied about the school-spirit business. But then I saw a red ribbon in her hair. The others wore only tiny red accents.

Claudia grinned what I assumed was a phony smile. "Feeling better?" Her only red seemed to be lipstick.

"Swell," I said. *Imagine it and you can be it*—I'd read that in *Mademoiselle*.

Gracie stepped out of her circle and took my hand to bring me to a good-looking boy at a neighboring picnic table. "This is my Buck. Buck, Ruth."

"Hey now," Buck said. He had sunburned cheeks and an easy smile. An even-easier smile belonged to the boy sitting next to him, a boy with a single dimple and a white oxford shirt with rolled-up sleeves.

"We're off to physics, Bucky and me, but find us at lunch." Gracie twirled and pointed at the half-moon of picnic tables. "Our posse sits under the big tree."

"It gets pretty crowded there." Claudia came over to hang on the arm of the friend of Buck who'd met my eye for a half second.

Thurston-Ann, in a red patent-leather belt, sidled up to me. "She's a walnut, Claudia is," she whispered. "Tough to crack."

I laughed, but it came out like a snort. "Can you point me toward"—I glanced at my schedule—"Lenox Hall?" All the brick buildings looked exactly alike.

"Claudia just told me that her first class is in Lenox. Claud!" Thurston-Ann yelled, her ringlets dancing around her shoulders.

I was struck then by a certain sameness in hair color. Everyone in sight was on the blond spectrum, from nearly white to deep honeycomb. I might have been wearing the right spirit color—too much of it—but my hair was defi-nitely the wrong shade, unless or until I made a weekend date with Miss Clairol.

The back of Claudia's head flounced to the right, along with the boy, but once inside the building I lost track of them in the sea of blond. The doors were marked with names (Archer, Beauregard) instead of numbers.

The bell rang before I found Greer, my homeroom/history class. I slid through the door and to the first available desk as "And to the Republic for which it stands" boomed over the intercom.

I flung my hand over my heart, promised "liberty and justice for all," and sat down.

But the voice over the speaker continued. "Our Father who art in heaven—"

I jumped up. Of course I'd heard the Lord's Prayer before; Fontaine and Mr. Hank had always said it on Christmas Eve when we'd visit. But the words had never left my mouth, not in the right order. I said the "kingdom come" part loud. The rest I mouthed along, religion by ventriloquism, until we were delivered from evil, power, and glory.

"Amen," the class said.

Ah-mein, I said to myself. Certainly, Fontaine couldn't object to my sounding Yiddish-y if I did so only in my own head.

"We continue, now, in *sighhh-lent* prayer," the teacher said, his voice slow and low. "Y'all may take a seat."

I kept my head down but let my eyes drift up. A row over, the white-shirted boy with the dimple didn't even pretend to bow his head. He folded a piece of paper into an elaborate airplane, a marvel of notebook engineering.

After a moment so long it must've been three, the teacher, a balding man with round glasses and a bow tie, tapped his pencil on my desk. "In my room, girls sit to the left."

"Oops," Claudia said from across the room.

"I'm sorry," I said, feeling my cheeks flush. "Sir," I added belatedly. I grabbed my binder and moved to what I now clearly saw was the girls' side.

Mr. Sawyer quickly glanced at an attendance sheet. "Of course, I had nearly every last one of you as second-years. No need for a drawn-out prelude. We will begin our work where we left off—at the cusp of the War of Northern Aggression."

I aligned my binder with the top of the desk and willed my face to look less hot and bothered.

Mr. Sawyer inched his glasses down his nose and looked around. "What happened in this country one hundred years ago? Miss Starling?"

"I have no earthly idea," Claudia said.

He nodded to me. "Maine—Maine is your clue. You are from the North, are you not, Miss Robb?"

I had no earthly idea how he knew I was a northerner. "I know Maine became a state in 1820—" I remembered the sign we passed on the way to sleepaway camp.

"Off the point." Mr. Sawyer's tone soured. "Mr. Jefferson, perhaps you can enlighten us."

"Sir?" the cute paper-plane boy, Mr. Jefferson, said. The cute boy who—*of course*—must be Claudia's Davis Jefferson. "A hundred years ago were the Lincoln-Douglas debates, before Mr. Lincoln became president. They were a preview of Mr. Lincoln's views on slavery, sir. And the state of Maine, sir, was somewhat divided on the issue of slavery—little-known footnote of Yankee history there." He turned my way with his wide-open smile and his single dimple.

The dimple did me in, even though his New England facts seemed suspect.

"Indeed," Mr. Sawyer said.

I raised my hand. I was a hand raiser. Being in the South didn't make it less so.

"Yes?" Mr. Sawyer bounced a piece of chalk in his palm.

"Before the Civil War," I started. The paper-plane boy turned to me, his tongue punched into his cheek.

"Miss Robb," Mr. Sawyer said. "When you spend a little more time with us, with people who lost their homes, who buried their silver and their loved ones and their livelihoods, you will see there was no *civil* war. The war was most *un*civil.

We refer to it as the War of Northern Aggression, or if we are feeling more generous, the War Between the States. Is that clear?"

No. "Yes, sir," I said. "It's just I remembered Lincoln's first vice president was from Maine."

Mr. Sawyer didn't say anything. He turned to the board and wrote—*The Three S's: Slavery; Secession; Fort Sumter*—then launched into a lecture about the first shots of the Confederacy, looking over the tops of our heads at some invisible spot out the window.

"Hannibal Hamlin," I added, feeling a current of northern aggression course through me. "The vice president."

While Mr. Sawyer stayed at the board and listed delegates from the first states to secede, Davis Jefferson stood up. He pinched the fold of the plane and let go.

It sailed onto my desk. I stuffed it in my lap and unfolded the missive. Inside, Davis Jefferson had written: "Welcome to the nineteenth century."

When the bell rang for the next period, the pilot swooped in to retrieve his aircraft. "Hey, I'm Davis."

"I figured that out," I said.

"Oh, she's Rude," Claudia cooed over his shoulder. "I mean Ruth."

I checked my schedule. "I've got English in Lawton. Why's everything here a name?"

"For the Civil War generals," Davis said.

"The War of Northern Aggression generals?" I volleyed back.

"It's for the big donors, actually—as Davis knows," Claudia said. "There's a Starling Hall in the lower school."

Davis looked at me, his confident hair swooping my way, a kind of hello. "I like a smart-ass, Ruth."

At lunchtime, Gracie was sitting, legs in an S, under the tree, as promised, along with Claudia, Thurston-Ann, Buck, and two boys from English.

"I heard you ended up on the boys' side in first period," Thurston-Ann said.

"I tried to tell you," Claudia said, which was a fatso lie. She took a sip from a bottle of Coca-Cola, holding it so casually it could slip right through her fingers.

Davis leapfrogged a bench to join the posse. "Ruth can sit on my side. Why not? Hey, Ruth," he said with his single dimple and sunbeam smile.

"Hey." I was only three letters away from "Say hey."

"Hey yourself!" Claudia stood up and looped her arm through Davis's.

"Girls, girls, girls," Buck said, leaning back and clasping his hands behind his neck. His elbows framed triangles of

50

blue sky. "Will one of y'all go on into the cafeteria and find me a pineapple Jell-O?"

"Did someone take away your ability to walk?" Gracie asked, but then she got up and headed through the double doors of the cafeteria.

Thurston-Ann swung her skirt over so there was room for me at the end of the bench.

The talk was regular lunch talk about homework and Elvis and weather, and whether *The Blob* was scary or stupid (both, I said). If I were in New York, inside my old caf, we'd be having some version of this same conversation.

"What'd the doctor say about your shoulder, Davis?" Claudia bit down on her straw.

"Out for the season." Davis windmilled his arm around. "Buck'll have quarterback all to himself."

"Well," Claudia said, drawing out the l's. "Now you can watch the games with the rest of us."

Davis took an acorn or such from the ground and chucked it from hand to hand.

Gracie returned with a scoop of jiggling Jell-O in a metal sundae dish. I decided against eating my lunch, knowing Mother had likely packed a note in there, as she had since I was in second grade—an aphorism or a few lines of poetry from Zora Neale Hurston, her favorite—and knowing my sandwich, a slab of cream cheese on rye bread, looked different, like *something*, not like the Twinkie Thurston-Ann was torpedoing into her mouth.

Buck sucked down the Jell-O. "Too bad you can't help us slay Ansley Academy on Friday." He had very white teeth, Buck did.

"Do you have plans this weekend?" Davis asked somebody, maybe me.

"I thought you'd never ask," Claudia said. "Davis E. Jefferson, will you accompany me to the year's first mixer?"

He smirked. "Year's *only* mixer."

Claudia stomped her loafer. "You and your wit."

"Course I will, Claudia," he said.

"Do you need a date to go to the game?" The question popped out of my mouth before I thought twice. Apparently, I was now the type of girl who was smart-ass-y in history and flirty enough to hint around to boys with dimples—a single boy with a single dimple who'd already said yes to another girl—about going to a game.

Davis's smile was wide as a Buick. "Anyone can go with anyone to a game."

"You're some ball of wax, Ruth," Claudia snipped. Before she could say more, we were interrupted by the authoritative *clap-clap-CLAP* of Mrs. Drummond, the Home Heck teacher who'd taught us how to tell lamb shank from lamb shoulder

in third period. "Ladies! Ladies only! Time for the Awesome
Blossom!"

She moved on to the next picnic bench. "Ladies! Ladies
only! Awesome Blossom!"

I looked to Thurston-Ann.

"It's a first-day-of-school thing," she said by way of
explanation, taking out a compact and reapplying her lipstick. "We line up and look pretty for pictures."

Mrs. Drummond stood at the edge of the quad and yelled
stage directions. "Tall ladies first. Claudia?"

Claudia situated herself on the top step in front of the
chapel, her swan neck stretching skyward. From this angle,
it looked like the steeple rose straight out of Claudia's scalp.

Thurston-Ann and the majorettes were next.

The boys—Buck, Davis, and a few others—stayed at the
picnic tables, our audience.

Gracie and I were in the front with the shorter girls. At
least I wasn't the shortest. Next to me was a girl with a non-
red sweater, who sat in the backy-back row of history.

"I'm Geraldine," she said.

"Ruth."

"I heard." It occurred to me Gracie and her friends had
the snazziest outfits, the loudest laughs, and the tightest circle, one that didn't, perhaps, ripple out Geraldine's way.

Mrs. Drummond assessed us. "Angle to the side for the most slimming silhouette." She walked over and repositioned Geraldine's hips. "Better!" she announced. "Now, the blossoms."

"Awesome!" Buck yelled.

"Blossom!" Davis added.

"Gentlemen!" Mrs. Drummond said, but not in a voice that would give anyone pause. She started on Gracie's side, offering up carnations from a picnic basket. When she got to me, I looked in the basket and paused.

"They're exactly the same," Mrs. Drummond said. "Don't be fussy."

They weren't the same. Some looked like they'd been imprisoned in wicker for weeks. I took a blossom that wasn't too brown around the edges, along with a straight pin.

All down the row, the silhouette of flowers poked out from girls' chests. I pinned the bloom over my left breast, which reminded me of putting my hand over my heart, which reminded me of the pledge, which reminded me of the Lord's Prayer, which reminded me I wasn't in New York.

I sneezed.

Mrs. Drummond patted my unadorned breast. "Pin to the right."

"What?"

"Wrong bosom," she said. "Right is *right*—that's a way to remember it."

I must not have read that page of the pink book. A flush rushed up my neck, and I repinned the flower. I shot a look at Davis, but he was goofing with Buck.

While the photographer clicked away, what drifted into my mind without my permission was this: I wanted to kiss him. There was something so nice, so warm about the sunny smile that lived on his face.

Afterward, Mrs. Drummond collected our flora. "I'm sorry to call attention to you, Miss Ruth."

"It's fine, ma'am," I said, the honorific coming almost naturally.

Mother was always telling me to stand *out* from everyone else—to skip the girdle, to open my own car door, to be an individual. Like being part of the crowd was the worst thing imaginable. I think she missed the point. It felt good to be part of a whole, even something flowery, even something brown around the edges.

"So, Ruth." Davis bounded up the stairs like a golden retriever. "I'll see you at the game then."

"Ruth'd be bored out of her gourd at our game—she's lived near Columbia *University*," Claudia la-di-dahed. "Has she worked that into conversation yet?"

Davis grinned. "Not yet."

What was wrong with dreaming about a boy's lips, even a boy named, of all things, Davis Jefferson? A small sting of something—guilt, I'd guess—fluttered behind my right eye. But it was shockingly easy to blink away the idea that Claudia thought Davis was divine, mainly because she herself was so undivine.

"See you there," I said.

"Careful you don't get her bombed." Claudia threaded her arm through Davis's. "Evidently, New Yorkers can't hold their liquor."

"Oh, *good*," he said, giving his hair the quick flick of someone who knew he was a charmer.

Consider me charmed.

5

Shut the Oven Door

Mother rolled up twenty minutes late to pick Nattie and me up after school, her window down, a cigarette dangling from her hand like a sixth finger. Evidently, it had been a while since she'd read the pink booklet and its advice about puffing in public.

I called dibs on the front, per usual, and slid Mother's typewriter, a portable, to the floor, running my fingers over the keys, wondering what she'd typed today. "Couldn't you be on time for our first day?" I said instead of hello.

"Got stuck covering the world's most tedious school board meeting, a half step up from reporting on rose blight," Mother said. "And you girls? How was day one?" She swiveled from one of us to the other.

"It was bad," Nattie said. "Boring and bad."

I cranked down the passenger window and angled the side mirror so I could keep an eye on Nattie in the back seat.

"It's okay, Nattie," Mother said. "No day is harder than the first. You, Ruthie?"

"We're all going to the game on Friday."

Mother turned onto West Paces Ferry, the road that cut across the Buckhead section of Atlanta, from the nice part to our part, the even-nicer part. "I didn't mean the social life. I meant the classes."

"Those were fine." I kept the Uncivil War business to myself.

She braked hard at a stop sign. There was no coasting with her—just lurch, brake, brake, lurch. Mother had a scarf with anchors on it tied around her neck, even though we were hours from the ocean. I momentarily missed Manhattan, which was not only an island, legitimately surrounded by anchors, but also a place where Mother never had to drive if she so chose.

As we lurched into the motor court of the main house, Fontaine was out front, something glinting in her hand. She was perfectly turned out for a Monday afternoon: a bias-cut skirt, an ivory blouse with a floppy bow, and coordinated ballet slippers. She had a flock of flats, a pair for every shade on the color wheel.

"Girls!" Fontaine said. "Come with me and tell me everything, everything about your day. Mr. Hank needs to talk to Alice."

Mr. Hank was reading the paper in his porch rocker. "Not especially, I don't."

"Let's say you do," Fontaine said.

It was a crown—with a center stone and sparkling leaves—in her hand.

"Well, Alice, I guess I could show you what came over the Teletype about Arkansas," Mr. Hank said, rubbing his palms against his khakis before getting up. My favorite of his canes, the one with a cobra handle, was hooked over the back of his chair. "Little Rock, big problems. We hired some hotshot from New York to cover the story. Suddenly the South is a beat people want."

"You could send me, Daddy." Mother pointed to the crown. "Make me Queen of News."

The Daddy reference caught me off guard. I hadn't heard her call Mr. Hank—whom, for whatever reason, we never called anything but Mr. Hank—Daddy in a jillion years. And it temporarily swamped me with grief for my dad/daddy. I closed my eyes and a picture of him floated up, settling in next to me with his coffee, an elbow to my ribs and a crooked smile for Fontaine. I swiped at my eyes with the sleeve of my bolero.

"Can't remember the last time you wanted to be queen of anything around here," Fontaine said.

Mr. Hank let out a laugh. "Al, it's what we call a galloping story. We need a guy to hop on and gallop along. But come on, let's see today's disaster."

Mother followed Mr. Hank into the study, where he'd recently had the boys from the paper install a Teletype machine, big as a radiator. It clanged like mad every time a story came across. Mr. Hank had told us three dings meant an advisory (something newsy was coming); five dings meant a bulletin (news was happening); ten dings meant a real news flash (a humdinger, in his words). In the month-ish we'd been here, most of the dings had been related to football scores and tornado warnings, or the occasional integration fight.

"Was it ten bells?" Nattie asked, but Mr. Hank didn't hear or didn't answer. "I guess I'll go walk Frooshka," she said, shoulders in a slump. "I want to feel her fuzziness."

"Go on with that ridiculous beast." Fontaine turned back the cuffs on her blouse to reveal a lining of pale stripes. She knew her way around the perfect fashion detail—a sweater that buttoned up the back or a ruffle that was shiny when the rest of the dress was not. To me, she added, "We'll get you a crown of your own, but first we'll bake."

"Bake?" I asked.

"Your mother rather conveniently forgot any southern recipe in her repertory. But you're of the perfect age—you need a go-to dessert you can whip up in a pinch."

The kitchen of the main house stretched along the screened-porch side. It was always cool, even when the air conditioner wasn't plugged in. Birdie was watching something on a little television with a fuzzy picture. She flicked it off as Fontaine clanged around. "Where do we keep the bowls?" Fontaine asked.

"Want me to make something for you?" Birdie said, taking out a glass bowl, measuring cups, and a whisk. Her hair was curled under in neat rows.

"I've got it, Birdie," Fontaine said. "No need to keep us company."

"I'll catch the ironing then," Birdie said before descending to the basement.

"What were you watching?" I asked. But she was already gone.

As I washed my hands, Fontaine said, "Tell me more about this first day of yours."

I flipped through possible responses about the wrong side of the classroom and my wrongly pinned un-awesome blossom but decided on the news Mother hadn't cottoned to. "I'm going to the game with Davis Jefferson. Do you know him?"

"Of course. His brother is a football s-t-a-r. You're off to a good start." Fontaine flashed a convincing smile. Her brooch flashed, too, catching the sun.

"Except I think he has a girlfriend."

The Teletype clanged from the other room—three sharp ding-a-lings.

Fontaine laughed and lit the oven's pilot light. "Girls around here trade beaus like baseball cards. Go on and crack a couple eggs into the bowl."

I cracked, then whisked. "I've never owned a baseball card in my life."

"That's enough with the eggs, dear. We don't need a custard." Fontaine sifted the flour and plopped it in the bowl. She folded in a heap of cocoa powder, added a cup of sugar, a small scoop of Crisco, and a fat pinch of salt. Then she beat the batter, poured it into a square pan, and slid the brownies into the oven.

Fontaine spun to me, a smile forming on her lips. "Why don't you come with Mr. Hank and me to church on Sunday. The services are almost exactly an hour, and afterward there's mingling. You're half Christian, lest you forget."

"Thurston-Ann goes there—she's a cheerleader," I said.

"All the better."

But something about the notion of churchgoing made my eyes flick out to the window, to the beautiful pool where neither my sister nor poodle was in view. Our background was half Christian, but also half not—*more* than half not, since Mother had already converted. And I wondered, for a brief, not-breezy moment, if Fontaine was disappointed in more than half of me.

The Teletype clanged again—another three-dinger.

"Can you turn that *inaaaaane* noise off," Fontaine yelled to Mr. Hank.

"The news doesn't care what you think of it," he yelled back.

Fontaine shook her head. "You go ahead and give it some thought, my worship overture," she said to me. "On to more fashionable matters." She fished two bobby pins out of her skirt pocket and handed me the tiara. It peaked in the center. "Everything is better with sparkle. This one was from Holley Ball." I thought of Mother's reference to the superfluous "e." She'd likely think a tiara of any kind was superfluous. Fontaine settled the crown on my head. "You're more beautiful than your mother."

That was an absolute fib, and for a second, I questioned how many other fibs Fontaine had tucked in her pocket. It's not that I wasn't pretty. It's that Mother (and, for that matter, Fontaine) were impossibly pretty. Maybe with the addition of a crown, I'd suddenly inherit their southern beauty. Or maybe I'd inherit Fontaine's happiness in this place, with the help of some sparkles atop my head. Or maybe I'd inherit something I wanted even more—a sense I was part of the Fontaine-and-Alice crown continuum.

"While those brownies bake, I've got an idea," Fontaine said. "Come along."

I followed her up the back stairs, to Mother's old room. There, hanging from the bedpost, was a pale-blue gown with a jewel neckline, narrow sleeves, and a smattering of embroidered leaves, each more ethereal than the next. It was the very dress Mother wore in her portrait, the one hanging over the mantel in Fontaine and Mr. Hank's library.

"Give it a whirl," Fontaine said, unzipping the back and threading crumpled tissue paper out of the sleeves. "She wore it for the 1933 Magnolia. The year she was queen."

I stripped to my slip and stepped into the gown. It was Cinderella-y chiffon.

Fontaine wiggled the zipper up. "*Magnifique!*" she said, scrunching up the sleeves so the chiffon didn't droop down my wrists. "Let's get you a higher heel."

I sashayed over to the big mirror. The dress was perfecto, the kind of gown made for starry nights and gin gimlets. The kind of gown I wouldn't mind spending a year in.

Fontaine was back with a pair of her heels—gold T-straps a smidge too big.

I swished left, then right, chin up, chin down. In the

mirror, I saw the dress first and myself second. I saw who I could be and not who I was or wasn't.

For what seemed like a long time, Fontaine and I stood, arm in arm, elbow in elbow, like we were posing for a prom picture, her perfect chignon and my imperfect curls boinging out all around the crown.

"Ruth, I want you to love life here," she said, pressing her hand into my arm.

Dimpled Davis and flippy Gracie and sparkles and pink books—that's what came to mind. I nodded.

Fontaine unlinked her arm from mine. "Better check those brownies."

I followed her down the stairs, careful not to step on the chiffon.

Back in the kitchen, when I peeked in on the brownies— still gooey—the tiara tipped forward.

Fontaine straightened it. "You'll have your own opportunities," she said. "So many crowning opportunities."

"Should I take notes?" I asked.

"Notes? Just like your mother. The peach doesn't fall far from the tree."

I pushed the cuffs of Mother's dress up and dug my notebook out of my binder—Mother's favorite kind, with a spiral across the top and "EZ on the Eyes" green pages.

Fontaine looked at me for a second before speaking,

like she was taking in the whole shebang. "All righty. So, first there's the mixer, where no crown is proffered. Then the Chrysanthemum Ball, which everyone calls the Fall Ball. Old-timers call it the Mum, but no one calls it the Chrysanthemum, because, I suspect, no one can spell it. Got that?"

"Yep."

"You mean to say, 'Yes, ma'am.'"

"Yes, ma'am."

"The Fall Ball is a Covenant-only affair. Not even three weeks later, we've got the Magnolia, which is citywide."

"Fall, then three weeks later, the Magnolia," I repeated.

"Don't glide over the Magnolia without recognizing its significance." Fontaine tapped her manicured nail on my notebook. "There are flower balls all year long. But for debutante purposes, the ones that count, the ones that gather one hundred well-bred girls from all corners of the city, are the Magnolia in autumn and the White Rose in the spring."

"*Pre*-debutante, Mother says."

"*Pfff.* The point of the debutante—'female beginner,' from the French, of course—is to introduce young women to a . . ." She paused for a second. "A like-minded circle."

I imagined a circle of blond and briefly wondered if my pen should take note of something other than the rules of the balls.

"You're recommended by established members—like, say, a grandmother. You attend a dozen lessons in comportment and etiquette, as you've started to do on alternate Thursdays."

"Yes, ma'am." Standing there in Mother's ethereal dress, I was struck by a quick and brutal truth: I couldn't wait for comportment, whatever comportment was, and for every ball in my future.

Fontaine gave my chiffoned arm a squeeze. "That's why we don't dwell on the Jewishness. The Jewish people have their clubs and such, and I've heard they're lovely. But they don't have the balls and the debs—those are only at the best clubs, which just so happen to be restricted." She folded a dish towel on the counter. "Unlike your mother, the debutante group doesn't drift outside its circle. I want the very best for you, Ruthie, and people here, well, they won't understand. I want your dance card to be full, full, full."

I nodded. I couldn't wait to dance with boys with single or double dimples, to see Fontaine beam down on me, a crown on my somehow magically unfrizzed head.

"Won't understand what?" Mother asked. I flicked my head and saw her in the doorway.

I went back over my part of the conversation and decided I hadn't said anything I regretted, not out loud. "Why no one calls the Chrysanthemum Ball the Chrysanthemum

Ball," I said, flapping her favorite kind of notebook around for emphasis.

"Because no one can spell it," Mother said.

"Listening in long?" Fontaine asked.

"Long enough." Mother reached into the bowl and swiped a smidgen of left-behind batter. "Ruth, please go take off that relic."

"What about the brownies?" I asked, yanking the tiara off, or trying to. A few strands of unruly hair wound around the sides, not wanting to surrender.

Fontaine opened the oven door a crack and quickly shut it. "Nope."

Smoke snaked out the sides of the door, curlicuing toward the ceiling.

Nattie was back with a panting Frooshka. They both sniffed at the air. "What's burning?" Nattie asked. "And why are you so fancy?"

"Don't touch that oven door," Fontaine instructed. "We're forgetting about the baked goods for the moment. We're keeping it shut."

"We're not." Mother grabbed the dish towel and took the brownies from oven to sink.

Fontaine pulled the chain to get the ceiling fan going.

"Take it off now, Ruthie," Mother said, her short hair winging up in the breeze.

"How about we dip them in milk?" Nattie asked.

"Lost cause," Fontaine answered.

I went upstairs to change, and their words drifted up behind me, along with a whiff of scorched chocolate. Mother's voice was clipped. "Why put Ruth in that dress and talk up these balls at clubs that won't let her in? No daughter of mine is falling for southern cotillion if it comes with a whisper of hate."

"Your fight is not Ruth's fight," Fontaine said, which contradicted the peach and the tree. "She wants to fit in. She wants to take on the opportunities."

"She doesn't know what she wants," Mother said.

I couldn't let that one go. "I know," I yelled down the stairs. "I know exactly what I want, and it includes dancing and crowns."

"Don't yell, dear," Fontaine yelled. Then quieter but still audible, she said to Mother, "And I told her she could come to church with me."

"Church?" Nattie's voice was squeaky. "We're Jewish."

"Half," Fontaine said.

"I converted, Mother. The girls are Jewish."

I hung Mother's dress just so, threading the tissue paper back through the sleeves.

By the time I came back downstairs in my too-red school clothes, Fontaine had thrown the dish towel over the brownie fiasco, Mother was at the kitchen table with Nattie on her lap, and Frooshka was sacked out, front paws crossed, on the linoleum.

"Ruth—good news," Mother announced in a voice that said otherwise. "Keep your Saturdays free."

"Saturdays, plural?" I said, imagining pool parties and gown shopping with the pastel posse. "I think my dance card will be full." I shot a look Fontaine's way.

"I think not." Mother's lips flattened into a line. "Starting this week"—she circled her hand around the table—"our Saturday mornings will be spent honoring Shabbos."

"Oh, for heaven's sake," Fontaine said.

I brushed my fingers over my wrists, where Mother's dress had recently draped itself on and over me. "Why? We haven't gone once since Dad—"

"I've been hearing good things about the rabbi on Peachtree," Mother said over me.

"He's an integrationist," Fontaine said.

"Ruthie," Mother said, and I looked at her. "You want to go to all these pre-debutante festivities, then you spend time at temple. One for one."

And I thought: Fine, I could be Jewish on Saturday mornings as long as my dance card was full, full, full on Saturday nights.

6

Score Squeeze

The home bleachers were packed. *Fweeeeee, wheeeeee.* I followed the sound of a two-finger whistle to see Gracie waving. "Over here!"

In Gracie's world, a few rows up, smack in the center, she'd spread a sunny patchwork quilt over the bench. "Say hey!" she said, handing me a pom-pom. "When Thurston-Ann gives us the signal, we swish this around."

Claudia and her fashionably long legs and circle skirt sat nestled against Davis, a pair of pom-poms at her feet.

I'd worn a tricolored shift of red, black, and white. I was glad Gracie had told me to dress up, because girls and guys were decked out like they were on dates. Davis had on a blue blazer, as though it weren't approximately a jillion degrees.

71

"Scoot," Davis said to Gracie. He moved left, and Gracie moved right.

Before I could second-guess the lineup, I squished between them. Davis smelled good, like soap and sunshine and beer. Claudia sat on his other side.

Amid growing hoots and applause, the majorettes took the field.

"Which one's Thurston-Ann?" I yelled to Gracie.

"T-Ann is always front and center. She cheers like no other. Go on, wave your pom."

Wave, I did.

I spotted T-Ann's pink cheeks under a red-feathered hat and thought she must be awfully hot under that plumage.

On the field, Principal Chalmers walked out to the microphone. Everyone settled down. "We are honored"—*ahhh-nod*—"to have Coach Parker to start us off."

A short man in short sleeves stepped forward. "Bow your heads."

Even though I was still ticked that Mother had thrown a fit over her Magnolia dress, as a tiny tribute to her and my promise to attend temple, I raised my head slightly.

Coach cleared his throat. "Oh, Gracious Lord. Shine your goodness on our boys. Light the way so that they may play with vigor. Together we say . . . 'Go, Crusaders!' "

The band struck up "The Flight of the Bumble Bee," which I recognized from excruciating piano recitals of the past, both my own and Sara's.

Davis shifted his weight, and his shoulder grazed mine. "Fun so far, Babe Ruth?" I felt his words slide down my eardrum. I nodded. I was somebody's Babe Ruth.

He reached inside his jacket and extracted a bottle of beer from a hidden pocket. I wondered how he felt about being up here instead of down on the field. With a quick *thwack* on the bleacher, he popped the bottle's top and tipped the beer my way. I took a sip, and he knocked back the rest. He reached into a second pocket and pulled out a second bottle. This time, he popped the top and handed it to Claudia, even steven.

Claudia handed the bottle back without imbibing. "Mr. Jefferson, you are late to the party. Jimmy fixed up some manhattans." From farther down the row, Jimmy, who was cute in a big-guy-goofy-grin way, wagged a shot glass. "He didn't even know we have a Manhattanite in our midst," Claudia said.

Davis pointed to Claudia's glass and asked me, "What the heck's in a manhattan?"

I spotted a maraschino cherry of the most garish color. "Cherries," I said.

The sun hung low, casting shadows that made everyone on the field look eighteen feet tall. From the grass, T-Ann picked up a red Covenant flag—a giant C surrounded by small crosses—and swished it overhead. The brass segued into a rendition of "Oh! Susanna." Thurston-Ann waved the flag, faster and faster until, *whoosh*, she took off down the field. The team followed behind. Buck appeared last, clapping his hands up to the bleachers, inviting everyone to return his applause.

Gracie was on her feet, clapping loudest of all.

After the coin toss, which we lost, the people in front of us sat down and we did, too. Ansley Academy didn't score on the first drive. Once we had the ball back, Buck threw a long pass. "That's my beau, my Buck," Gracie announced. "He's mine!"

From behind, someone yelled, "We *know!*" The tone was kind, though, because who didn't love Gracie?

But then Buck threw an interception, and the crowd let out a collective groan. I parked my pom under the seat.

"Know what happens when we score, right?" Davis asked.

"I know. Seven points. Well—six points plus the kick." Over the years, Dad had drilled me on the basics. We'd listened to Sunday games in the kitchen, our heads bowed to the transistor, rooting on the New York Giants and their MVP, the fearless Frank Gifford.

Davis shook his head, and his hair flopped forward. "Nah, Score Squeeze. It's a tradition. You hug the person sitting next to you. Can't turn your back on tradition, right?"

Unless you're my mother, I thought.

I shrugged and Davis chugged, but inside I wondered about the squeeze: When the time came, would he squeeze Claudia or me? And if me, should my hands stay by my side or go around his back?

"I need the ladies'," Claudia announced. "Gracie?"

"I'm staying put," Gracie said.

"Davis?" Claudia asked. "Would you be a gentleman and walk me over?"

Davis got up and held Claudia's elbow, all chivalrous, down the bleachers.

Gracie pulled me into a whisper. A few stray strands of blond had worked free of her ponytail. I ran my fingers over my own increasingly crazed curls. "If you were to ask me about Claudia and Davis," Gracie said, "I'd tell you that just because she's sweet on him doesn't mean he's sweet on her. Sweet isn't always a two-way street."

"Oh, good. I was—"

"But she has claws, our Claudia. Keep an eye out." Gracie reached into her bag and swiveled up her lipstick. "You want to refresh?"

I swiped on a little.

A few minutes later, Davis was back. "You have a little

red on your chin." He brushed his pinky finger below my bottom lip, right in front of Claudia. Claw-dia.

That little touch unbuttoned me—unbuttoned the worry, anyway. That place in my chest that felt shruggy two minutes ago moved over to make room for a boy with floppy hair and soft lips. Well, I imagined they were soft.

On the field, Buck circled his arm around in big loosening-up hoops. He completed a few passes, and we were in field-goal range.

Soon the ref raised his arms and yelled, "The kick is *gooooooood*."

I got ready for a squeeze—sanctioned by southern football, even.

Davis didn't move one inch in my direction. I uncrossed and recrossed my legs, hoping a slight jostle might remind him he had a certain tradition to keep alive, but Davis kept his eyes locked on the game while guzzling down a third beer.

Ansley Academy marched down toward the end zone, but—rah!—we sacked the quarterback.

Claudia stood up and screamed, "Go, Crusaders—*charge!*" with such vigor it looked like she might have a stroke.

The wind picked up. All those pennants held by all those boosters in the first row fluttered, the Covenant C flapping, a sudden impromptu parade.

The power of cheer worked. Buck spiraled the ball, and number 83 on our side nabbed it as it whizzed by. Davis jumped up, and I did, too. I looked over at Gracie, but she was staring at the field, hands folded in prayer.

On third down, Buck dropped back, cocked his arm, and released the ball into a soaring arc.

Boom.

Davis threw an arm around my shoulder. "Remember, touchdown equals this," he said into my hair as he squeezed me.

"Touchdown? Oh! That's why you didn't—"

"What?" He leaned closer. "It's hard to hear you."

"Nothing," I said.

His hand slid off my shoulder to my back, just above my bra strap. After the cheering died down, he ran his fingers down my arm.

I shivered in my head, if not in factuality.

"Told you it'd be fun," Davis said. His eyes crinkled into a smile, and I noticed he had the faintest freckles sprinkled across his nose and eyelids.

Claudia gave me her best glower, but I didn't much care.

"Team was better *before*," a guy in front yelled. He stood up and faced the stands. "Hit harder, played smarter." The guy had on a yellow cap, like the man next to him, two sunny dots in a sea of Covenant red.

Davis flicked a bottle cap at the guy, and he saluted back with a raised middle finger.

Davis and I squeezed in three more Score Squeezes, each more shivery than the last, on the way to winning the game in a blowout.

———

We all waited by the field house for Buck to come out: Davis, Claudia, Gracie, and me, plus Jimmy and the two yellow-caps—the younger one was super handsome, and the older was skinny-skinny and wearing an untucked shirt.

T-Ann and her majorette friends waited too, holding bouquets of red balloons. Davis pinched one from the center of the pile and yanked it free.

"Davis E. Jefferson!" T-Ann yelled. "That is not your rightful property."

"Yeah, but I have an immediate need for a corsage." Davis tied the thin ribbon around my wrist.

"Davis!" Claudia protested. "Are you not taking *me* to the mixer? Any corsage you have a need for would be headed this way."

"Claud," Davis said, his eyes fixed on me. "*You* are taking *me* to the mixer."

The younger yellow-cap spoke up. "Zap-zap. The brother is a magnet." He reached deep into his pocket and took out a lighter. He flicked it and held it against one, then another of T-Ann's balloons until they burst with a loud *pop, pop.* Everyone laughed. Everyone but Davis.

Davis closed his eyes for a half second. When he opened them, he said, "Ruth, meet Oren Jefferson. My football-star brother. O, this is Ruth."

"And me," the older man said, stepping forward. I saw then that he was forty or fifty—definitely not football age.

"And Cranford Parnell," Davis said without enthusiasm. "My uncle."

Buck banged out of the locker room, hair wet, smile huge. He whirled Gracie around with the confidence of a winner. "Oren! Cranford!" Buck said, slapping Davis's uncle on the back. "Thanks for coming."

"Good, good win," Oren said to Buck. "Full-speed, all-out end-zone playing."

T-Ann stuffed the balloon carcasses in the trash without missing a beat, then led the group toward the parking lot.

Oren fell in next to me. He snapped a twig off a maple—or maybe it was an oak—as we passed by. "You're not from here, are you?"

"Not exactly." I held tight to my balloon.

"She's a New Yorrrrker," Claudia said like she was doing vocal exercises. "And Ruth, Oren is a football legend."

Oren was gorgeous—maybe even more gorgeous than

Davis. Everything about him—flecky blue eyes, wavy hair, immaculate white shirt, muscle-y arms—was a little bigger, bolder, more intense. Even his dimple was grander—he had two, double the charm.

"Legend where?" I asked.

"Georgia Tech. We have a bye this week," Oren said, with a tip of his cap, which I now saw was embroidered with a GT.

"Oren has a bye for the season, it turns out," Davis added.

In the parking lot, we stopped at a truck that belonged to Cranford. He lowered the tailgate, and even though it was dusty and we were dressy, people started climbing into the bed. I couldn't figure out how to manage it gracefully, so I waited until last and then heave-hoed myself up.

Gracie spread her quilt over the hump where the wheel poked up, and she opened her pocketbook. "Knew you'd be starving." She handed Buck a sandwich in waxed paper. "Chicken salad, no almonds."

"It's wrong to have a picnic in the dark," Cranford said. He picked up a few stalks of hay from the truck and snapped his lighter. The thin bundle crackled, then flared orange.

"Not here." Davis grabbed the hay bouquet and jumped from the truck. "Won't be able to see stars through your stupid smoke." He stomped the sparks out with his loafer.

Oren whispered to me, "As I am to football, Davis is to stars—a genius. That boy knows his sky. Here's a tip."

Oren flashed a not entirely winning grin. "If he ever asks you—"

"I can hear you, O. Shut up." Davis kept grinding his sole into the pavement even though the hay was now a billion flecks of dust. I slipped down from the truck, careful not to let my dress ride up, and stood next to him.

Jimmy took T-Ann's hand, and they hopped off the back and headed toward the woods.

Oren inched over to Claudia, and they got to talking, leaning against the back of the truck's cab. "Davis," Claudia announced, her arm linked through Oren's, "I am reminded you are not the only Jefferson with charm."

"When you're right, you're right, Claud," Davis said. He batted my balloon. I batted back.

The air was still warm, but drier, friendlier. "So, you're some kind of astronomer?" I said.

"Amateur." Davis kicked the dirt. "Oren and Cranford and booze—they can be bad friends." He leaned over and whispered in my ear. "Boom."

A shiver shot through me, lips to hips.

He cracked open a beer from one of his mystery pockets—he must've stashed a whole six-pack in there—and I had a sip, then two. At some point, I glanced Claw-dia's way. She was throwing her head back in laughter, possibly fake, while Oren leaned into her, smile wide enough to light the night.

"I have to go," I said to Davis. "My grandfather is picking me up at ten." I'd briefly considered some kind of lie about who was fetching me, but I wasn't quick enough to create one on the spot.

Davis walked me back to the bleachers and waited with me.

Unlike Mother, Mr. Hank was right on time. He had a glass on the dashboard, a whiskey for the road.

The news blared on the car radio—a murder in Cobb County, an integration protest in Decatur—but none of the names were familiar, none of the news touched my Score Squeeze night.

When we pulled into the motor court of the main house, I got out of the car, the unpopped balloon tied to my wrist, and floated through the front door.

7

Shalom, Y'all

The balloon was wilted by morning, but I tied it back on my wrist anyway. It was the first corsage I'd been given, improvisational or otherwise, and I was in the mood to show it off.

"How was the game?" Mother said, when I joined her in the kitchen. She had a knife in hand, ready to scalpel a cantaloupe.

"Good—for us." For me.

"I tried to wait up," she said, "but Mr. Hank had me writing up the police blotter last night, and it wrung me out."

Nattie shook cornflakes into a bowl. "What's that old balloon on your arm?"

"This?" I asked, aware my voice jumped. "It's from a boy named Davis."

Mother ate her melon over the sink, careful not to drip on her blouse. She sighed her sigh. "Services start at ten. We'll drop Fontaine off at the Club first. You might want to change." Nattie was in her bathing suit, and I was in pedal pushers and a tie-up blouse.

"Oh," I said. "Services." I'd somehow—temporarily—forgotten.

"Let's both wear green. Minty green," Nattie said. The thought of us matching, which we hadn't done in centuries, seemed to cheer her.

"All right then," I said, even though mint might be my least favorite hue in the hueniverse.

———

We rolled all the windows down, but the air in the Savoy didn't move—not out or up or around. Fontaine, in a dress with buttons on the diagonal, occupied my usual front seat. Nattie and I were back-seat buddies.

The traffic took a cue from the air. It didn't budge. Mother flicked her pearl lighter open, shut, open, shut, then lit her cigarette.

"We'll be late," Nattie said, drumming her fingers on the seat between us.

"Life will go on," Mother said.

"Y'all could spend Saturday swimming at the Club,"

Fontaine said. I imagined that was how Gracie and T-Ann and Davis might spend the next few hours. "You're always welcome."

"Are we? Are we *always* welcome?" Mother said. "Will you be telling your Club friends that your daughter and granddaughters are spending the morning at temple?"

Fontaine twisted around to the back seat. "I've been there—to temple. Once with Pastor Douglas and the ladies of Wesley Methodist. The place is splendid."

"We're not talking about you being welcomed in a synagogue," Mother said. "We're talking about Ruth—all of us—being welcomed into a restricted club. And until then, we'll be going forward, not backward." Mother punched the accelerator just as the traffic broke.

"Don't you make me or the city of Atlanta out as narrow-minded," Fontaine said, still facing us. "Covenant has Jews."

"It does?" Nattie asked. "Where?"

"But," I said, "I thought you said people don't drift—"

"There's a quota, I believe, and the Jewish girls are perhaps not—" Fontaine stopped and readjusted her smile. "The girls who're going to the Magnolia and such, those are not the Jewish girls. Of that, I'm one thousand percent sure."

"On that, we agree," Mother said, grinding out her cigarette.

My legs felt glued to the Savoy's upholstery.

"It's the five-o'clock shadow—and I'm not referring to facial grooming," Fontaine went on. "Jews are well accepted at the banks or the law offices or the hospital or whatnot. But after dinner? After five o'clock, people like to socialize with their kind. I'm not saying it's right, mind you. But if you're—let's take a for-instance—socializing with Gracie Eleet, and you were to tell her your religious preference—"

"Not preference," Mother clarified. "Religion."

"You've changed religions once—why not change again?" Fontaine twisted herself back around to the front. "Because the moment 'Jewish' leaves your lips, people'll adjust their reactions. Until that second, maybe they think you're Italian . . . or some Russian aristocrat—isn't that what Miss Natalie Wood is? But once they hear you're Jewish, it's the headline—the only thing people will remember about you."

"Enough," Mother said sharply. She whipped up the long drive to the Club, which Fontaine called "the capital-C Club." We lurched past the lawn mowed in a perfect criss-cross pattern, past the Negro valets in red blazers and white gloves, barely slowing to let Fontaine hop out, then lurched back to Peachtree Street (as opposed to Peachtree Park or Peachtree Battle or Peachtree Memorial or Peachtree Valley). Mother pointed us toward Midtown with nary a word.

The temple rose above its neighbors at the top of a hill, a kind of Jewish Tara with whizzy traffic at its feet. A discreet sign with gold lettering announced: TEMPLE SHIR SHALOM. We walked up the steep driveway, leaning forward so we didn't lean back.

"We're definitely late," Nattie said, ticking off the minutes on her watch. "Eleven minutes. The pink booklet says—"

"Nattie, by now you know I'm always fashionably late," Mother whispered as we approached the triple front doors painted lipstick red. She opened the right side with the quiet of a thief.

It was like going into a theater after the movie started; we had to let our eyes adjust. We stood in an entryway behind another set of doors. Part of me hoped it would be too late to go in at all, so I could sit poolside with the pastel posse at the no-sense-telling-them-I'm-Jewish Club, or wherever they might be.

A man with a frown-shaped mustache appeared from a side room. "Shalom, y'all," he said softly, opening the inner doors for us.

We were at the back of a big sanctuary. Except it didn't look like any temple I'd been in, definitely not our temple in New York, which was sleek with everything the same shade of wood. This room was fancy and gilded, a wedding cake of a place. Even the ceiling was grand and swoopy, with a field of flowers made of plaster frosting.

Shalom, y'all, indeed.

The frown man motioned to an empty pew. Most pews were empty. There were twenty worshippers here, tops. I thought about our home temple and all those bar mitzvahs—one a weekend the whole seventh-grade season—that packed the pews to capacity. I thought about sitting shoulder-to-shoulder with my Hebrew school friends in itchy slips, giggling anytime we thought the rabbi wasn't looking. I thought about feeling a part of something, instead of apart from everything, a part of something that went deeper than the awesomeness of a brown-around-the-edges blossom.

An older couple one row up pivoted to smile at us. It might have been phony—it was hard to tell, because people in Atlanta threw smiles around like confetti. The woman was accessorized to the nines, even though it was a swelter-y September Saturday. The ceiling fans groaned, trying to move a few molecules of warm air.

This rabbi was tall and tan, like he'd possibly be good at tennis. He had hair the color of a mushroom, parted swoopily to the side, and he was wearing a khaki suit—what Dad called a Friday suit—that looked out of place against all the gold on the altar: gold curtains, gold ark, and gold candelabras that could pass for weaponry. He cleared his throat and read a few prayers in English, fast. I was so used to the guttural *cccch*s of Hebrew, that the plain English sounded foreign, not the other way around.

"I invite you to try to stay awake as you take in today's sermon," the rabbi said with the confidence of someone who could hold an audience, even if it was twenty people.

A chuckle came from up the aisle, and that's when I noticed a guy my age, give or take. He seemed to be the only person—other than us Robbs and the rabbi—under sixty.

The rabbi launched into his sermon, but I kept looking at the guy. He wasn't wearing a jacket but a bright plaid shirt, skinny tie, and thick black glasses, like he thought he was Buddy Holly.

"Let me ask you." The rabbi's voice held a twinge of southern twang. "When was the last time you had a Negro in your home? When was the last time you stopped shopping at a store because it discriminates? When was the last time you sat in the back of the bus, even when it was crowded and blistering hot?"

The questions were rhetorical, I knew, but still the answer was never. For me, the answer—even though we were northerners, even though Dad and his ad agency had done work for the United Negro College Fund—was never.

Mother took a handkerchief from her pocketbook and dabbed her eyes. I loved that handkerchief, embroidered with orange tulips, like the ones Dad brought her from the corner florist on Valentine's Day, because red roses were cliché.

I leaned into Nattie. "Dad worked with the United Negro

College Fund." I wanted her to know everything about him that I knew. She huffed a breath in and didn't exhale.

The rabbi slapped his palm against the pulpit. The slap got Nattie breathing regularly again. "And if you think that *that* is dangerous"—his voice got louder and more urgent— "then I believe it's time you live a little dangerously."

"If *what's* dangerous?" I asked Mother, cursing myself for missing the good part.

"Button it," she said softly.

The sun shifted, and a shaft of light poured through the big stained-glass windows shaped in arches that were vaguely Ten Commandments-y. I'd always thought of stained glass as a Christ-on-the-Cross situation. I once spent most of a Christmas Eve at Fontaine and Mr. Hank's church, twenty or forty blocks north of here, watching Nattie count the number of glass pieces in Jesus's right foot (the answer: eighty-three). Here, the light was turning Nattie's ankle a delicate shade of lilac.

A man across the way had nodded off.

"This is my calling as a rabbi—a call to justice."

Mother fanned herself with a pamphlet of upcoming activities. The accessorized woman shrugged off a capelet.

"It's time we stand up. As Atlantans, and as Jews," the rabbi finished. "Amen."

"Amen," Buddy Holly said, loud.

"Ah-mein," I said, as Dad would have said.

As the service wound to a close, we turned in the prayer book—the same black *Union Prayer Book* we used in New York—to the Kaddish, the mourner's prayer. I didn't read it; I knew it. I said the words with Mother and Nattie, the Hebrew tripping off my tongue, coming from somewhere deep inside my skin. It was a prayer for the dead that didn't mention death. Our rabbi back home had made a point of telling us that before Dad's funeral, the last time I'd said this prayer, any prayer, silently or out loud.

I still wasn't keen on being here and missing who-knew-what with who-knew-whom among my shiny could-be friends. But these words: These were Dad's words, and they had the force of familiarity.

Mother traced circles on Nattie's back.

From behind the gold curtains, Oz-style, music rang out.

"What's with the organ?" I whispered to Mother.

"I like it," Nattie said. "It's quivery."

After the service, we followed a small parade of congregants down a hall lined with photos of girls in white dresses, as if everything here, even religion, were one big society occasion.

In a room appropriately named the Social Hall, Buddy Holly was shoveling egg salad onto a cracker. "New Jew?" he asked me, his eyebrows jolting off every which way.

"More like old Jew, new Atlantan."

"I'm Max. Want a Co-Cola?"

"Ruth. It's a little early in the day, don't you think?" I fell right into his rhythm.

A pregnant woman with the spectacular bone structure of actress/goddess Sophia Loren introduced herself as Dina Selwick, the rabbi's wife, and introduced her daughter as Leah. Nattie skipped right off, braids flapping behind her, to play with Leah.

"I figured you for a northerner," Max said, picking up where we left off. "Around here, we drink Coke for breakfast. Heck, I drank Coke from my baby bottle." He popped the cap off by angling the bottle against the tablecloth's edge, as Davis had last night, and handed it to me. That trick must be in the southern-boy repertoire.

I tipped my bottle back. "Who's forcing you to be here?"

"Not a soul." He rolled up the sleeves of his plaid shirt. "I'm helping the rabbi spread the integration message to college students."

"So it's a job?"

"No, it's a cause."

"Oh," I said. "Oh, that's swell."

He smirked with his eyes. They were nice eyes, brown, but the rest of him—hunchy shoulders, owlish eyebrows—was a lot less attractive. "Do you know the SCLC—the

Southern Christian Leadership Conference?" he said. "Or the Ministers' Manifesto? About integration? Rabbi Selwick helped draft it, and it's been signed by eighty-seven clergy."

I knew New York things. I knew every crack in the sidewalk on Amsterdam between 110th and 112th. I knew the air conditioner over the door of Harold's Shoes, a store for old ladies with bunions, dripped. "I—I do not." I felt like I'd swallowed a rock, and I took an instant dislike to the know-it-all with smirky eyes. "Are you in law school?"

"Prelaw. Emory." A few congregants jostled around the nearby coffee urn. "People here don't care about—"

"We don't care about what?" asked the man who accompanied the caped woman I'd seen in the sanctuary. "I'm Mr. Silvermintz, by the by," he said with a smile that didn't show his teeth.

"Ruth Robb."

The man turned to Max. "You bending this young lady's ear about how we don't care enough about the plight of the Negro? Always with the civil rights? Apparently," he said to me, "this young man is on a mission to make us the most unpopular place in Atlanta. We've been threatened, you know."

I didn't know—how would I know? And threatened with what—boredom?

"Miss Robb, please excuse this rebel." Mr. Silvermintz nodded before wandering off with his coffee cup and saucer.

"Rebel," Max said. "That's a compliment. Follow me, Ruth Robb."

"Why would I follow you?" I asked, though I knew I would. Max's chinos were lassoed with a beat-up leather belt, and his shirtsleeves were rolled willy-nilly—every part of him oblivious to how he must look to the world. And yet he had a whiff of that familiar New York intensity—and that was sort of great.

He jangled a fat set of keys. "No one else is going to show you the best part."

I glanced around to see if Mother was ready to go, but she was sitting at a table with the rabbi, leaning on her elbows, looking rapt. Nattie and Leah were playing a game of tag in the foyer. Nattie looked one "You're it!" away from making a friend.

"I guess I've got a few minutes," I said, polishing off my Coke.

"This way, then."

We walked behind the behemoth of an organ. Back here, in the not-for-congregants area, things were plainer. Max opened an ordinary wooden door, no gold in sight, and started up a narrow flight of stairs.

"I hope you aren't planning something nefarious," I said,

going for that jokey tone Davis and his friends used, but it felt off, like I was suddenly smug.

Max walked backward until he shared my step. "I don't have time for a girlfriend."

"Ignore me," I said. Still, he was close enough that I was glad I'd brushed my teeth well.

At the second-floor landing, Max unlocked a metal door to reveal a fire-escape-steep ladder. I gripped the railing on either side, wondering about the wisdom of being here. When we ran out of stairs, Max pulled a rope from the ceiling. A trapdoor swung down, and a fat square of sunlight poured over us. He climbed up into the air.

I inched myself to the top of the ladder and peered out.

Pure sky—the opening was the roof.

I didn't mind heights—not when I was on a diving board and there was a lake under me at camp. But a roof I didn't know and a boy I didn't know? Nope. "I'll stay here," I said, white-knuckling the metal ladder.

He kneeled on the roof, his chinos grinding into the tar, and stuck his head back inside. "C'mon," he insisted. "Are you scared?"

"I'm not scared. I'm not petrified." It was suddenly a jillion degrees.

"You don't have to do this—lots of people turn around right here."

That did it. I hauled myself up to the roof, which was flat, at least. But it was gusty and loud up there in the great expanse of air. The rotunda looked a mile away.

"Just stay away from the edge, Ruth Robb," Max said.

"Helpful." I took a step, intending to take another. But then I lay down on the surprisingly smooth pebbles on top of the tar. I imagined I was sunning myself, trying to feel familiar and safe. Even perfectly prone, the breeze was biting. I closed my eyes. The sun looked purple from the inside of my eyelids.

"Okay, we can sit for a second." I could hear Max settle next to me. I picked up a bunch of pebbles, letting them run through my fingers while looking for my not-afraid-of-heights strength. The sound was pleasing, rhythmic, and then a different sound filled the air. It started quietly, and then it was clear the sound was coming from Max. He was singing. He was singing something soft and smoky and bluesy. I let it wash over me, there on the pebbly, too-open roof. I didn't want to ask Max what the song was; surely, I should already know. But then I sat up and asked anyway.

"Good, right?" he said. "McKinley Morganfield, better known as Muddy Waters. I've worn his album out."

That bit of honesty, and that bit of blues—it was a push. I stood up and followed Max over, way over, to a swinging ladder with toothpick stairs that led to a rotunda with a copper cherry on top.

And then we were inside the dome, ringed by stained glass, miniature versions of the beauties below.

It was a View-Master view, not like New York at all. In New York, everything was foreground. You couldn't step back and see it all. Here, there were medium-sized buildings of medium-sized shapes—no jaw-dropping Empire State, no glittering Chrysler.

Here, there were treetops and sky, wide brushes of green and blue, oceans of openness. Here, there was room in the air for clouds, for possibility.

"It's pretty," I said.

"Not underneath, it's not. Underneath, it's repugnant," Max said.

"You're so irritating," I said, though possibly not out loud.

"Look down at the Fox Theatre." He pointed slightly to the left, where I couldn't actually see a theater, just a bunch of rooftops through a shaft of cobalt blue. "Did you know the Fox has a Jim Crow balcony?"

"I'm not even sure who Jim Crow is."

Max ran his hands through his in-need-of-a-cut hair. "Tell me you're kidding."

"I've *heard* people talk about it," I said. "Of course." I'd bet a hundred bucks my ears were turning red.

"Jim Crow is based on an old blackface caricature, not an actual person." His tone was know-it-all again. "Jim Crow laws deny basic rights to blacks. It's 'separate but equal.' Do you think whites and blacks can't share the same movies, restaurants, water fountains, elevators, parks, schools, streetcars, buses? Do you think that's equal?"

"I think that's idiotic." My fingers were sweaty—the heat, maybe, or the lecture, or the truth of Jim Crow, which I'd known about only by osmosis before; no one had spelled it out so clearly, ever. I rubbed my hands up and down my minty dress, leaving little splotches. "But you like hearing your own voice, don't you?" I said.

He laughed a truly great laugh—loud and low and long, like a blues song. "The rabbi is doing good work. He's ruffling feathers," he said.

For some reason, Max was ruffling me.

He went back down the toothpick ladder, and I followed—one foot, then the other.

On the traffic-free way home, Mother said, "Someone at the paper should be covering the rabbi and his work with the alliance."

"Ruth went off with a boy," Nattie singsonged.

"He says he's a rebel, helping the rabbi with . . ." With what? Was it desegregating the movies, or was that a metaphor? "College students, I think." I wondered if Sara would join the cause if she were here, which she clearly was not.

Mother patted my thigh. "Keep Thursday free."

"Can't—there's a debutante meeting at the Eleets' house."

"Not debutante, *pre*-debutante," Mother said. "No one has invited you to cotillion land yet. You're in preparation mode. And if the girls hear you're a synagogue-goer, you'll be in blackball mode."

"I can miss only two meetings," I said like it was the law.

"Ruth's right," Nattie piped up. "That's in the pink booklet."

"I don't recall the pink booklet offering advice on how to pass yourself off as someone you're not," Mother said.

I rolled the window down. "It's one thing to be dragged to services . . ."

Mother lit a cigarette and took her time breathing in the first drag. "It's our deal: your dances, this temple. Fontaine can show you how to write a regret."

"Regret?"

"We're back to Thursday. We are joining the temple and the cause. The rabbi and your rebel are coming for supper. And Nattie, the rabbi is bringing his daughter."

Nattie leaned forward so her head was between us. "Shalom, y'all."

8

Sh-Boom, Sh-Boom

Norma opened the door and called up the stairs to Gracie. "You have a visitor."

"Helloooo!" Gracie yelled down. She had invited me over this afternoon, post-Shabbos services (not that she knew it was post-Shabbos), so we could get ready together before the girls–ask–boys mixer.

I followed Gracie's voice up the curving staircase to her nearly all–pink room. Gracie herself was seated in front of a vanity mirror, eyeliner in hand, hair in rag rollers, face dotted with dabs of Clearasil.

"You're already bouffed," Gracie said, by which I think she meant I'd back-combed and sprayed my hair into submission.

"It's not a pretty sight otherwise," I said, taking in just

how comfortable Gracie was covered with unlovely pimple cream, in her lovely room.

Gracie bounced on the bed, one eye done up in winged eyeliner, the other naked. Her four-poster bed was festooned with a wondrous number of horse ribbons, arranged in neat rows of like colors—all the blues, then reds, then yellows, whites, pinks, greens, purples, and browns, an equestrian rainbow. We sat side by side, as if on a parade float. I scissored my fingers over a ribbon—white, fourth place. White for white lies.

"I don't ride horses," I said, surprised this was what popped into my mind and out my mouth, but also somehow inspired by Gracie's ability to be so herself.

Gracie laughed. "Who cares?"

"I haven't ridden ever. Not once, even though I said I did on your porch. I wouldn't know a horse from a pony."

She laughed again. "One is much smaller than the other." Her tone was relaxed, uncomplicated, and that ease made my chin quiver. "Don't let some silly pony make you sad. You need a nip of So Co?"

Gracie boinged up and opened her top dresser drawer, digging around under the mounds of sweaters—featherweight cashmere, most likely, just right for Atlanta nights—to extract something. A flask, of course.

I took a sip, tinier than I had at T&E, wanting to keep the booze down this time around, and laughed.

It was the kind of moment I would have shared with Sara. I flirted, for a half second, with letting more truths gallop around the room. I could blurt out I was Jewish or not *not*-Jewish, but I thought it best to stop sipping and nipping before spilling this bit of news.

Gracie went to the mirror, took out the curlers, and stabbed at her un-made-up eyelid until she was more symmetrical. She dipped a cotton ball in witch hazel to swipe off the pimple cream.

I ran my hand along the embroidery on Gracie's coverlet, feeling the scrolled monogram, wondering if someone had stitched the whole thing by hand, and if so, thinking what an act of love that would be.

"Your turn," Gracie said, coming toward me with her eyeliner. "Don't twitch."

Matching eyeliner wings in place, we entered the Covenant gymnasium, where Mademoiselle Tremblay, the French teacher who always wore a French braid, was positioned by the hi-fi. She cued up the doo-wop-y "Sh-Boom."

Life could be a dream—sh-boom.

Not that there were so very many kids at first. Not that there were Claudia and Davis, specifically. I wondered if the whole mixer was going to be a sh-bust, but then, somewhere during the fourth song—*whoosh*—a whole crowd waltzed in, filling the gym with girls in twirly dresses and boys in blue blazers. Davis and Claudia made an uneventful entrance, her leading, him following, and Buck and Gracie waited not even a second to hit the dance floor. It was then, oddly enough, that I noticed there were enough red balloons hanging from the folded-up basketball hoops to float every boat on the Chattahoochee. And I thought of the now-shriveled balloon, given to me by Davis, occupying a place of honor on my closet doorknob.

Mademoiselle Tremblay tapped the microphone when the song ended. "*Bonsoir*, students. Shall we do the Stroll? Girls on the right, boys on the left, *s'il vous plaît*."

I joined the lineup of girls across from the lineup of boys. Claudia stood next to me, a gold cross nestled in her décolletage, and ballet flats—authentic Capezio, I'd bet—on her skinny feet. I imagined a zipper running from my ankles to my thighs, as suggested in the pink booklet for optimum posture purposes. *Zip*.

Mlle Tremblay cued up a stroll-y ballad. First-in-line Gracie and Buck came together, held hands, and dipped and kicked their way down the center aisle.

I quickly counted off, calculating who my partner would be. Six down was Vernon and his high-water khakis; he wouldn't have been my first choice but wouldn't have been my last either. Claudia had clearly and fiendishly calculated where to place herself for a perfect Davis partnership.

One by one—really, two by two—impromptu couples came together to stroll down the centerline of the gym. Geraldine, the only girl wearing bobby socks instead of stockings, stepped on the toes of a boy I didn't recognize, and he dropped her hand like a hot potato. Thurston-Ann and Jimmy, who hadn't arrived together, of course, ended up across from, and mooning over, each other. The makeup phase of their most recent breakup seemed well underway.

Next up: Vernon and me.

But!

Vernon ducked out of line at the last second, and suddenly Davis was in his place.

Davis just—*just*, sigh—laced his fingers in mine and led me down the line. I looked over my shoulder to Claudia, who'd scotch-taped a smile to her face.

Instead of going back around for another Stroll, Davis and I went over to the snack table. He passed a bowl of chips my way, then bounced a few into his mouth.

I shivered.

"Cold?" he asked.

Before I could answer—not cold, smitten—Davis shrugged off his jacket and draped it over my shoulder like another skin. His jacket was him. Part of me wanted to string my arms through it so he would be holding me, but the other part of me thought of Claudia. I shrugged off his jacket and handed it back with a gracious southern thank-you.

Davis and I stayed like that, our backs to the snack table, shards of potato chips greasing our fingers, as Mademoiselle Tremblay segued to regular music. Gracie and Buck moved as one on the dance floor.

I didn't know what I'd have been doing at a dance in Manhattan, but it wouldn't have involved a boy with a dimple or a blue blazer. I didn't even try to say anything. There was no way to land a clever line. Clever didn't seem to be the point.

Davis nudged me. "You're supposed to ask me to dance."

"Why aren't you saying that to Claudia?"

"Any girl can ask any boy. Haven't you ever been to a girl-ask-boy mixer?"

I hadn't. I scanned for Claudia and saw she was doing a rather vigorous Twist. "Okay," I said. "Do you want to dance?"

"Hell, yes," he said, dimple fully deployed.

Out on the crowded dance floor, I focused on the weight of Davis's arm against my waist. For once, I was glad I'd wriggled into the girdle.

He was too tall for me to rest my chin on his shoulder— that's what Gracie was doing with Buck—but I was the right height for him to rest his chin atop my head. And that, I decided, was even better.

Claudia knocked on Davis's back the second the song was over. "Hey, you," she said, cheeks So Co flushed. Before Claudia could say more, she gave a loud belch, much louder than my Eleet tea gaffe. And by now I knew the pink booklet advised against ladies eructating in public.

———

As the music wound down, the posse drifted out the double doors and took up residence on the big set of steps toward the field.

Davis sat down next to me, not an inch between us. He lit a cigarette and blew a smoke ring that floated boldly into the air. "Good clear night. Stars out to the horizon."

My head was up, but my eyes were to him. "I can't do that—blow a smoke ring."

"You can." He put his cigarette in my mouth.

I hated smoking, but I wasn't thinking that. I was thinking this ciggie had been in his mouth and now it was in mine.

"Hold a little smoke in your mouth and then ooo it out—like you're thinking of something great," he said.

"I doubt Ruth smokes," Claudia said, bending down between us.

I tried it—the breathing in and ooo-ing out—but I coughed. "I'll practice," I said, though I wouldn't.

"What's your favorite constellation?" Davis asked someone, possibly me.

"The Dipper?" I said.

"Big or Little?" Claudia asked. "I'm guessing you don't see many stars in New York with those skyscrapers lit up."

"Little." I was little, so why not.

"Orion used to be my favorite," Davis said. "It's so easy to find in the winter—"

"Mm-hmm." Claudia leaned forward, her hair a velvety curtain across his shoulder.

"But now it's Cassiopeia," he said, disentangling himself from Claudia.

T-Ann stood up. "I have to go undecorate the gym."

"I'll help," I said.

"Stay here and help me look for Cassiopeia," Davis said. "Wouldn't that be nice? Nicer?"

It *would* be nice/nicer. It would be nice/nicer to be together with this boy with a wall-to-wall smile and a naturalist's knowledge of the sky.

"Fireworks time," T-Ann's Jimmy announced. He'd emerged at the edge of the woods, a lit twig in one hand, Oren by his side.

I squinted in the direction of the trees and saw the faintest of faint orange glows.

"What are you going to light, Oren?" Claudia giggled

and fell against T-Ann, who straightened her back up. "A football? A cross?"

"Claud," Gracie said, "I think that's your flask talking."

Claudia reached in her pocketbook and tugged out her monogrammed-with-a-wreath flask. She held it up to her nose. "Flask? Are you talking?"

"Cross lighting—like cross burning?" I said to Davis, because he was the one I was next to. The Teletype at home had been dinging out cross burnings, announcing fires on the lawns, the houses, the storefronts of Negro families.

Davis scuffed the step with the toe of his loafer. "What are you doing here, O?"

"Just having a little fun," Oren answered.

"Lightings are a celebration of southern spirit." Claudia nearly hissed. "Don't pretend you don't like a flame."

"I'm not pretending a single thing," Davis said.

And I thought: Speak for yourself. I'm pretending so much—hiding the Jewish situation along with my general New York neuroses—someone should give me a Tony.

"I'm not waiting for you, mealymouthed Davis Jefferson," Claudia said, pushing between us and jumping down the steps. "Come on, Oren!" She swayed toward the light, looking fierce.

Buck and Gracie drifted after her, and T-Ann had already gone to undecorate the gym, leaving Davis and me behind.

"Let's fly," Davis said. I flapped my wings and followed.

108

We walked, almost close enough to hold hands, through shoulder-high thickets and a clearing in a patch of tall trees—pines, perhaps—that ringed the edge of the gym.

"Good kindling." I picked up a couple of sticks, not more than an inch around. "We built a lot of fires at camp," I said. Except we had s'mores instead of s'alcohol.

"You trying to impress me with your pyrotechnics?" Davis asked.

"Are you impressed?"

"Very much," he said, snapping one of my sticks in two and putting a piece behind my ear like a flower.

But then we came to the clearing, and this fire wasn't like one I'd seen or set—ever.

In the middle of a circle of tamped-down red clay was a pyramid of sticks taller than Nattie. A giant cone of flame licked the twigs and seemed inclined to burn the woods down.

"Good one, right?" Oren said. The fire stretched his mouth into a wild grin.

All around the fire, the sky looked charcoal, the flames sucking the light from the sky.

Every sense I'd ever had was head over heels. The crackle, the heat, the smoke lodged in my molars. I felt safe and warm, even though I was already safe and already warm, given I was at a school dance on an eighty-degree evening. Still. *Still.*

On the other side of the orange, Gracie waved to me, and

it was like her hand was on fire, sparking light, reminding me she was, this place was, full of luminescence. All I had to do was wave back to be part of the fireworks. And wave I did, though some inside part of me knew I was still something of an outsider.

Claudia, her skin a perfect copper in the gleam of the fire, trickled what was left in her flask over the flame. It flared blue for a second but then petered into nothing before Claudia swanned off on the arm of Oren.

***

And that was how Davis came to drive me home.

He cut the engine in front of the main house. "I'm dying to kiss you," he said. "But even northern girls probably don't do that on a first date."

I didn't say: Is this a date? I didn't say: I would have kissed on this date/not-date if you hadn't warned me I shouldn't.

"Here's what we're missing." Davis leaned over and put his hand under my hair. I could feel all five fingers whisper-touching my neck.

He was so close to me I only had to exhale. "Just so you know, I kiss on the second date."

9

The Southern Mount Rushmore

"Are you up? Are you up now? Wake up so we can go swimming." I opened my eyes to find Nattie standing over me, staring.

"Stop that! Don't be a weirdo." I turned over and listened for her to walk away. And she did.

But it was hot and I felt bad, so I got up anyway.

Nattie, already suited up, was gulping her cornflakes in the kitchen. I made my usual coffee, creamy and sugary.

Mother walked in from the main house. "Oh, good— you're up." She smoothed Nattie's hair, which was a mess. "The society editor called in sick, so I'm covering a wedding on Stone Mountain. What do you say? Come along? It'll be ten degrees cooler."

"I'll stay here. I want to swim," Nattie said.

"Actually, it's not a choice, honey. I want you both there," Mother said. "Unpleasant things happen on Stone Mountain, and I want you to see it."

"Where there're lightings?" I asked. Stone Mountain was prominent in Mr. Hank's news roundups.

"Lightings?" Mother said. "If you mean cross burnings, then yes—that exactly."

The coffee sloshed around my tongue. "Lightings are supposedly a celebration of southern spirit—that's what this girl Claudia says."

"I sincerely hope Claudia is not a close friend," Mother said.

"Oh, she's not."

"Are we going to see a cross on fire?" Nattie asked. "I don't want to."

"It's good to see what happens even when it's not happening." Mother ran her fingers through Nattie's hair, somehow wrangling it into a respectable braid. "And, Ruthie—bring your notebook. I could use you on the fashion aspect. You know I can't tell organza from organdy."

"Organdy is usually cotton," I said, but Mother had ducked into the bathroom to put on her face.

Nattie and I changed into what I now thought of as tea dresses—soft of color and swingy of skirt. Soon we were off in the Savoy, lurching east, past the outskirts of Atlanta along a four-lane road, then a two-lane road—Mother driving, me front-seating with an eye on Nattie in the back. Nattie had brought along a pocketbook filled with rainbow index cards to make her precise notes; she was now organizing them by color.

———

A half hour later, we pulled into the parking lot, and I was surprised, for some reason, to see Stone Mountain was an honest-to-goodness mountain, an eerie, nearly naked hunk of granite erupting out of the ground. Even more surprising: On the side facing us was the start of a carving chiseled into the stone.

"Why's there half a horse on the mountain?" Nattie asked.

"Let's have a look," Mother said. We walked to the edge of the lot and stared up.

The carving wasn't so very big. Almost people-sized. And it wasn't only horses or half horses—two half soldiers were atop them.

"Are there carvings on every side?" Nattie asked.

"Just the one," Mother said. "From everywhere else, it looks like a gray egg of a mountain. Some call it the great southern Mount Rushmore."

"Great?" I asked. Nothing about it seemed especially great.

"When I was Nattie's age," Mother said, "the Daughters of the Confederacy commissioned it to honor the Confederate troops. The group ran out of money after Robert E. Lee, but I hear they're back on a fundraising tear and the state is set to buy the place. Stonewall Jackson and Jefferson Davis may make it yet."

Jefferson Davis, Davis Jefferson—once I thought of Davis and his tribute name, transposed though it might be, I couldn't forget the feeling of his fingers cradling the back of my neck. I held my hand on that spot and craned to get a better look.

The mountain sat against a perfect sky, a riot of wildflowers bloomed nearby, and the strong sun warmed our shoulders—it was a postcard for how gorgeous Atlanta could be. Except. Except: Carved Confederates were half blasted into the mountain, and beyond the wildflowers there were clearings used to host cross burnings once the strong sun went down.

"I can't decide if it looks real or looks phony," Nattie said.

"It's real, honey," Mother said. "But now let's find the other reason we're here. The more joyful reason." We followed Mother to a fancy inn on the far side of the parking area. "Looks like a wedding setup to me," she said without much oomph, pointing to a garden with a gazebo festooned with roses.

"Why's this news?" Nattie asked, not caring that her Mary Janes were sinking into the red clay. I high-stepped it to avoid the same muddy fate.

Mother smiled. "It's for the society page. All the vows that are fit to print."

"What makes a wedding society-worthy?" I asked, but even as I said it, I bet the answer was in the pink booklet.

"Depends where you are. Here in Atlanta or thereabouts," Mother said, gesturing to the grounds, "if you're the bride, it's a matter of what club your family belongs to, and what church you go to, and what your daddy does for a living or what his daddy before him did. And if you're the groom, it's a matter of where you were graduated from—University of Virginia, Duke, Ole Miss, Emory, more or less in that order, plus, of course, Georgia, not the most original choice, and the occasional Princeton for the real intellectuals."

"Was your wedding in the paper?" Nattie asked. "In the society pages?"

"Your dad and I eloped."

Which was something I had not known. I could picture their black-and-white wedding photo in a carved wooden frame, Mother beaming in a light suit and Dad looking at her adoringly, his mouth to her ear. It never occurred to me no one else was in the shot.

"What did Fontaine have to say about that?" I asked.

"Not a lot, and that was the point." Mother spun a button of her blouse around until I thought it might fly right off.

I wondered if they eloped because of the Jewish situation, and the wondering made my stomach hurt.

"C'mon, let's find a spot to observe," Mother said. The up-front rows were filled with fetchingly dressed guests. We settled into chairs in the past-last row, and Mother gave Nattie and me assignments while we waited for the service to begin. Nattie had the job of recording little facts on her index cards. "And, Ruth, take in what people are wearing. Write fast," Mother said. "We can make sense of the notes later."

"I don't write fast, though." I thought fast but wrote slow.

"There's a trick," Mother said. "Find me a blank page in your notebook."

I took my EZ-on-the-Eyes notebook out of my pocketbook and flipped past the list of clothes I'd wanted to buy and the books I'd wanted to read and the boys I'd wanted to like me (I'd have to add Davis) until I found a blank sheet, and handed the notebook over.

Mother scribbled. "What's this say?"

"Let me see," Nattie said, grabbing it first. She scanned the words. "Gibberish."

I peered over her shoulder. Mother had written: *Th KKK cn hld mtngs hr fr prptty.*

"The Ku Klux Klan can hold meetings here for . . . pretty? For property?" I said. I'd heard more about the Klan—and what Mr. Hank called its riffraff ways, against not only Negroes but Jews and homosexuals—than I'd ever heard in the North.

"Perpetuity," Mother said. "The Klan considers the mountain sacred ground. But that's not my point at the moment. My point is: Leave out the vowels and you'll write fast as a fox."

"You know what else has no vowels?" Nattie said. "The Torah."

I remembered that—the rabbi taught us that the Hebrew letters were the word's body and the vowels were its soul. The reader had to add the vowels, the soul, to breathe life into every word.

"You always teach me something new." Mother gave Nattie's braid a tug.

As Mother started taking her vowel-less notes, I found myself twisting around in my chair to check the Stn Mntn summit for any inkling of crosses. Some of the trees tapered at the top in a way that made me think of pointy hoods, and I wondered if Davis, Mr. Naturalist, would know the species. I tried to imagine the summit dotted with actual white hoods poking up like bleached thorns.

I rubbed my arms, feeling those thorns poking right up through my skin.

A string quartet struck up something string-y, and a line of bridesmaids in sky-blue dresses walked down the aisle partnered with guys in gray suits. Later, one of the bridesmaids, who had on enough hair spray to asphyxiate the bridal party, told me the bride's dress had seventy-seven buttons.

The musicians started up the wedding march, and the bride entered on the arm of her father. Her dress was an organza (not organdy) tea-length number with a sweetheart neckline and a short-sleeved organza jacket with a dramatic collar. Said another way: *swthrt nck wth orgnz jckt.*

The bride looked twenty, tops—about the same age as Sara, though there was no evidence Sara was of the marrying mind. Still, the back of *Seventeen* and *Mademoiselle* were filled with ads for china and silver patterns—Fontaine had been asking which ones I liked; "A girl should know her own taste," she'd said—and it gave me a fizzy feeling in my throat to see this organza girl and think she could be Sara or, someday, me.

"Who gives this bride in marriage?" the minister asked.

"Her father does," the man said. He placed a delicate kiss atop the bride's veil.

I reached out for Nattie's hand, and I saw she was holding her breath something fierce, her cheeks puffed out, her eyes fluttery.

"You want to take a walk?" I whispered, and she exhaled. "Or should we wait until they kiss—the bride and the boy?"

"Kiss?" she said. "Ew, let's go now."

Mother gave us permission with a nod.

We didn't have the right shoes for an actual walk, so we headed under the low canopy of a tree that might have been a willow. I held back a branch, delicate and swoopy, so Nattie could cross under, and we stood together amid leaves and tall grasses that left little bits of dew on our dresses.

"You okay?" I asked.

"Look at that." Nattie pointed to a small brass plaque nailed into the tree, listing the mountain's height and such. "No one would ever see that hiding here."

I picked a leaf from the tree and started shredding it into skinny green matchsticks. "Why do you hold your breath?"

She shrugged, copying the wording of the plaque exactly on one of her index cards: "The carvings on Stone Mountain are three times as big as Mount Rushmore. On a clear day, you can see more than forty-five miles from the top of the mountain."

"Don't stop breathing, okay?" I said.

"That's what happened to Dad." Her fingers were inky. "He stopped breathing."

My eyes instantly welled up. "He did."

She nodded, slowly at first and then sort of frantically.

We stood together in the shelter of the willow, or whatever it was, watching the leaves sway, hiding us, then not-hiding us, then hiding us.

———

By the time we wound our way back to the roses, the ceremony was over, and the bride and groom were smiling for photos. The bride's gown had collected twigs in its hem.

Mother was still scribbling. "Let's see what you girls got," she said, and we handed over our notes. She scanned quickly, a pencil behind her ear keeping company with a pearl earring that must have been Fontaine's. "Good, good."

"Dad won't be here to walk any of us to our weddings." Nattie held on to her braid.

Maybe Mother teared up, or maybe the sun was in her eyes. "I'll be there." She said it right away. "I'll walk each of you down every single aisle we find."

Nattie leaned into Mother the way Frooshka leaned into me.

Mother looped one arm around Nattie and scribbled

away with the other. "That's the other reason I wanted you to see this place."

"Because you needed to cry?" Nattie asked.

"I cry every day, Natalie. No, I wanted you to see the beauty side by side with ugliness. If one of these nights you see a flicker on this mountain—not that you could really see it from Atlanta, but putting that aside for the moment—you need to know that along with organdy and happiness, there's a hatred we can't look away from. Two years ago, thirty-five hundred Knights of the Ku Klux Klan stood on this mountain, lit three large crosses, and declared that being white—not Negro, not Jewish—made you as solid as Stone Mountain."

That sent a chill straight down my throat. "Can we go to the top?" I asked, shading my eyes and looking up. "Is there a trail?"

Mother put down her notebook. "There used to be, on the other side. I'd sometimes climb here with girlfriends on a sunny afternoon."

"Did it seem strange?" I asked. "To hike among the half-carved Confederates?"

"We didn't give it a second thought. But we're not exactly dressed for an expedition today."

You'd think I would have cared about that, but what I cared about was seeing the spot where the hate happened.

Back in the parking lot, we dropped our pocketbooks in the Savoy and found a wooden sign carved with yellow letters for the Walk-Up Trail—one mile to the summit.

***

We climbed single file—Nattie, then me, then Mother. The ascent was gentle to start, skipping over smooth stones, but the trail soon turned heart-thumpy. The ground was strewn with rocks, with tall grasses, their roots forced up through the stone, and with little yellow daisies that were impossible not to love. It was hard to keep our footing, Nattie in her slick-soled Mary Janes, and Mother and me in low-heeled pumps. I tried to imagine hauling a pine cross and a jug of kerosene up this path. I tried to imagine hating someone enough to strike a match.

Nattie hummed a ditty over and over and over, and Mother was silent for what must've been twenty minutes.

At the top, there were giant depressions in the stone, little ponds filled with water, filled with life, filled with shrimp—of all things to be filled with. The rest of the summit was moonlike. There were no signs of burnings. Maybe the ash had floated off the mountain into the ether of constellations.

Maybe, but I couldn't really tell because it was foggy at the top. We stayed a few minutes, then reversed ourselves, silently sliding back to the security of the Savoy.

In the car, we took off our shoes; Mother drove back stocking-footed.

She filed the story from home, banging away on her Underwood portable typewriter, the carriage dinging every time she got to the end of a line, announcing her progress. My seventy-seven-buttons detail led off the piece, and Mother worked in Nattie's best fact—about how very far you could see from the top of the mountain. Even though that day the promised view was nowhere in sight.

10

Lemonade with Communist Overtones

Just before four that same day, I headed to the main house and pulled Fontaine's trick—knocking and walking right in—ready to learn the fine art of writing a regret.

"Hey there, sugar—in here," Fontaine called from the garden room. She was straightening a pile of stationery at her writing desk, its leather surface the color of an avocado. While the guesthouse was light and white and spongy with carpet, the main house was shade and shadow and hardwood. "Sit," she commanded, and I thought of Frooshka, who was in the backyard with Mr. Hank. "The point of a regret is to make the hostess sad you are unable to attend—so sad she'll keep you on the list for next time."

"I don't need to say the reason, right?" I had checked the pink booklet.

"Nope. It's always—*always*—about next time. Keep that in mind." Fontaine tapped her forehead.

I hadn't told Fontaine why I needed to decline the Eleets' next T&E meeting, but I assumed she knew—knew about Mother and the rabbi and his cause. Fontaine had a way of knowing things without anything being said. There was a lot of unsaidness in the air. Maybe it had something to do with the air-conditioning, which was groaning in the late-day heat. Maybe the air chiller, as Fontaine called it, took all the hot air molecules and made them more agreeable, rounding the hard edges off the truth.

I pulled a petite wooden chair alongside Fontaine. In the center of her desk, next to a cup of fountain pens, she had a stack of thick note cards with a leaf motif. I ran my finger over the leaf, feeling its ridges.

"That's engraved, as proper stationery should be," Fontaine said. "Use your best cursive and don't crowd your letters together."

I took a fountain pen in hand and wrote:

Dear Mrs. Eleet,
    Thank you for your invitation for Tea and Etiquette on the tenth.

Fontaine took the card out of my hands and ripped it down the middle. "No one likes a girl with bad handwriting. And never start with 'thank you.' Totally unoriginal, and we both know you are an original, Ruthie."

I tried again, concentrating on the down stroke of each letter, imagining Fontaine was my third-grade teacher who'd made me stay inside from recess one day and write an entire page of capital Q's. I would use no capital Q here, that was for sure.

Dear Mrs. Eleet,
    How kind of you to invite me for Tea and Etiquette on the tenth.

Fontaine tucked my second attempt away. "Why don't you try to work in the word 'generous'—everyone likes to be thought of as generous. And create some enthusiasm."

I took a third card, lamenting that Fontaine seemed to have an endless supply.

Dear Mrs. Eleet,
    How I wish I could attend the etiquette dinner on Thursday. I am certain it will be a delightful evening of conversation and education, and I

only hope you can forgive my absence. I thank you for your generosity.

"Lovely," Fontaine said. "And by the by, Millie may be the T and E chair, but real southern tradition is passed down generation to generation. We have five generations in the ground here. There's nothing Millie Eleet can teach that I can't tell you better myself. As a for-instance, if you're wondering about the placement of an oyster fork, it goes to the right of the spoons."

"I've never had an oyster," I said. I didn't add: Oysters aren't kosher. Though Dad had been known to order a BLT once in a blue moon.

"You will. No doubt you will have an oyster, and soon. Millie Eleet can help with that kind of minutia. But opening your world like an oyster? That's my job." Fontaine smiled so genuinely. "And I relish it."

I picked at a thread on my skirt. "I learned velvet has a season, and this is not it."

"Clear as a bell. Here's a less obvious one: Don't serve pink lemonade. It has communist overtones."

"You're kidding."

"Only a very little bit." Fontaine smiled. "Let's have a nip of Dubonnet. It's not a bad thing to learn to sip in the privacy of your own home." She went to a side table, where two small glasses were already set out. "Or mine."

"Did someone tell you about the Southern Comf—"

"Of course. Whatever your question, the answer is of course. Of course someone told me."

We both laughed, and the Teletype rang out—three dings, not a big story—like it was in on the joke. She poured us each a thimbleful of liquor from a deep-green bottle.

"To you, dear Ruth." Fontaine downed the drink in a long sip and poured another.

"And to you, Fontaine," I said, taking a minuscule swallow.

Fontaine was three thimbles in when she said, "You're a Landry, even though you're masquerading as a Robb. Your father, the bighearted Arthur Robb, was a good man—yes, he was. I'm sorry he's gone, but I'm happy you're here." She clinked her empty glass into my full one.

And I felt both, side by side—sorry to be here and happy to be here.

"We will meet again for Dubonnet and Landry family lessons. In the meantime, you walk your note over to Mrs. E. Off you go. And take that dog of yours."

———

Frooshka was sprawled out poolside. The whole scene—the pair of chaises, the pitcher of (not-pink) lemonade, the striped umbrella—was perfection, as if it had been lifted from a photo of a vacation the Robb family had never actually taken.

Mr. Hank sat in the shade, his glasses pushed down his nose, a stack of Teletype bulletins at his side, his cane at his feet.

"How'd Stone Mountain strike you?" he asked. Before I could answer, he said, "Scratch that. Let me ask you—how many Negroes did you go to school with in New York?"

"I was going to say strange—for Stone Mountain. But for Negroes—a few." Our school integrated before I started kindergarten, long before it was law.

"Don't think the South has a monopoly on racism."

"I don't." But a clang in my chest made me think maybe I did.

"Still, no two ways around it, it's worse here." He lit up a cigar. I half gagged.

"The Supreme Court ruling a few years back to desegregate—Brown versus Board of Ed in '54? People called it a day of mourning."

"Not Mother and Dad—they went to a party to celebrate."

He blew out a puff of smoke. "I wrote an editorial praising the decision. Got invited to a few less golf games, not that I'm a fan of golf. The kicker was a good one."

"The kicker? Are we talking football now?"

Mr. Hank laughed, but in a not-mean way. "At a paper,

the kicker is the last line of a piece—the one that kicks the reader in the teeth. The one they'll remember."

"Oh." I thought not for the first time that Dad, with his word-li-ness, would have made a great reporter. "Do you remember it, your kicker?"

"Course. I spent an hour on it." He cleared his throat and recited: " 'There's a new math in town—separate is no longer equal, and we must right our wrongs, rumor by rumor, school by school.' "

"That's good—the 'rumor by rumor.' "

"I thought so. But you know how our neighbors here responded? Our neighbors who favor 'gradualism'—gradually bringing the races together over God knows how many years? Our neighbors . . ." He brandished his cigar in the direction of the magnolias. I followed the lit end and saw nothing but loveliness—the flowers, the pool, the sky. "They built a pernicious academy—a *private* academy—that didn't have to follow the federal law."

"You mean Covenant?"

He nodded. "It's not the only one, but—"

"Then why send us there?"

The smell of Mr. Hank's cigar mixed with something too ripe in the garden. It settled into a sour taste in my throat.

"It's hard to argue with Fontaine." He swung his cigar this way and that. "And the truth is, we're a long way from integration. You know, the University of Georgia, our own UGA, doesn't accept Negro students? I hear there's a plan afoot to offer scholarships to send them out of state."

"Fontaine says there are Jews at Covenant, but I haven't met any." I wasn't going out of my way, of course.

He shrugged. "The whole integration climate inflames the Klan. There was a time the Klan had local politicians and businessmen as members—not that I agreed with them then either, not that I'd ever agree with a white Christian supremacist organization. But now? Now it's riffraff and more riffraff. Couple months ago, a Klansman in Marietta announced he couldn't decide if he wanted to blow up a Negro house or kill a Jew."

I snapped a leash on Frooshka, not feeling so great about going to a school built solely for segregation. I ruffled Froo's crazy-curly hair, not so very different from mine. "The poodle—the Jew-dle—and I will be back."

"That right there," Mr. Hank said, finally stubbing out his cigar, "is a damn fine kicker."

The heat radiated up around Frooshka and me as we strolled to the Eleets'. I was in my knock-around clothes—an old bandana-print skirt an inch (or two) too short, a white blouse tied at the waist, and tennies. There was no one else out and about, just the distant sound of a lawn mower as we turned the corner to West Paces and then Arden.

I was about to slip the don't-start-with-thank-you note in the mailbox when Gracie yelled "Say hey" from the columned porch.

Froo dragged me up the steps, and I saw Gracie wasn't alone. Sprawled on the wicker chairs were Davis and Buck in red Covenant T-shirts and shorts.

Davis jumped to his feet. "Hey, Babe Ruth."

I worried a little that liking Davis was like thinking Elvis Presley was hubba-hubba—too easy, too predictable. But like him I did.

"What are y'all doing here?" I asked, letting that "y'all" slip right off my tongue. Davis might live right next door, for all I knew.

"We're here a lot," Buck said. "What are *you* doing here?"

"Dropping this off." I put the envelope down near Gracie's drink, hoping she wasn't inclined to open it now and see my not-up-to-par handwriting.

A ceiling fan with varnished wooden blades beat at the air.

"You want a drink, Roo? Can I call you Roo?" Gracie asked. "It fits you better somehow than Ruth." She slipped her fingers into her empty glass and fished out an ice cube for Frooshka, who gratefully chewed it up.

"Sure," I said. "Sure to both."

Gracie got up and stretched her legs, slipping the note into the pocket of her fern-green skirt. Her fern-green skirt that was, of course, the proper length.

"Hey," Davis said, now standing exactly next to me. "I'll keep the dog out here while you refresh the drinks." He was close enough I could see that group of freckles, a constellation of them, on his eyelids.

I handed over Froo's leash, and she leaned right into him. He passed the poodle test.

Once we were inside, Gracie said, "Y'all are kind of cute together."

"The poodle and me?" But I knew what she meant, and I liked what she meant.

"You and Davis. The game, the mixer, the porch." Gracie handed me a Coke.

I took a sip. "What about Claudia? She'll hate me. She'll hate me more."

"That die was probably already cast. I should tell you, though, the last girl who tussled with Claudia transferred to public school."

I thought of Mr. Hank's comment about how, why, and when Covenant sprang to life. "That wouldn't be the worst thing in the world, would it?"

"Well! Depends who you ask on that one." Gracie tilted

her head and looked right at me. "I'm glad you're here, Roo." She said it in this very straightforward, non-sugarcoated way—like it was simply a fact. And I was struck that in one afternoon two people had told me the same very lovely thing.

"Let's talk about something other than Claudia—or Davis Jefferson," I said.

"Agreed! Enough with boys, boys, boys."

"*Garçons, garçons, garçons,*" I echoed. Gracie and I had French together with French-braided Mademoiselle Tremblay.

"Is French harder here or in New York?" Gracie asked.

I shrugged. "It's easy in both places." I didn't add: I'm good at languages—for instance, Hebrew.

"I want to spend a year in Paris like Jacqueline Bouvier Kennedy." Gracie closed her eyes like she was dreaming in French, and I took note of her admiration for another former New Yorker, like *moi.* "Jacqueline spent her junior year at the Sorbonne and said it was the high point of her life. Not marrying the handsome senator. But studying in Paris—by herself."

"I wonder if *Mademoiselle* started in Paris? The magazine, not the person."

"Most likely."

"Maybe I could work there in Paris. Why not?" Who would have guessed I'd be living in Atlanta. Paris was as likely/unlikely.

"Doesn't that sound *incroyable*?" Gracie said.

It did sound *incroyable*, but before I could add my *deux* cents, someone—Davis—yelled: "Wait! *Stop!* Dog! Poodle!"

I banged through the screen door to see Frooshka in full sprint.

"Chipmunk!" Davis said, by way of explanation. He ran after Froo. I ran after him.

Frooshka, in hot pursuit of a woodland creature, took off toward a tall stone fence and scampered up and over.

"Shitshitshitshitshit!" I screamed.

"I'll get her," Davis said.

I backed up a few steps and bounced up and down on the balls of my feet. Then I charged the fence.

I got my hands on the ledge and hoisted myself up, hoping to get at least one foot on top before throwing myself the rest of the way over. It wasn't pretty, but I made it.

"Holy smokes," Davis said behind me before he veered off somewhere.

On the other side of the fence was a large, fancy garden. It took a second for me to see that many of the shrubs were sculpted into cones and spirals and such. And there was Frooshka, fiercely sniffing the grass under the shade of a giant orb.

I yanked her leash.

Davis had walked the long way around and was leaning against an impressively tall tree. It turned out I needn't have done my hurdler imitation. The fence ran only in front of the house, not on the sides. The grandeur was just for show.

"Who clips all their ivy into shapes?" I asked, still catching my breath.

"The Harrises do—this is their place. And it's not ivy— these are yews. English yews."

"How can you possibly know?" I said, smoothing my skirt back down and walking back in the direction of the street. I wondered how much of my slip and gunders were on display when I'd hopped the fence. "I didn't mean for you to see all that."

He paused to look at me. His eyes were a good blue—not intense enough to look fake. "You New York girls know how to chase down your animals."

Froo trotted faithfully beside me, unaware of what I'd done on her behalf.

"The yew," I said, even though I didn't care about it. "How do you know the name for some bush?"

"It's a tree, a conifer. I spend a lot of time outside." He pinched off a leaf with a cluster of purple berries. "Beautyberry," he announced. "There are lots of specimens here. Black walnut, loblolly pine—" He stopped again and looked at me. "I can't believe you. You're not like any girl around here, that's for damn sure."

"Because I swear? And run after my dog?"

He shook his head, and that hair of his flopped forward. "Didn't you say you kiss on the second date?"

"Are you saying this is a date?" Then I remembered I wanted to think about something other than boys. What came out of my mouth without my permission was: "Do you know the story behind Covenant?"

"Who cares?" The sun streamed down in little fingers through the trees, whatever species they might have been. Right there on the Harrises' brick walkway, surrounded by shrubs—trees—clipped into odd shapes, Davis laced his fingers under my hair. Who cares, indeed.

Even though it was a jillion degrees out, a chill ran down me, nose to toes.

Then he leaned down, confident hair and confident boy, and kissed me. He tasted like Coca-Cola.

He broke off to look at me a minute and pull a sprig of something out of my hair. And we kissed again for five seconds, five minutes, Frooshka lying on my feet the whole time, like my kissing this boy was an everyday occurrence.

"I've got to go," I said, thinking too much of what Mother—or Claudia—would say.

"I have an idea for our third date. Ruth, go to the Fall Ball with me."

I thought about Fontaine, who'd be pleased as non-communist punch.

I thought about how many Saturday services I'd have to sit through in exchange for the dance. I thought about how I'd break the news to Mother that I was falling—fast and deep—for the frippery after all.

Then, of course, I said yes.

11

The Rabbi and the Rebel

Mother was in a panic. The rabbi and the rebel were coming to dinner, and somehow she'd forgotten she didn't cook. Dad had always made dinner in New York—well, Dad and Shanghai Palace, which we'd had delivered twice a week—and since arriving in Atlanta, we'd been living off the leaning tower of frozen casseroles. Two days ago, someone had left a "Lazy-Day Lasagna" on our doorstep, and the week before, we got a delivery of Hawaiian chicken with pineapple and paprika.

Apparently, it was bad manners to serve frozen food to company, so Fontaine had sent Birdie over to fix up her fluffy meatloaf. The way Birdie was slamming drawers around, she seemed none too pleased.

Nattie didn't much notice. She still looked gloomy more than any of us liked. Nattie's sole request was that we change into plaid—a skirt for me and a jumper for her, in like-minded tartan. The dress-alike thing cheered her a bit.

Birdie had moved on to stabbing cubes of cheese with frilly toothpicks when the doorbell sang its Dixie song.

Mother quickly fastened the hook and eye of her skirt—paisley, A-line—then opened the door.

"Bienvenue."

"What does that mean?" Nattie whispered, standing so close to me our two plaids melded into one.

"It means Mother is nervous."

The rabbi shrugged off his blazer and fisted it, all casual. His daughter, Leah, handed Mother a jar of peach preserves and Nattie a brand-new deck of cards. Max, no respectable jacket in sight, smiled and, for some reason, my heart sped up a half beat. Then I thought of Max and his "I don't have time for a girlfriend," and Max and his arrogance, and Max and his too-big glasses, and—*and!*—Davis, of course, Davis and our upcoming Fall Ball, which I'd yet to mention to Mother. I slid Max to the side of my mind.

Nattie sat next to Leah on the too-white carpet, shuffled the deck, and started a game of Spit.

Mother squeezed past the card table I'd helped Birdie set up, half in the foyer, half in the kitchen, holding her own gin and tonic in one hand and a tray of cocktails in the other. Perhaps with the help of Beefeater, she'd regained her composure—even her pageboy had put itself back in place.

The ceiling fan lifted the rabbi's hair straight up. "If we're going to talk about an alliance to integrate Atlanta, let's start tonight. Let's come together for a common cause."

Birdie came in with a platter of appetizers.

"Do you want to sit and join us?" Max asked Birdie, helping himself to a Triscuit. "Join our conversation? About integration?"

Birdie tilted her head. "I'm working, thank you."

Mother took a long sip of gin.

"And at my church, we're having plenty of conversations," Birdie said.

I saw then that the rabbi's shirt was blotched with sweat at the collar. "Reverend Ingram and I are allies," he said.

"Mm-hmm," Birdie said, mouth tight. "I'm sure you are great allies, sir."

The conversation made me wish I could take a long sip of Mother's drink, too.

The rabbi stood up and shook Birdie's hand. Her eyes flew to the ceiling for a second, but she shook back. "I know some people think this is not my fight," he said. "I feel—and my conscience feels and my teachings tell me—it is. We've been fighting for ten years to live justly in unjust times, and we keep on fighting."

Birdie stepped back into the kitchen without another word.

Max cupped a handful of peanuts. He offered a few to Nattie, who popped them in her mouth. She didn't even like peanuts, but she seemed to like Max. I tried to see Max like Nattie did—to look past the owlish eyebrows to see the charm of a guy who was generous with snacks and working to make the world a fairer place.

The rabbi nodded. "It's the goal—should be—of American Jews—"

"Nattie?" I said. "Kitchen." I'm sure the rabbi was a good man and he was saying things I agreed with—*of course* I agreed with him—but my debutante deal with Mother didn't include sitting through lectures, and anyway I wanted to go see Birdie.

"I'll help," Leah said.

"And me," Max said. He whispered, "I've heard this before—a hundred times."

Birdie was unmolding the Jell-O ring, topping it with dollops of mayonnaise with a hard flick of her wrist.

"Miss Ruth, cut the flowers on the angle," Birdie said. "Miss Natalie, you and your friend can help."

Nattie handed me dahlias from the garden. I snipped the

stems while Max peppered Birdie with questions. Where did she live? Did she have children? Were they in school? What was her church? Did she have a mister?

I listened for the answers. It said something not very nice about me that I had seen Birdie every day for the five or so weeks we'd been here and didn't know important things about her (I knew she had kids, of course, but I was blurry on other key details). And it said something about Max that he felt entitled to breeze into someone else's house and ask whatever popped into his head of a Negro woman, who might have felt compelled to answer.

"You're being presumptuous." I pointed at Max with the garden shears.

"No violence, Ruth Robb," he said, smile in place.

Meanwhile, Birdie answered Max's questions without fuss but without looking at him either: Southeast; two daughters; one at Spelman College and one working for the phone company; Ebenezer Baptist with Reverend Martin Luther King Sr.; and she did—but he passed a year ago.

"Sorry to hear," Max said.

"Like us," Nattie said, turning to Birdie.

"Exactly, sugar," Birdie said, squeezing Nattie's hand.

"Sorry about your dad," Max said to me. He was down on the floor scratching Frooshka behind the ear. I crouched and took the other ear, wondering if Birdie went home to an empty house, wondering how she could afford to send her daughter to college, wondering what she would be doing if she weren't employed by Fontaine and Mr. Hank.

"I'm making place cards," Nattie announced, and I realized I hadn't worried about her all night, and that made me not-hate Max even more.

"Why ever?" Leah asked.

"We'll be squished, Nattie." I took Max's offer of a hand up from the linoleum. "I don't think we need to bother with place cards."

"We do! More than four people and we have to have them," Nattie said. "We find our seat and bon appétit." To Leah, she added, "It says so in this pink book." Quoting the pink booklet was serious business for Nattie, but she surprised me by busting into giggles.

I hoisted myself onto the kitchen counter. Max hoisted himself up next to me.

"Who knew fomenting a little revolution could be so funny," I said.

Birdie was spooning a lemon sauce over the asparagus—fomenting a little hollandaise—and I stopped laughing, because my comment might not seem so very funny to her. As if Birdie could hear my thoughts, she shook her spoon toward Max and me. "Do not park yourselves on the counter, especially while food is being prepared."

In my mind, I added: Especially while food is being prepared by a Negro housekeeper for a group of white people
discussing integration.

I hopped right down, my neck astonishingly hot. "Thank
you, Birdie," I said, my usual refrain.

"Thanks for preparing dinner, ma'am," Max added.

In all the years I'd been visiting Fontaine and Mr. Hank,
I'd never before heard anyone in the house address Birdie as
"ma'am."

⸻

After a dinner during which the rabbi talked about the
"two" of everything—two drinking fountains; two places to
sit at the movies; two Bibles in a courtroom; two schools—
that he wanted to change to one, Mother brought out the
peach melba for dessert, and I brought out coffee and sugar
cubes.

The rabbi scooted his chair back from the table, gearing
up for another lecture. "So, Leo Frank," he said. "Does the
name ring a bell?"

Mother grabbed her EZ-on-the-Eyes notebook off the
counter.

"Mr. Frank was a Jew, raised in New York, as it happens."
The rabbi tied his napkin into a knot. "He was accused of
beating and strangling a thirteen-year-old girl named Mary

Phagan when she came to collect her paycheck at the pencil factory where he was a supervisor. This was some forty years ago."

"Strangled," I said, hand to my throat.

Max interrupted. "He was framed. His crime was being Jewish."

"It's rather a long story," the rabbi said.

I liked the rabbi well enough, but he didn't seem to know a short story, and I wasn't sure this was a story I wanted to hear, no matter its length.

The rabbi didn't pause. "The case had many twists in the testimony, and that, along with a whole lot of anti-Semitism, led to a conviction. Mr. Frank was sentenced to death," he said. "People lined the street, yelling 'Hang the Jew.' The governor, who believed he was innocent, reduced the sentence—"

"Remember—framed," Max repeated.

"—to life in prison." The rabbi tested the knot he'd tied in the napkin, and that was when it hit me that it wasn't a knot he'd tied. It was a noose. "Seven carloads of men calling themselves the Knights of Mary Phagan broke into the prison and took Mr. Frank, bound and gagged, to a park north of here—near where Miss Phagan grew up."

"Nattie," Mother said, "why don't you take Frooshka out for her evening stroll."

"I know the end," Leah said. "Dead."

The heat of the night, of this talk, snaked up my neck.

"Frooshka," Nattie called, her voice crackly. She stood up from Dad's chair, and the pillowy plastic deflated with a hiss.

"I'll come, too," I said, quick to my feet.

Mother shook her head almost imperceptibly. "I need you to know this, Ruth."

I was glad Birdie was gone. I didn't want her to hear us talk about lynching. But then I thought Birdie probably knew a lot more about it than I ever would, and probably knew about people who were closer to her than this man I'd never heard of who died decades ago would ever be to me. I sat back down.

"These men tied his ankles," the rabbi said.

I uncrossed mine. Mrs. Eleet's "What letter should a lady's legs make?" question popped into my head. Who cared about the curve of a calf if your ankles were tied together?

"They tied a hangman's noose," the rabbi said, fingering that noose in his napkin.

"Had Mr. Frank step up on a table. Threw a rope over the branch of a tree. An oak. Kicked the table away, and his head fell backward. He broke his neck."

None of us had touched our coffee. The air was sharp with chicory and dread. I palmed a sugar cube.

The rabbi nodded. "Not long after, those men, those Knights of Mary Phagan, who had been quiet for years, resurrected the Klan on top of Stone Mountain. Not twenty miles from here. In their white robes, they burned a cross fifty feet tall to celebrate the lynching of Leo Frank."

"We were up there," I said, something unpleasant bubbling up my throat. "We were just there—for a *wedding*. Did you know about Leo Frank?" I asked Mother. "Did you know?"

"I knew," she said, scribbling notes, her voice shaky. "Not everything, but I knew."

"Here's what I think is the worst part," the rabbi said.

Max put his hand next to mine for a second, then seemed to think better of it.

The rabbi reached into the front pocket of his shirt and pulled out a faded postcard. "People sold souvenirs."

That was the worst thing? Wasn't death the worst thing?

Mother picked up the postcard, then put the card on the table, facedown, so it was a blank, so it could be anything.

I turned the card over and shut my eyes nearly all the way. Through my squint, I saw a nightshirt and thin legs off the ground. Birdie's meatloaf rolled around my stomach.

"Now, the Frank tragedy is especially close because he was a member of our congregation," the rabbi said quietly. "He sat in our sanctuary." I imagined the light in the temple, the gold ark, the frosting flowers on the ceiling. "But all throughout Georgia," the rabbi continued, "from before Leo to after, six hundred Negro men were lynched. Some so close by, on roads we drive every day. Some castrated or set afire— then lynched."

I hadn't said anything in minutes. "I'm sorry," I said. "I'm sorry, I'm sorry," I said again.

The rabbi stood up. "The long shadow of Leo Frank leads us here, to helping with civil rights. We have much more work to do."

"What can we do *now*?" Mother flipped to an empty page in her steno book. She was ready to make a list.

"I've kept y'all too late for a school night," the rabbi said. "This will be the topic of my sermon for the High Holidays, but in the meantime, let's start with something simple," he said to Max and to me. "Every time you're thirsty, take a drink out of the colored persons' water fountain."

I thought: Birdie does that every day, and it's not a choice.

Nattie put herself to bed while Mother and I cleaned up—me washing, her drying, same as always.

I flipped on Dad's transistor radio. "Wake Up Little Susie" kept us company.

"You know, I've been letting you figure things out here,"

Mother said, elbowing me and shutting off the hot tap. "But it's time we talk, the two of us, no bullshit."

I'd only heard Mother swear once, when Dad dropped the Thanksgiving turkey on the floor and proceeded to pick it up with two spatulas only to drop it again.

"I thought we would talk when you went to *pre-*debutante training. Then I thought we'd talk when you went to a Christian school where, God knows, you must pray every day. Then I thought we'd talk when we went to temple." Mother got up, rooted around her bag, and lit a cigarette.

A throbbing started over my left eye. "Davis taught me how to blow smoke rings."

She stubbed out her cig, her disapproval implicit.

"Forget Davis and his smoke rings," Mother said. "I have a question." I almost expected her to grab her notebook to jot down my vowel-less answer. "How many people have asked if you're Jewish?"

"Not one. It's not like I've lied." The whole night—the rabbi, the napkin noose, the lack of Dad, all of it—sat there, between us. I added, almost apologetically, "I'm going to the Fall Ball with Davis Jefferson."

"The boy with the balloon?"

"You said I could make a trade—temple time for deb time."

Mother switched off the radio. "Sit down, Ruthie."

I sat in Dad's place, letting the plastic stick to my legs.

"You're passing—you're trying to pass," Mother said.

"Pass what?" I asked, eyeing the salt and pepper. Just last night, Nattie informed me, courtesy of the pink booklet, one should pass the salt and pepper together, as a pair.

"Don't bend who you are to fit with the pre-deb girls or this boy with the balloon."

Frooshka started barking her head off at something outside.

"Froo," we both yelled.

It gave me time to figure out what I wanted to say. "You think I shouldn't bend? You brought us here. You moved us in with your parents. You sent us to Covenant." I caught my breath galloping right out of my chest. "What do you expect me to do now? Bring a menorah to homeroom? It's never going to happen."

"Ruthie, I did what's best for us." She puffed her cheeks out, full of air, and then oofed all her breath out. "Everything is hard here. Everything is blue. Nattie, with all her bubbling underwater, knows this better than we do, I think."

"It doesn't feel that way at *all*." Dad—definitely blue. The lynching of Leo Frank—blue. But the mixer, Davis, Gracie and her sweet tea and sweet dresses and *sucre* talk—not blue, not blue, not blue.

Mother reached across the table to me. "To lose a husband—so young! So young there was no plan to think about losing him. To lose the father of your children. To lose—for all of us to lose—the city we call home. And to arrive here to the hatred of segregation."

"There was hate in New York, too," I said. "Mr. Hank reminded me of that."

"Not like this." Mother lit a cigarette again. The ash grew and grew before she took a drag. And then she surprised me with her throaty laugh. "And you're right, too. Not everything is blue. The only light in the sky can't be from the cross burnings—it can't."

I knew we couldn't see Stone Mountain from here, but I checked out the window anyway in case the sky was orange. It wasn't.

Mother turned off the fluorescent overhead. The glow of her cigarette made the room half-light/half-dark, both things at the same time. And that in-between-ness made the distance—between her and me, Dad and not-Dad, Manhattan and Atlanta—as fleeting as a flick of ash.

12

VistaVision

I had Sara on the phone, assessing wardrobe options. "There's the red-and-white rose dress, but those're school colors. I don't want to look too rah-rah." I kept my voice low. The phone sat on the built-in shelf in the little foyer, open season for eavesdroppers. Mother would be ticked I was talking about fashion and boys; one or the other was bad enough, but both together would confirm my superficiality.

"Believe me, it doesn't matter if you wear red or purple or poo brown." Sara exhaled, and I wondered if she was smoking a ciggie, which she'd promised Dad she would stop. "Keep David waiting. Seven minutes is my rule. If you come out too soon, he'll think you're easy."

"Not David. *Davis.*"

After the briefest pause, she added, "You could go to a movie by yourself, you know. I hope you have a good time, but you don't need a boy to have fun."

I could hear the distance pulse through the receiver, a reminder that Sara was there and I was here, and vice versa.

"I've been having fun," I said, in a tone I feared had taken on a shade of Mother's blue.

"Really?" Sara exhaled long and slow. Between Nattie's inhaling and Sara's exhaling, I couldn't get away from audible breathing.

I corkscrewed the phone cord around my finger. "Fontaine had me try on Mother's Magnolia gown. Did you know she was queen of everything here?"

Sara was quiet for a second. "She was a queen in New York, too. The library committee and the poetry readings. And the temple stuff. She just didn't have a crown."

"Are you trying to tell me I'm shallow?"

She laughed. "You *are* shallow! But you can be shallow and deep at the same time. Water is water."

"What does that mean, water is water?"

"Is that a Gertrude Stein poem?" Sara asked herself. Oh, please. She and Max were pretentious peas in a pod. "Nope, don't think so. I mean, even if you're in the shallow end, you're in the pool. Not the literal pool. Well, the literal pool, but also the pool of—"

I heard the *click-click* of Mother's heels from the kitchen. "Gotta go!" I whispered.

"Wait! Don't let him feel you up yet!"

The receiver was innocently cradled in its base by the time Mother walked in. She tilted her head. "Are you on the telephone?"

"No." I wasn't currently.

Mother followed me to our room and sat, legs akimbo, wearing one of her many pairs of black capris, while I changed into a dress with a pale-blue peplum. "Tell me about this boy." I think she said this without judgment, but it was Mother, so I couldn't be sure.

"He's—" I wanted to say what was true. That he was handsome. That he didn't torpedo his tongue around when he'd kissed me amid the topiaries. That he had an impressive knowledge of plant life. That he and his vines had wound their way into my dreams, in English and French. I settled on, "He's smart." That was definitely a way to get in Mother's good graces. "He'll probably design some feat of engineering one day—maybe a bridge." I had no idea if this was in the realm of possible, but his brother was at Georgia Tech, so it might well be. I had no idea if he even liked his brother. In the last few weeks, ever since Oren had started regularly attending Covenant games, Davis had stopped going altogether.

Mother fluffed up my hair with both her hands.

"Don't touch!" I'd just finished pressing the ironing wand over sections of my hair to singe the wave right out of it, à la *Mademoiselle*.

"I love these curls," she said. "I can't abide the thought of you taming them for a boy, no matter how smart you say he is. Anyway, I care more about your erudition than his."

"I'm not doing it for him. I'm doing it for fashion."

"Ruthie," Mother started. But I was saved by the Dixie doorbell.

Mother answered while I tried to fasten pearls around my neck. Fontaine had said she'd buy me real pearls for my birthday—her motto, as she'd announced on more than one occasion, was "no pearls, no power"—but in the meantime, Nattie had cut fake ones off a vaguely Victorian doll she'd found in Mother's old room. They didn't quite fit around my neck, so I looped them twice around my wrist.

"Go talk to him," I told Nattie, who'd had her nose in the pink booklet this whole time. "I have to wait seven minutes."

"Why? There's nothing about that in here," she said, waving the book around.

"Sara said so."

"Remember page thirty-seven when you're at the movies," Nattie said.

"Thirty-seven?"

" 'Beware the derriere'! Don't scoot down a row with your backside in people's faces."

"Am I supposed to put my face in people's faces?"

"Maybe," Nattie said, already in the hallway.

I stood in the doorway and listened to Davis come in. I couldn't see, but I could hear just fine.

"These are for you, ma'am. Momma cut them from the garden."

"How lovely," Mother said in her cocktail-party voice.

"And I'm sorry to hear about your . . . about Mr. Robb."

"Let me find a vase . . ." Mother's voice trailed off.

"Do you know about Leo Frank?" Nattie asked.

"What?" Davis said. "Who?"

"Say hey!" I sure wasn't going to wait the whole seven minutes now. Maybe I was a little easy after all.

"Hey!" Davis said back. He stood and rubbed his palms on his khakis. His pants had an exceptionally sharp crease down the front, and I wondered who had pressed them—if his family employed a Birdie or a Norma at his house, smoothing and creasing everything over. "You look *gooood*," he said in a way that made my blood thrum. "Your hair—it's terrific."

Davis opened the front door and I started to walk through it, but suddenly Mother was at my elbow, her voice low but not low enough. "Home by eleven," she said. Then she amended: "Make it ten."

I tossed my terrific hair.

Once we were outside, Davis said, "I don't get it. Parents always like me."

"It's her," I said, reknotting my cashmere cardigan, which was really Fontaine's cashmere cardigan, around my shoulders.

"Okay," he said with his great smile. "Okay, good."

We drove in Davis's banged-up Rambler down the spine of Peachtree, past the Steakery, the place kids went after school for Coca-Colas and onion rings, past a few churches, and past the lone temple, my family's temple, where six hours earlier I'd been saying Kaddish for my father. A mile or so later, we pulled up to the Fox Theatre. Everyone called it the Fabulous Fox (everyone but Max), and now I knew why.

The theater had the razzle-dazzle of Radio City Music Hall, where I'd actually been exactly once, since it cost a fortune to see a movie there.

A zigzag line of Negro men and women, boys and girls, queued up outside the building—*up* the building, really. "What's going on there?" I asked, nodding my chin to the left.

"Colored-only ticket line," Davis said without a hiccup in his voice. "Leads to the Crow's Nest."

"It's not that way in New York." But even as I said it, I wasn't sure it was true. There was no colored-only line, but I honestly couldn't remember sitting next to a Negro person at the movies, and the last time I took a train to Harlem to see a movie at the Roosevelt, even though Harlem–Lenox Yard was only three stops north on the IRT, was never. I didn't want Max and his know-it-all-ness to be on my mind, but he popped in against my will.

Davis opened an elaborate carved door in the front of the building, and I walked on an actual red carpet into an explosion of gold (not so very unlike the temple, really): gold walls, gold lights, a gold railing, and gold stars painted on the cobalt ceiling. This was my kind of sky—glittery and entirely indoors.

While I freshened up in the bathroom, reapplying my brand-new and as-yet-unmelted Fire & Ice in front of a giganto mirror, Davis stood in line for refreshments. One Coca-Cola, two straws.

Davis led me to an empty row toward the back of the theater, so there was no need to put Nattie's posterior advice into action. Before I sat down, I fingered the fancy uphol-stery on the cushion, a six-pointed star, like a Jewish star, with a monogrammed F in the middle. The whole place was so swell, I couldn't help thinking everyone, including people in the (Jim) Crow's Nest, should be in the cushy seats.

159

I glanced up there, but my angle was off and I couldn't see a single face.

When I looked back to our section, I saw a short man in a gray suit seated ahead of us. Something about the curve of his shoulders made me think—for two seconds—it was Dad. In those two seconds, I'd convinced myself Arthur Robb could have gained twenty pounds. Or aged twenty years. Or acquired a tan or a sudden need for glasses. Or a new gray suit. I remembered how I'd been wearing a gray jumper the day he died. I hadn't wanted to take it off; if I took it off, the day would be over, along with the possibility of a different ending.

I scratched under my Fontaine cardigan. My skin was one big prickle. And then I stopped scratching, because Davis looped his arm over the back of my seat. Not around me per se, but at the ready. It could drift down and make contact with my skin at any moment. My taffeta rustled.

"Thirsty?" Davis angled a straw my way.

I took a sip at the same moment he did. Two straws, two noses, two mouths. The sip was perfect. The sip was happiness.

"Have you seen Hitchcock?" Davis asked. "*Rear Window*? *To Catch a Thief*?"

"All so far. My dad loved him, loved the writing. You know the thing Thelma Ritter says in *Rear Window*? It's something like, 'When two people love each other they come together—wham—like two taxis on Broadway.' He loved that. Every time we'd see two taxis on Broadway, he'd say that line. Every time."

"I'm sorry about your dad, Ruth."

"People always say, 'Sorry about your dad.' And I always say, 'Oh, it's all right.' But I miss him. He would have loved this theater. He was a sucker for glamour."

The lights dimmed. "I miss him so much," I added under my breath.

"I bet he was something. I wish I could have met him, your dad."

"I know," I whispered, and I flooded with emotion for this dimpled boy who said the right thing to a briefly blue girl. "I *know*."

The opening cued up in VistaVision. The screen filled with the image of Kim Novak's lacquered lips and, just like that, Davis's arm dropped into place—a nickel in the juke-box. My eyes stayed on the screen, on the giant spiral now circling Miss Novak's eye.

He leaned in so slowly I wondered if he was going to actually kiss me or if he was merely evaluating me for my kissing potential.

Then he swooped in that last bit and we were legiti-mately necking.

Right away, we got over the awkward moment where you don't know whether he's going to the left or right, and you don't know whether you should close your eyes or not. Right away, it felt like we'd been kissing for a year.

And the rest of the movie was more of the same. I wasn't entirely following the plot, distracted as I was by the holy-smokes of the kisses. It flitted through my mind that the movie seemed to be about lies, and I hadn't exactly been telling Davis the whole truth. But then he'd lean my way and my eyelids would flutter, and I'd think maybe the whole truth was overrated. If everyone told the whole truth, then Hitchcock wouldn't have a career.

Still, when the movie ended and a velvet curtain fell over the screen, I was stuck thinking of what I wasn't telling Davis. I was stuck thinking—of all crazy things to be stuck thinking—of the rabbi and the rebel up the street and the man who was not my father.

Davis whispered to me, "I'm going to jet to the bath-room. Meet you in the lobby?"

"Sure," I said.

And I waited for a while, in the red-carpet, gold-walled splendor, but then I didn't. As people wandered out of the theater, I followed. Without really planning to, I wound my way to the colored-only entrance, taking the outside steps two at a time. The stairs were wide enough not to be panic-attack-y, but there were an awful lot of them. I passed only a few people coming down on my way up, and I didn't stop to hear what they might be saying about the white girl in a hurry. Five flights, forth and back, until I got to the door at the very top.

Up in the Jim Crow balcony, I expected to be the only white person, but I was the only person, period, since the movie had ended what must have now been ten minutes ago. That meant I could keel over and catch my breath without having to explain anything. I didn't sit. The wooden benches had no backs, and I imagined if you were taller than me— as most everyone was—you wouldn't be able to stand up straight. I was so close to the painted gold stars of the ceiling I could have caught one, caught two, in my hands.

I pressed the button on the drinking fountain on the back wall. No water came out. I leaned on the button harder— and tried not to focus on the cracked porcelain and the rings of brown—and watched the water slowly, slowly burble. I lowered my head and took a drink. Even as I sipped, I felt like a fool. Who was I really helping? Yes, I was sipping in solidarity with Birdie and other Negroes—although I'd yet to meet so very many other Negroes. But I wasn't sipping the way Birdie would—because in thirty seconds, I could walk back down the colored-only stairs and drink from any fountain in the city.

On my way down those stairs, I met Davis, skipping up the steps, two at a time. "What the heck?" he said, slightly out of breath. "I looked everywhere. What are you doing up here?"

I wiped my mouth on the back of my hand. "Getting a drink."

"There's a fountain downstairs. This one—"

"There shouldn't be two fountains," I announced. Even though it was true—that we shouldn't be in a city, in a state, in a part of the country that separated people—I didn't love the way I sounded. I was afraid I sounded like Max—like I wasn't just doing something good but wanting everyone to know how good I was.

"Oh. Oh, right." Davis grinned. "I've never met someone like you, Ruth."

Back on the crowded street, he said, "What are you doing next weekend? There's a swim-and-dinner party at the club on Sunday."

I slanted toward him, looping my arm around a fancy streetlight in front of the fancy Fox. The metal was scroll-y and solid. "I'm free," I said to Davis. Free and easy, Sara might've said.

Davis ran his hands down my sides. He could count my ribs, if he were so inclined. "Ruth Robb in a swimming suit—now there's a fourth date. And how about the

Magnolia? Come to the Magnolia with me. There's a fifth date. Or maybe, by then, a sixth."

I nodded then tiptoed up for a pressed-in kiss, not waiting for him to make the first (or the fifth or the sixth) move.

———

We went the long way home. Davis held my left hand with his right, threading his fingers through mine so I was half spinning the steering wheel. We pulled into a parking lot behind a ball field, in the shadow of a pine, or what have you. Davis reached under the seat and, in one practiced move, slid the front seat toward the back.

Honestly, if it were up to me, I'd have kissed him all night long. The kissing—the anticipation and then the actual, factual action—flooded sunshine into every corner of my mind. The kissing made me feel less tangled. The kissing made me feel like I could waltz right into a happy, uncomplicated southern life.

But instead of kissing, Davis pivoted toward me and turned on the overhead light.

I squinted and futzed with my hair.

"I like you, Ruth."

I thought: You barely know me.

A few wayward petals from the roses he'd brought Mother

had stuck to the seat. I picked one up—pure velvet—and ran my finger over and over it.

"What do you like?" he said. "Besides me. And besides roses."

I threw the petal his direction. "How do you know I like you?"

He smiled. "Empirical evidence."

"I like Hitchcock," I said.

"Me too. Bet you like one of the Janes—Eyre or Austen."

"Please. Give me some credit. I like . . . I love . . . Truman Capote." Actually, Sara liked Truman Capote. But last year, *Mademoiselle* had published one of his short stories, so that was something.

"I should read him then."

The thought of Davis doing something because I loved it was sort of exhilarating. "I don't really *love* him," I said, wanting to tell the truth when I could. "I just read one story of his about Christmas, and it was depressing as dirt."

"Ah, so in the neighborhood of true." Davis one-dimpled me. "That's what we say when something's close enough."

I might have puzzled over this, but suddenly we were kissing full tilt.

When we broke to grab a breath, Davis tipped my chin to look out the windshield, which we'd fogged up. He cleared a spot so I could see the stars—the real stars, as opposed to painted ones on a ceiling.

Somewhere out the window were the constellations or the cosmos, if those were even two different things.

I whispered, "*Sainte, sainte merde.*"

"Not a constellation," he whispered, his fingers drumming my collarbone.

"It means 'holy, holy shit' in *le francais*."

And he laughed a laugh that might be my new favorite sound.

"Is that what you want to do with your life, beyond falling for me—to live in France and swear like a sailor and wear fancy clothes?"

"France-y clothes," I said, laughing. "No, that's Gracie's plan—to go to the Sorbonne like Jacqueline Bouvier Kennedy."

He smiled his thousand-watt smile. "What about you? What's your plan, Babe Ruth?"

No other person—outside my immediate family—had ever asked about my future, with or without a southern drawl.

If he'd asked me a year ago, even two weeks ago, I would have said I wanted to be an editor at *Mademoiselle*. The magazine had guest editorships for college girls. But instead, I said, "I want to be a reporter. Like my grandfather and my mother." I imagined taking vowel-less notes, finding the perfect detail to start a story, pounding away on the Underwood, coming up with a last line that would kick a reader in the teeth.

He nodded. "Ambitious."

"And you? What's the Davis Jefferson plan?" I tried to strike the same jokey tone, but I had to hiccup the words out. I suddenly cared so much, too much.

"I'm hoping Georgia Tech. Like my brother, but not like my brother," he said.

"I told my mother you wanted to build a bridge."

He grinned. "Why?"

"I thought it would impress her."

"My dad wants me to study forestry, but I want to be a test pilot—like the Mercury astronauts. To see constellations from space."

For some astonishing reason, I felt a tear slide out of my eye. I quickly wiped it away, unseen, and cranked the window down.

Davis started the car. "It's nearly ten. I better get you home so your mother won't hate me—hate me more."

"My dad wouldn't hate you," I said, which may or may not have been true. It was, perhaps, in the neighborhood of true.

Before he shifted into drive, Davis reached up to flick the light off but then flicked it right back on.

I breathed in, ready for an earth-defying kiss. I wanted to go through that trapdoor, like the trapdoor to the temple roof that let in all the light. I wanted to blow that door wide open and expose the wonder of the sky.

But instead, Davis looked at me, the light still on. He didn't move for a long, long second. "You," he said. Just that. Just perfect.

13

One Hundred and Forty-Two Bricks

Nattie and I waited, waited, waited for Mother and the Savoy to turn up at Piedmont Park. We'd taken Frooshka for a Sunday afternoon romp.

Nattie was hopscotching on an imaginary grid when finally—twenty minutes late, natch—the car pulled up, Mother's ciggie dangling out the window, waving us over.

Except it wasn't Mother behind the wheel. It was Sara.

Nattie screamed. Okay, I did, too.

Sara slammed the car in park and came out to squish us both to her like we all shared the same skin. Froo jumped up and put her paws on Sara's shoulders, slow-dance-style.

"I've missed you weirdos," she said, driving us back to the guesthouse with the help of Mr. Hank's road atlas.

It turned out Sara, in her beatnik all-black, had taken the Greyhound from Penn Station—twenty hours chugging south. She was here for fall break and for the Ten Days of Repentance that started with Rosh Hashanah and ended with Yom Kippur. Holy days I hadn't planned on observing. That was the other reason Sara was here. She'd been summoned by Mother following the rabbi-and-rebel dinner to "remind Ruth who she is"—Mother's words, according to Sara.

That night, after a roast beef dinner in which Fontaine questioned Sara's political and sartorial choices, Sara shoehorned herself into my bed. It wasn't the first time we'd shared a twin bed, but the first time in, oh, twelve years. Nattie asked Sara to sing a lullaby Dad used to croon when we were little—and then, the second Nattie fell asleep, Sara and I whispered about her Jerome and my Davis.

It felt so good to talk—to not think and rethink and rehearse, but to talk in the dark. To not have to hide the Jewish part of myself from the pastel posse, or the T&E part from Mother. To talk about how I loved feeling popular, even tangentially, and how I ached to earn a crown like Mother and Fontaine. "I want it, even though I don't know why," I said, and that felt good, too—to admit how much I didn't know.

"What do you have to do to get it?" Sara shifted to her elbow. "The crown." I could see the vaguest outline of her hair, calmer, saner than mine.

171

"For the school dances, it's pretty much popularity. But for the debutante—" I caught myself. "*Pre*-debutante balls, which are the Magnolia and the White Rose, I have to attend Tea and Etiquette meetings, be recommended by an established member—a grandmother, for instance—and beat out some hundred girls in Atlanta."

"Eh, you can best ninety-nine other girls."

"You don't approve."

"I'm not Mother—I don't approve or disapprove. If you want it, go get it." What Sara wanted for herself, she then told me, was to actually finish James Joyce's *Finnegans Wake*, which she called "an experiment in incomprehensibility," and to bop Jerome like a bunny on a near-daily basis.

For sixteen years, Sara and I had shared the same air, the same air-shaft view from our bedroom window, the same family jokes, list of words, and favorite books, and I drifted off to sleep now so very happy to have her elbowing me in the ribs.

The next morning, Mother, Nattie, and I were on our second bowl of cornflakes when Sara surfaced.

"Is that your temple outfit?" I asked her.

Sara pirouetted—black headband, black leotard, black capris, black ballet flats. She looked like Audrey Hepburn in *Funny Face* without the beret.

Frooshka leaped her floofy black self into Sara's lap like she was part of the ensemble.

"Black is my color—the color of bohemia," Sara said, as if she'd read it in *Mademoiselle*, which I guarantee she had not.

A smile formed on Mother's lips.

"Black is for funerals," Fontaine said. She had knocked and walked in without missing a beat. She unclasped her pearls and held them out to Sara. "You know what would look great—these. 'No pearls, no power.' That's what I say."

Fontaine, bless her, had been only too happy to call Covenant's school nurse earlier to report I was feeling queasy. I was surely queasy about anyone finding out why I wouldn't be in school. Fontaine promised to make the same call for Yom Kippur.

Mother poured Sara coffee—black, of course.

Sara sidled up to Fontaine. "Thanks, but I'm not a fan of adornment."

"There's nothing that can't be made better with a little adornment," Fontaine said.

"We better adorn ourselves and change," Nattie said to me. I was still in my pj's, and Nattie was in her bathing suit; she'd slept in it.

"Ruthie?" Fontaine offered the pearls to me.

I'd coveted Fontaine's pearls—and her motto—every day

I'd been here. I nodded, and she made a production of lifting my hair and nestling the strand around my neck.

Fontaine stood back and assessed. "They're daytime pearls, cultured. But they're lovely—even with pajamas."

We were seventeen minutes late to services. The usually deserted parking lot was packed, and we pulled into one of the last open spots.

"I love this place more than New York," Nattie said out of the blue. It was like one of those analogy tests: Nattie was to temple as I was to Davis—completely, extremely smitten.

"New York will always be special—you can love both," Mother said.

Nattie paused for a second. "Dad would let me bobby-pin his yarmulke on."

"That's right, honey."

"His hair was sort of sproingy," Nattie said.

Sara shouldered between Nattie and me, locking arms. "Super sproingy." We were back to being a trio—the girls.

As we approached the lipstick-red doors, I wondered if Sara would hate it here—the red, the gold, the plaster flowers on the ceiling, the stained glass that turned ankles lilac. Would she think it was too much, too gussied up, compared to our sleek and modernist temple in New York?

Mother stopped short. "I can't believe it, on this day of all days."

Sara dropped our arms. "Holy shit."

"Sara!" Nattie said. But then we all saw.

On the brick wall above the lipstick doors was a scrawl of black paint—*JEWS ARE NEGRO LOVERS*—with one giant swastika for emphasis.

Mother dug out her notebook and jotted down the exact wording. "This is what happens. The rabbi speaks up for what is right, and people get scared."

"Those bastards," Sara said.

"We don't see this all the time." My voice cracked. "Don't think we see this all the time."

Nattie kept staring. "Who would do this?"

"I can't believe you have to live here among this"— Sara looked around at the loveliness of the building, the loveliness of the long, graceful lawn that swelled from the street, the loveliness of the pale-blue sky, light as chiffon— "evil."

Somehow, Mother had her arms around us all. "Let's go in," she said.

"It ruined one hundred and forty-two bricks," Nattie whispered. She'd been counting—not staring, but counting. Cataloging what was lost.

There was room in the back row, where Mr. Silvermintz and his peacock-hatted wife were in residence. We squeezed past them on the aisle and entered the row in our usual order: Mother first, then Sara, then Nattie, then me. But instead of Dad next to me, I had Mr. Silvermintz.

He leaned over. "Ruth, meet Mrs. Silvermintz." She smiled one of those could-be-sincere smiles and went back to thumbing the prayer book.

Every man in the place had on a white yarmulke—rows and rows of white satin circles perched on the heads of men who were not our father. I scanned the pews, looking for Max, but I couldn't find his head among all the others.

The choir, in shiny gold robes, sang out. And Nattie sang out, too.

In the special High Holiday prayer book, I flipped through pages of Hebrew words that looked, that sounded, familiar. I fingered Fontaine's pearls, turning them around one by one on the knotted string.

After nearly an hour of all of us standing, sitting, standing, praying, standing, singing, the rabbi took a step back from the podium and cleared his throat. We were in for the sermon. From our way-back row, I could see only the top half of the rabbi. Instead of his usual rumpled suit, he wore a white robe with gold trim. He looked vaguely royal.

"These are sacred days," he began, "but even amid the sacred, we are compelled to acknowledge evil in our backyard."

Mother leaned over to Sara. "Hand me my pocketbook."

"You're taking *notes*?" I whisper-asked.

"Habit," she said, pen poised in her lap.

The rabbi's voice rose. "Shortly after the discovery of the words on our walls, a neighbor, a Christian, came over with a large white bedsheet."

The congregation seemed to suck in its breath.

"He wasn't a Klansman, if that's what you're thinking," the rabbi said. "He just wanted to hang a sheet over the words to cover them up, but I turned him down. If we cover up the hate, we are only brave in theory. The KKK makes no secret of its hatred of many races and religions. Is there comfort in not being the only target?"

"No," Sara said, not even pretending to be quiet.

"No," the rabbi echoed. "We're sometimes fooled into thinking hatred doesn't happen here because the magnolias are in bloom. But hatred cannot be hidden."

Mother scribbled discreetly.

The rabbi's voice gathered in volume and righteousness. "Isaiah chapter six, verse eight tells us: 'I heard the voice of my Lord, saying, Whom shall I send? Who will go for us? I said, Here I am. Send me.'"

He sat down in one of the thronelike chairs on the side of the bima, and I knew what was coming—the sound of the shofar, the twisted ram's horn blown on the High Holidays. A regular man, in a regular suit, picked up the horn.

I held Nattie's hand, and she squeezed back. Some years, blowing the shofar had been Dad's job, which was an odd thing for a man with little musical talent. It didn't take regular talent to blow the shofar, Dad had said—it just took someone showing you how. And his father, who'd been dead long before we came along, had shown him how.

The man who definitely wasn't Dad blew three short piercing cries, like an alarm, like a battle cry, followed by a long, anguished wail.

My heartbeat turned up in my stomach.

Sara reached into Mother's pocketbook for a hankie. I thought she'd dab at her upper lip, where she had a frown of sweat, but she wiped her eyes.

I stood up, scooting past Mr. Silvermintz, past where Dad should have been sitting—completely ignoring the pink booklet's advice about putting my posterior in the face of others—and left.

I opened the lipstick door to the shock of daylight and nearly tripped over a bucket and rags on the lawn.

Max rounded the corner, balancing a ladder on his shoulder. He was dressed up, for a change, in a tie and jacket, a yarmulke askew in his overgrown hair.

"Hey, what are you doing out here?" He checked his watch. "Services aren't over for an hour."

"What are *you* doing out here?"

He clanked the ladder against the brick and started to climb. "I'm cleaning this up."

Right then, in my tea-worthy dress, I climbed behind him, like climbing to the rotunda but without the panic. I needed to touch the paint, the ugliness, for myself. I ran my fingers over the letter L, following the heavy brushstrokes, and landed on a black bubble, still wet. I pressed in, dimpling the paint.

"You'll ruin that dress," Max said.

I'd worn it to the last T&E, where it got a big "Terrif!" from T-Ann. "I don't care," I said.

"Then grab a rag and help me get it off."

I took a rag from the bucket on the grass and soaked it with turpentine, which smelled of pine trees and licorice, but with even more vim.

I climbed back up, leaning left while Max leaned right. We worked until services ended, until we'd rubbed off the "Jews Are" (me) and the "Negro" and the swastika (Max). Only "Lovers" was left, and when Max said he'd take care of it, I believed in him.

14

Frock Around the Clock

That Saturday, Sara and I joined Fontaine, in her short gloves and lampshade hat—as chic as a pillbox but more flared at the bottom—as she bombed down Peachtree, passing every car on our way to Lumet's department store. She must've been going sixty.

"Fontaine!" I yelled.

She turned to me in the back (Sara had claimed the front) and nearly careened onto the lawn of one of those majestic houses on Habersham. "Never got a ticket!" she said.

We were approaching the dip in the road before the temple. "Can you slow down here?" I said. "I can't tell if they've finished cleaning up the words."

"The mischief," as Fontaine had called it. She'd heard the news from Mr. Hank, who knew it from the Teletype, before Mother, Sara, Nattie, and I even got home from services.

Fontaine slammed on the brakes. I jackknifed forward.

I rolled down the window and stuck half my body out to get a better look. Leaning over the gearshift, Sara gazed up at the building. The bricks looked good, if a bit splotchy—the V of "Lovers" faintly visible if you knew where to look.

Fontaine stepped on the gas, and I rocketed back into place. "Whatever happened there has nothing to do with now," she said. "Don't dress today for yesterday's weather."

I saw the corner of Sara's jaw tighten. "Fontaine, I'm happy for everything you're doing for our family, but please don't tell me to keep being Jewish quiet. That may work on Ruth, but . . ."

The rest went unsaid. I knew what Sara meant. She meant she was in the approval/disapproval business, like Mother, after all.

A few fast minutes later, we pulled in front of the green-and-white-striped awning of Lumet's. A valet in an emerald jacket greeted us with a smile. "How are you doing, Mrs. Landry? Will you be long?"

She gave the valet her key case. "A few hours, Walter. Park me in the shade."

"Yes, ma'am."

"Thanks, sir," I said, but only Sara seemed to hear me.

Fontaine linked her arm through Sara's—Fontaine's pale-pink sleeve against Sara's severe black, the embodiment of their differences right there in cotton poplin. "Miss Sara, I am liberally spirited," Fontaine said. "Here we are at Lumet's, owned by—founded by!—Jews. And I'm one of their biggest customers."

Walter, who hadn't yet pulled away, laughed. "Oh, that she is."

"Is this the kind of department store with books?" Sara asked, taking her arm back. "At Macy's, the entire basement has been turned into a book cellar."

Fontaine's tone cooled ever so slightly. "Some of the best writers of this generation are southerners."

"On the fifth floor," Walter said. "Opposite the elevator."

"Thanks," Sara said, and I noticed then that sometime in the last two months, without mentioning a word to me, Sara had pierced her ears. She wasn't wearing earrings, but there were faint dots, like the faint V on the bricks, marking the place earrings could slide in if they were so inclined.

We walked through Lumet's doors—Fontaine, then Sara, then me—and I felt my mood lift right up. The store was my kind of swell, with gilded ceilings and mirrored columns. And there, lined up on marble benches near the glove counter, were Gracie and Mrs. Eleet, Thurston-Ann and Mrs. Vickery, and Claudia and Mrs. Starling.

Fontaine was the only grandmother of the bunch. Mrs. Eleet had offered to take us dress shopping along with our mothers. But when Mother conveniently announced she'd be working, Fontaine had leaped—literally, did a grand jeté—to take Mother's place.

"Y'all," I said, "this is my sister Sara." I made quick introductions. Three blond heads and six blue eyes stared at Sara and her bohemian mien.

Claudia took her kid gloves off one finger at a time.

"From New York," I added unnecessarily.

"You're as chic as Ruth, with your all-black," T-Ann said, less enthusiastically than usual, and I remembered she wasn't allowed to go to New York on account of all the commies and Jews.

"It's the ultimate funeral choice. Isn't that what you said, Fontaine?" Sara asked.

"Sara's looking for books. Fifth floor, I hear," I said.

Gracie, all business, stood up and said, "Let the shopping begin."

With Sara and her *insouciance*—a favorite word of Mademoiselle Tremblay's—out of the picture, it was surprisingly easy to shift my thoughts back to fashion and frippery.

We were at Lumet's in search of two numbers—a less

dressy frock for the Fall Ball and an honest-to-God gown for the pre-debutante Magnolia. In under an hour, we dispensed with the former, all four of us in tea-length variations of a fit-and-flare with tulle: coral for me, celadon for Gracie, teal for Thurston-Ann, tart lime for Claudia.

When it was time to go to the higher, fancier floor in search of higher, fancier dresses, the whole posse rode in an elevator with shiny brass walls, each panel embossed with a foxhunting scene. The brass did strange things to our faces, stretching our smiles too wide. It hit me that somewhere along the way, I'd stopped comparing every single thing to New York. I couldn't even conjure up an image of the elevator at my beloved Saks.

The better dresses at Lumet's spanned an entire floor. It was frock around the clock, as Dad might have said, with dresses displayed my favorite way: by color (not unlike Gracie's bed, the equestrian edition). All the ivories on one rack. Then the golds. The silvers. The oranges. The pinks and reds. The purples and greens. And the blues—there were enough of those, baby to indigo, to take up two racks.

Gracie and Mrs. Eleet gravitated to the ivory selections, and Thurston-Ann and Mrs. Vickery beelined for the peach sequins.

"Why don't you try something with lace, Ruth?" Fontaine held up a tea-toned gown with a narrow bow at its empire waist.

I peered at the price tag pinned to the satin hanger and kept flicking through the dresses. "I'm fine with something less lacy."

"My treat, Ruthie. It's your first Magnolia," Fontaine said.

A *Mademoiselle*-ism popped into my head: *Great minds wear simple design.* I held up a plum shift with a round collar that cost twelve dollars. "This is Audrey Hepburn–esque," I said.

"So it is," Fontaine said. "And that is about the worst thing I can think of, sending my granddaughter, daughter of a queen, off looking like a waif."

"Do you think the better Mr. Jefferson will like this?" Claudia asked the air. "Oren asked me to the Magnolia with a bouquet of lilies."

"You'll have Oren wrapped around your pinky before long," T-Ann said.

"C'mon, Ruthie, try a few lovelies on." Fontaine lifted a gold dress from the rack. In that second, the years whirled off Fontaine's face, and she looked like a girl herself.

Claudia tilted her head as if she were posing for a picture. "Already called it."

A saleswoman nodded. "Yes, I put the very dress in her room."

The voice made me look up. I'd heard it before. I followed

it to the face that belonged to Mrs. Silvermintz, of the peacock-plumed hat, in the back row of the temple.

"Ruth! Lovely to see you outside the usual walls. And, Fontaine, always wonderful to see you."

Fontaine blinked—fast—as if she were sending a distress signal.

"You know Fontaine?" I asked.

"Of course," Mrs. Silvermintz said. "We go back to Johnston Grammar School."

"Rose," Fontaine said without much energy. "We're looking for a Magnolia dress for my granddaughter."

Mrs. Silvermintz—first name Rose, I supposed—smiled. Everyone in the store seemed to know Fontaine, but the fact Fontaine was related to a Jewess, well, not a soul here knew that except three of us: Fontaine, Mrs. Silvermintz, and me. Four, if you counted book-loving Sara. Five, if you added in Nattie. Six, seven, if you included Mother and Mr. Hank. This little addition exercise made me grin, because Sara and Mother were wrong. It wasn't that nobody knew I was Jewish. It was just that not everybody knew.

With the slightest shake of her head, Fontaine turned her attention back to Claudia. "Aren't you a dear?" Not a minute later and a rack away Fontaine raised her voice. "Oh, Ruthie. This is exquisite!" She spun a delicate dress in the chicest pink. "This with your hair."

She had flawless taste, Fontaine did. The dress, embroidered with tiny dots, was lovely. Not as stunning as Mother's impossibly stunning Magnolia gown, but close.

We all trooped off to the dressing rooms with an armful of gowns. Even the try-on spaces were glorious—little rooms radiating out from a floral lounge, spokes in a glamorous botanical wheel.

"Share a room? More fun, right?" Gracie said to me.

"Let's do," I said. There was a step-up platform for posing purposes and an array of high heels waiting to partner with any number of dresses. I tried on some duds—too floofy, too va-voom-y—before slipping on the pink. It was long. Still, I twirled. I knew twirling was a cliché, but it was a dress built for clichés, for spins that would take you somewhere.

Gracie modeled a few cream-colored variations before ditching them all for a crimson-red dress she swished to an imaginary song.

Out we went to the dressing lobby, where the mothers, plus Fontaine, were arrayed.

"Ruthie, you knock me out," Fontaine said from her perch on the rose-festooned sofa.

"Oh, Gracie—imagine it with Maw-Maw's earrings, the rubies," Mrs. Eleet said.

Thurston-Ann had chosen a multicolored sequin sheath

that knew how to catch the light. It was very Hollywood. T-Ann's mother nudged her stomach. "Pull in, dear."

And Claudia, shining brightly in the gold charmeuse Fontaine had eyed for me, swung her golden hair for maximum attraction.

"Like it was made for you—like you are a gen-u-*ine* goddess," T-Ann said.

Mrs. Starling came up next to Claudia in the mirror. "Well, this—this will not work."

"I think it will, Momma," Claudia said. "You love things made of gold."

"Too low here," Mrs. Starling said, pinching the fabric by Claudia's impressive cleavage. "And too tight there." She plucked the fabric by Claudia's hips. "I believe this would favor you better." She held up a prim silk number in dishwater yellow.

"Not for the Magnolia," Claudia said.

"You'll shine in anything you wear, Claud," T-Ann said quietly.

"Go on—put on the buttercup," Mrs. Starling said, swinging the dress to and fro, as if trying to hypnotize Claudia into thinking it was worthy.

Dress in hand, Claudia slunk back to her changing room.

"The prettier Claudia gets," Gracie whispered in my ear, "the more ordinary Mrs. Starling likes her to look."

Mrs. Eleet went off to summon the alterations gal, who then turned her attention to Gracie first, as people tended to do.

Claudia came out in the new dress; it looked like something a fifth grader would wear to a father/daughter dance.

"Muuuuuuch better," Mrs. Starling said, fluffing up Claudia's unflappable hair.

Claudia bristled and stood straight as a model.

Thurston-Ann focused on wedging her feet into very high heels. Even she couldn't find something positive to say.

I was on the alterations block when Mrs. Silvermintz came by to start hanging up the not-today gowns. "Very lovely, Ruth."

I thought of seeing her yesterday. I thought of all of us yesterday. I braided, unbraided, then rebraided a hank of hair.

"Please, miss, no wiggles," the seamstress said, setting my hips straight.

By now the rest of the girls had gone up to the Tea Room with their mothers. Fontaine offered to stay with me and wait for Sara, but I told her to head on up; she'd been talking about the chicken almondine with frozen grapes for a solid week.

The seamstress packed up, and I stared at my pinned-up self in the mirror. I imagined wearing this perfectly altered dress—among my new friends, and the new boy who was a dreamboat—and then I imagined something else.

Maybe it was the light. The hopeful light of the dressing room was my New York light, the light of trying on someone else's clothes, someone else's possibilities. I sailed my hand through those waiting-to-be-returned gowns, and who should join me in my fashion reverie but Dad. I knew he wasn't there, of course. But something of Arthur Robb was before me. It was his bigness even though he was a small guy. His big smile, big laugh, big intellect.

And then Sara—not Dad but not *not*-Dad—was in front of me, a shopping bag of books at her feet. "What are you doing?" she said.

"Try on a dress with me."

"Not my scene." Sara thumbed through the rack where Mrs. Silvermintz had hung the castoffs.

"It used to be—when we played dress-up with Bubbe's clothes." I knew I had her then with those memories of us in Dad's mother's Shabbos-best dresses, always with some silly adornment—ruffles or pin tucks or feathers or all three.

From the rack, I plucked an orange dress with a feathered hem, a T-Ann reject.

"Maybe just this one," Sara said. There was a hint of a smile.

We went into the dressing room and Sara stripped down. I caught sight of the two of us in the mirror. I had on full armor—a cross-your-heart brassiere, girdle, and garter belt. And Sara had on gunders that looked like a bikini, and no brassiere whatsoever.

"Can you zip me?" she asked.

I eased the zipper over Sara's ribs. The feathers undulated across her knees. She ruffled them. I bumped her hip with mine just to see the feathers quiver. "Divine," I said, drawing out the word like T-Ann might.

"Dee-viine." Sara exaggerated the drawl even more. "May I have this dance, Miss Ruth?"

I gave her my hand, and instead of the fox-trot or what have you, she whipped me around. Thank God the dressing room was huge. Sara leaned back and I leaned back, and we spun, spun, spun, our fingers barely holding on to each other, like we were pulling all the air in the room into our sister orbit. We were floating. We were flying. We were so much like our childhood selves that I had to stop before I might have done something else, like cry.

Sara bent over to catch her breath. "Those girls—are they really your friends?"

"They are," I said.

"Do they know you were at temple yesterday?"

A trickle of sweat slid down my nose. "Unlikely."

"You don't have to wear your Star of David every day or anything, but it's who you are."

"I lost it, the necklace." I checked Sara's face, trying to tell if she was mad at me—for being a chicken or a liar or both. "Okay, I have it—I just don't want to wear it." I was flooded with a sudden need for the truth, especially with the person I'd shared a room with nearly all my life.

"You heard the rabbi—if you don't stand up, you're only brave in theory," Sara said.

"I'm not even brave in theory. I'm only brave in my dreams. I'm only brave in my dreams when I'm standing next to Dad. And when I wake up and Dad is gone, and Gracie and Davis are here, breathing and spinning on the dance floor and sipping Coca-Colas, then . . ." I tried to capture the seesaw feeling taking flight in my chest—pushing up, gliding down. "I don't want everything to have happened *to* me," I said, which wasn't quite right but wasn't not-right either.

"You know who you're like right now?" Sara said.

"Who?" Dad—I hoped she'd say Dad.

"Yourself." She gave me something resembling a hug.

Mrs. Silvermintz's voice broke in. "Sorry to interrupt, girls." Her beehive peeked into the room. On seeing Sara and her plumage, her smile froze a bit. "Isn't that a look? Can I bring you a pair of tangerine pumps?"

"Thanks, but we're all set," I said.

"And you, Miss Starling," Mrs. Silvermintz asked. "Can I get you a shoe?"

"Oh, Claudia's upstairs in the Tea Room," I said.

"I am *right* here," Claudia la-di-dahed, her voice too loud.

I stepped out of the dressing room, half zipped. And there she was, not three feet away, hip thrust out like a mannequin.

Claudia looked at me from one direction. Sara looked from the other.

"Miss Starling," Mrs. Silvermintz said. "What of the gold dress? Do you have that in your pile?"

"No, ma'am. Mother chose the buttercup for me," Claudia said, not missing a beat.

"All right then." Mrs. Silvermintz went off, arms fluttering with cast-aside silks.

"Were you here the whole time?" I asked Claudia—Claw-dia.

"Ding, ding." Claudia's hair was tangled, her cheeks red. "I heard about your rabbis and your Stars of David."

"You're full of shit—and you're a thief." Sara pointed to the bottom of Claudia's neat, pleated skirt, from under which poked a very gold hem. Claudia hitched the glamorous gown, which she was clearly and unglamorously helping herself to, into better hiding. "Where we come from—" Sara said.

I picked up the line. "Where we come from, the truth is . . ." And then I stopped, because what did I know about truth?

"Let's agree you didn't see what you saw," Claudia said, "and I didn't hear what I heard."

Her voice made my jaw jerk shut. I so wanted to utter a Dad-worthy, Dad-word-y comeback and sling it her way. But I had no words—nothing clever, nothing sharp. Or maybe I had *only* something sharp—the stab of knowing Claudia knew exactly what I'd gone to great pains to hide. I ran my tongue over and over my teeth, which now felt like they were made of glass, ready to shatter without warning.

Instead, I walked to the register, standing rabbi-tall, to pay for my dress with Fontaine's metal Charga-Plate. I slipped it out of its leather pouch, tracing her signature engraved in the brass—FONTAINE ALICE LANDRY—while Sara went upstairs to let Fontaine know we were ready to leave.

The three of us, two Robbs and a Landry, two Jews and a Methodist, exited through the columned lobby with the gilded ceiling in time to see the actual golden sun sinking from the sky. The light slanted across the parking lot in fat stripes.

While we waited for the valet to bring the car around, Fontaine, none the wiser, put an arm around me, and I inhaled her scent, which I now definitively knew was jasmine.

Home we went, Sara and I together in the back this time.

Fontaine took the turn at Peachtree Battle on two wheels, and I cheered her on.

15

Country Club with a Lowercase C

I was under the bonnet dryer, my hair sizzling like a steak, before the pool-and-dinner date with Davis, when Sara knocked on my knee. I shut off the contraption and let the hose dangle down my side.

It was the last Sunday in September, but no one had told the sky. The predicted high was eighty-nine. I popped my top away from my skin to keep the sweat from pooling in my bra.

"Which bathing suit are you going to wear?" Sara asked.

I laughed. "You don't care."

She laughed, too. "I don't, but you do."

"The one-piece with the daisy," I said. "As in 'fresh as a.'"

"A cliché, don't you think?"

"Or the black-and-white two-piece with the ruffle."

"Always choose the ruffle."

Another *Mademoiselle*-ism floated to mind: *If you want to fly, you have to ruffle some feathers.*

"I don't want you to fly off—to bus off," I said, my voice suddenly an eggshell, thinking of Sara and the seven states between us, going on about her life without us.

"Is it Davis? Is that it?"

"No, he's a good one."

"Does he know your favorite book or your middle name?"

"He could."

Sara exhaled, and I imagined she'd light up a Chesterfield the second she got on the Greyhound. "I'm going to tell you something. It won't be Mother-approved. Do you want to fry the other half of your hair while we talk?"

"Can you put it in braids instead?" I sat down on Dad's chair and felt the plastic exhale. Sara stood behind me, parted my hair down the middle with a pencil, and started in.

"When you're ready—only when you're ready—it might help to spend the night with him, with this Davis." Her fingers flew through my hair, untangling knots and yanking the sections into some semblance of order. "Because this happiness won't remember itself."

"I've only been crazy about him for two weeks. Three weeks."

She started on the other side. "Being with Jerome? I'm not saying it helps, but it helps. If you want to be with a boy because you want to be with a boy, it's all right."

"*With him* with him?" I swiveled around, thinking about how kissing Davis pushed the melancholy out of my head. I wondered what Gracie would think.

"Turn around—I have to fix this side." She pulled to the right. "Yep, sleep with him. Back-seat bingo. Jump in the passion pit. I was eighteen, but I wasn't grieving. And, you'll be seventeen in a few months."

"I'm not saying I'm ready. But maybe it wouldn't hurt to send a few, you know"—I lowered my voice—"rubbers."

"Good! Lead the parade, Ruthie," Sara said, and we both laughed. That was a Dad-ism. He wanted us girls out in front, leading the charge. "And slinkies!" she said. "We call them slinkies. They'll be on the way."

———

We waited in front of the main house for Davis to pick me up so Sara could put her eyes—and stamp of approval— on him before Mother drove her to the bus.

Davis and the Rambler clunked up the motor court. At the sight of two Robb girls—three, if you counted the poodle—he jumped out.

I made quick introductions. Davis's dimple was on full

display. "Sorry I'm a few minutes late," he said. "I wound up deep in a tennis game."

"*Fore*," Sara said.

"That's golf," Davis said, "but I like your sense of humor."

"Right—tennis. *Love*," Sara said.

Davis grinned. "Agree with you there."

Frooshka licked Davis's tennis legs, and he leaned down to give her a scratch.

"Davis," Sara said. "Are you trustworthy? Can I trust you with my sister?"

"Jeez Louise!" I objected.

Davis left Froo and walked so he was exactly facing Sara. "I know your family has been through it, and I promise you—more importantly, I promise Ruth—I will be a southern gentleman through and through. And through." Then like some ridiculous politician, he shook Sara's hand. And that was pretty clever, because he was treating her as an equal. She gave a vigorous shake in return.

Before I got in the front seat, Sara said to me in a normal everyday voice so the whole world could hear, "I'll see you at Thanksgiving, Ruthie. Meantime, I'll send you that package. I approve."

Davis punched the accelerator, and we were off to the club, Sara getting smaller behind us. I knew she'd be long gone by the time I got back home, but I didn't dwell on that.

Instead, I turned my mind to the club situation. I'd learned there were many kinds of clubs here, thanks to Fontaine, who'd described the place near Piedmont Park where she and Mr. Hank belonged as the only Club worth a capital C. The club for strivers where we were headed was on the edge of the suburbs, the club for newcomers was near the hospital, the club for people who made their money yesterday was north of the city, the club for German Jews was in Brookhaven, the club for Eastern Europeans was near the Tech campus, and there was no club for Negroes unless you counted the Negro-only nine-hole course near Lincoln Cemetery or the newly deseg-regated North Fulton golf course, both of which Mr. Hank had mentioned (and Fontaine most certainly had not).

We drove out past the new houses on Howell Mill, the radio blaring Carl Perkins and his "Blue Suede Shoes," the windows rolled down, the breeze turning my braids cotton-candy-ish.

Ten minutes later, we pulled up to a white building with col-umns out front, tennis courts on either side, and a lawn mowed in what I now saw was the country-club-preferred checker-board pattern. The place didn't look so lowercase-c to me.

Gracie and T-Ann were out front to sign me in as their guest. They took me to the changing room to put away my dinner dress, then went out the deck door. We weren't allowed to walk through the lobby in pool attire, according to T-Ann.

Rows of chaises—white iron, white cushions, white towels

rolled just so—lined the deck. The jumbo pool glistened a welcoming turquoise, but as inviting as it was, I remembered it wasn't made to welcome people like me. I sighed a Mother sigh.

Claudia and her glossy maillot and glossy legs and glossy ponytail had already set up camp in the blaze of the sun near the deep end.

"Hey," I said, putting my tote bag on an empty chaise.

Claudia flicked her ponytail. "Ruth."

"Let me order you a Co-Cola," Davis said.

"Have y'all seen Jimmy?" Thurston-Ann asked.

"He's around." Claudia made a roof over her eyes with her hand. "Somewhere."

"How was tennis?" Gracie asked, scooting her chair closer to Buck.

"Davis and I beat the others silly," Claudia reported.

"You and Davis?" I said.

"Parents set it up—been on the books awhile," Davis answered.

I wondered if this was true, or in the neighborhood of true.

Davis whistled, low and cool, and a Negro waiter hustled over. All the service workers here were Negroes. I didn't want to think of Max and Jim Crow and the temple and turpentine, but I couldn't stop thinking—thinking if Davis and company knew my mother was fomenting a little nonviolent protest with the rabbi, knew I even *knew* a rabbi, I'd never be invited to the club or the Club again. At the same second, I had a different thought that made me feel both better and worse: All the porters at Grand Central Station were Negroes, too. I filed this away to discuss with Mr. Hank.

The Cokes came, and Davis signed for the bill—like at Fontaine's Club, no cash changed hands—and he circled his arm around me.

We settled into the white-white chaises.

Gracie took off her cover-up; she had on a gingham one-piece with ribbon straps.

"Perfection," Thurston-Ann said to Gracie, her hat and cover-up firmly in place.

I popped off my dress and squirted Coppertone on my shoulders.

"Oh, baby," Davis said.

The waiter was back with a shake of the head and a word for Davis. Next thing I knew, Claudia signed his check. "It's no problem," Claudia told Davis, but he looked like he'd swallowed a sardine.

"Whoa-etta, your suit is gorgeous! Black-and-white heaven," Thurston-Ann said to me, ignoring the kerfuffle. She adjusted her one-piece. "Hey, speaking of heaven, Ruth, when're you going to turn up on a Sunday morning? At church?"

Davis pulled off his shirt. It struck me as strange you

could lollygag by the pool almost naked—with someone you wouldn't mind seeing naked—and no one batted an eye.

"Ruth?" T-Ann asked again.

"Uh, my mother hasn't seemed interested in church," I said. A version of the truth.

T-Ann inched her chaise a few inches closer to me. "You could come on your own or with your grandmother. Church'd be better with y'all."

Jimmy turned up in plaid shorts and saved me from responding.

Thurston-Ann swatted at him with her hat. "Where have you *been*?"

"Around." Jimmy sat on the edge of T-Ann's chaise, and it seesawed up a few inches.

I slipped on my Hollywood sunglasses and pulled out last month's *Mademoiselle*—this month's issue hadn't come in the mail yet, though it must've been on the newsstand in New York for five days. The old issue was a dud—a whole article devoted to how to wash your face: *Don't slide a washcloth around and call your face clean. Friction is half the battle.* I wondered what Sara was reading on the bus ride home— whatever it was, it was probably existential.

Davis closed his eyes and held my hand, stroking my palm sleepily with his thumb. He could do that for a thousand years as far as I was concerned.

I wanted to whisper something encouraging about the payment situation, but I couldn't imagine what to say.

Buck yelled, "Davis, you in?"

I propped up on my elbows to see Buck on the high dive.

"Busy," Davis said, not looking.

"My middle name is Tarbell, by the way," I said, lying back down. "For the journalist Ida Tarbell—my mother's choice."

"Are you sleep-talking?" Davis said.

"Just thought you should know."

Gracie fluttered her feet in the shallow end. "Mine's Elizabeth, same as my mother and her mother."

With a big yell, Buck did an underrotated forward pike and splashed into the water.

Davis let out a whoop, and Gracie kicked her feet fast, like applause. But here was the thing. Hearing Buck hit the water—even on a terrible dive—made me homesick for Maine, even though I only lived there in summer-camp season.

I stood and readjusted my suit. Davis whistled, low, but I brushed him off.

I went up the metal ladder, stopping three-quarters of the way up to look down. I didn't have the hiccup of panic I'd had climbing to the temple rotunda. The steps were hot under my feet, and the sun bounced around, throwing prisms like buckshot.

At the top, I curled my toes under and tested the spring. A squeak. I turned around, my back to the pool.

"She's chickening out," somebody—Claudia, most likely—said.

"You don't have to go," Davis yelled up. "It's higher than it looks."

I raised my arms, pressed down into the board, and bounced.

I could tell it was a good push-off. I saw a zipper of sky, of clouds. I turned one and a half times and entered the water with a ripple.

When I surfaced, Davis was treading in the deep end. I did a quick bathing-suit check and tugged my top over my top and my bottom over my bottom. Davis wrapped his arms around me. I wrapped back, weightless, breathless. "Damn, Babe Ruth," he said.

We stayed in the water, foreheads together, limbs tangled, for a very long time.

***

All us girls changed into our finery in the locker room, spritzing one another with perfume and winging it up with eyeliner. I corralled my hair into an approximation of a bun.

On the perfectly crisscrossed grass, the garden party hadn't quite started. It flitted through my mind that it was now well after five; I'd overstayed my five-o'clock shadow welcome. Davis took my hand. "C'mon. I want to introduce you to my parents."

Mrs. and Mr. Jefferson stood across the lawn in a tight circle of adults, looking as though they were anticipating a round of cocktails. Davis tapped his mother on the elbow, and she spun around, putting a smile on her face a second late. "Ruth! How lovely you are. So happy to see you."

I knew this southernism—saying you were happy to see someone rather than happy to meet them, in case you'd already met them and had forgotten—although, of course, Mrs. Jefferson had never set eyes on me before.

"Happy to see you too, Mrs. Jefferson," I said.

She was as skinny-minnie as her brother, Cranford.

"You're Hank Landry's grandgirl," Mr. Jefferson said. He stubbed out a cigarette with a scuffed cleat.

"Yes, sir."

"I hear he's a good man, though can't say I'm a fan of his editorials. Have to read him *after* I eat breakfast, if you know what I mean."

I didn't want to say yes. I didn't want to agree that Mr. Hank was anything but perfect. "That's a good one, sir," I said. It seemed if not exactly polite, at least in the neighborhood of polite.

A waiter glided by with a tray of martinis. Mr. Jefferson took two.

"Have fun," Mrs. Jefferson said in a not-fun voice, then turned back to her circle.

"They liked you," Davis said, and I wondered how he could possibly know. "They were high school sweethearts. Could be us."

Could it be? Could Davis turn into his two-drink father in scuffed cleats? Could he turn into someone who couldn't stomach Mr. Hank's editorials?

Mrs. Jefferson was back at Davis's elbow. "Keep an eye on your brother, dear. He's a little wound up."

Davis kicked at the grass with his loafer. "I haven't seen him."

"Well, if you do." When she walked away, I saw her pretty dress had a safety pin standing in for a missing abalone button at the back.

The waiter presented a platter of cheese puffs. "Thank you, sir," I said. Since the rabbi-and-rebel night, I'd made an inside promise to address everyone whose job it was to wait on me with "sir" or "ma'am."

If Davis noticed, he didn't say a thing.

An hour later, after rounds of passed appetizers and glasses of lemonade with mint and a tip of the flask—the latter courtesy of Claudia—Oren turned up and joined our table. He was as handsome as before, wearing a white oxford shirt that set off his tan.

Claudia draped her arms over Oren's shoulders. "Finally, the original Jefferson."

"Claud, aren't you looking nice," Oren said, his dimples making a simultaneous appearance. "Tell me, what color would you call that?" he asked, nodding to the strapless dress she'd been hoiking up—a dress I'd bet the ranch Mrs. Starling had not approved.

"Emerald Envy," she laughed.

"That's his new line," Davis muttered. "'Tell me, what color would you call that?'"

Claudia laughed too loud, and her straight-as-a-ruler hair swung to and fro. "They added lights to the courts, you know." She set her glass on the lawn and spun her dress around. "Want to play?"

"Could do," Oren said, his arm loosely around her waist.

"Do you use a continental grip?" Claudia wrapped Oren's hand around her own.

"I'll use any grip you want me to," Oren said.

"Let's see what stars we can find," Davis said to me.

"Ruth, ask him about the Star of David," Claudia said, over her shoulder.

"What'd she say?" Davis asked me.

I answered/not-answered with what I hoped was a kiss worthy of distraction.

It took a minute for my eyes to adjust to the night sky as we left the tiki torches and tennis rackets behind and sat on the slope between the second and third hole of the golf course.

Davis put his arms around my waist and scooted me closer. I was half on his lap. He felt different, more substantial, without the buoyancy of the deep end.

"What if somebody comes out here?" I asked.

"They won't, Ruth Tarbell."

It was a beautiful night at a beautiful club—actually, it was cloudy and it wasn't the capital-C Club, but still. I was with a boy who now knew my middle name.

Davis tipped his chin back. "You surprised me with that diving."

"I've been diving at sleep-away camp since I was ten."

"Where's that?"

"Maine. Have you been to Maine?" And then I laughed, thinking it was Maine that had come up that first day in history when discussing the Uncivil War.

"Maybe you won't believe this, but I've never been to the beach," Davis said.

"Not even in Georgia?" I asked. "Or Florida?"

"It's a good five, six hours from here. And then we'd have to stay in a motel." He seemed to watch for my reaction.

"You'd love it," I said. "As a naturalist—the tides, the mollusks, the stars at night."

"We have a hunting lodge, and that's it. The whole legacy," Davis said. "Our family isn't like the Landrys. My father's father is basically carrying us along at the club."

"My family isn't like the Landrys either—my Robb family." I was so relieved to say something unequivocally true. Sara would be almost halfway home now—Roanoke, Virginia, or close to it—and I smiled, thinking that I was doing her proud.

"I know," he said. And I wondered how much he knew. Lots, I hoped. I sort of hoped Claudia and her golden gown and golden tongue had spilled her golden guts.

But then Davis wrapped his arms around me, and my breathing fell in line with his, like we were sharing lungs.

He ran his finger from the top of my bun, over my nose, and down, down, down my neck to, eventually, inevitably, my bra.

I unbuttoned his shirt.

He unzipped my dress, one inch, then another. I was suddenly aware of the sway of the pleats, and I liked the way they looked as they swooped and swooned around.

I stood up and shimmied the dress off, keeping my slip on. I was leading the parade, and anyway, it was more than I'd been wearing at the pool.

"This curve." He bent down so I could only see the top of his head, and he pressed his lips against my hip, just two layers of nylon between us.

I was glad I hadn't had much to drink. I wanted to remember every speck of this night, even the grass.

"I'm dying to be with you." He gave me a crooked smile.

Then we did what we did so well—semi-clothed, in the semi-dark.

When we broke for a breath, my eye caught a spot of orange in the distance, beyond the club, beyond our side of the city. My first thought was the bonfire after the mixer. My second thought was worse.

"Is that fireworks? Or a fire?" I stood up, feeling exposed in my slip and yet feeling like I had to walk in the direction of the glow. Even as I asked, I had a stomach-sinking sense of the answer. Mr. Hank had been getting five-dinger alarms about crosses going up in flames nearly every day. Birmingham. Tallahassee. And Atlanta. "That's not a cross, is it? A cross on Stone Mountain?"

"Nah." Davis was right behind me, his front to my back, and I was so happy he was on my side—well, on my back, but on my side. "You can't even see the mountain from here. It's probably a burn pile of leaves or something. It's probably nothing like a cross."

I faced him. "Thanks for being honest." Talking to Davis was like talking to Max but without the sanctimony—it felt good to ask a simple question and get a simple answer. I could see it in his eyes, even in the semi-opaque dark, that he was such a good guy. I thought about saying something more—thanks for being so handsome, or thanks for being someone I might fall in love with—but the question that fell out of my mouth had to do with crosses. It was the one T-Ann had asked me those months ago. "What's your church?"

"No church," he said, fingers twirling around some hair that had escaped my bun. "I haven't been in a long time."

"Me neither—I'm not religious." My hands, on their own accord, flew up to my eyes, covering them like I was saying the Shema or lighting the Shabbos candles, not that I'd done that in recent memory. I swallowed the Hebrew thoughts and stuck my hands on my hips in what I hoped was a provocative way.

"I believe in science and the sky—what I can see," Davis said.

"I'm not sure I believe in anything."

"I believe in you and me."

And just like that, I was ready to take Sara's advice and be *with him* with him. Hell, I thought, I'd do it tonight.

Then—ooooof—the mood was gone because Davis was saying, "It's not just Stone Mountain, the lightings." His voice was soft but other things tensed up—his arms, for instance, and my heart. "For some people, the hate is here. My uncle Cranford and his hunting buddies, they don't understand. They're so ready to hate Negroes or Jews or homosexuals—anyone who's a little different."

In my head, I said, Jews, Jews, Jews. Out loud, I said, "Different? Like Jews, like northerners?" I had a cold patch in my throat, and it wasn't the air, which was still summertime-warm. I should tell him right now. Claudia already knew—it was only a matter of time before she'd blab. He'd already asked me to the Magnolia. He'd already told me that he didn't go to church. He'd already told me his religion was the sky and us.

"Who wouldn't like this northerner?" he said, and his sunbeam smile was back in residence.

The door was open. All I had to do was walk through it.

"There are lots of Jews in the North," I said, for starters.

Thwack. The sound of a tennis ball—hit hard—broke the moment.

I put my dress back on, fast.

"Orrrrrren." Claudia's voice came from over the berm. "I think it sailed thisaway."

Davis tipped my chin with his finger. "Don't forget this moment."

"How could I?" How could I forget the fire in the not-distant-enough distance, the chin tipping, the unzipping, the unspoken Jewness as I stood beside him on the golf course of a club that didn't want me as a guest.

16

Driving Lessons

Mother shoveled Nattie and me into the Savoy to head off to temple. On a Sunday. In New York, Hebrew school was during the week, and Sundays were for churchgoers, but here religious school was a Sunday-only affair. It would be the fifth time I'd been at temple in two weeks.

Today, Mother had a meeting with the rabbi and a pastor from an AME church, Nattie had her usual Sunday school—and me, I was helping Max. I'd been volunteered by Mother to be his assistant.

I went for a plain-Jane (or plain-Ruth) look—a simple crewneck sweater and button-up skirt. I didn't even bother fixing my hair, and let the curls go cuckoo. It was sort of a relief to dash out the door with Mother and Nattie. It was only Max. That was sort of a relief, too.

When I walked in, Max was discussing today's songs—Noah's Ark–themed—with the choral director. Before leaving, she handed us a couple of choir robes, the blindingly gold ones she said she'd special-ordered from a place in Boston for the High Holidays.

I zipped in and gave myself a static shock. "I hate polyester," I said.

"What did polyester ever do to you?" Max put his robe on over yet another plaid shirt, sleeves rolled up to his elbow. He put one foot on the chair and tuned his guitar in a way that said: I'm at home here.

"I'm sure you'll tell me there are more important things to hate." I busied myself straightening a pile of construction paper.

"Hate? I'm not agitating for hate; I'm agitating for action. I've been helping the rabbi organize student boycotters," he said. "We're starting with segregated lunch counters, and then—"

The kids bounced in. Nattie and Leah, in matching hair ribbons, and a girl named Judy, in teal cat-eye glasses, circled Max, a sixth-grade fan club. He greeted all the kids by name and handed out instruments—triangle, maracas, cymbals, and such.

Max strummed, and I snipped. He sang "Rise and Shine"—*The animals, they came on, they came on by twosies-twosies*—and I cut out gray elephants and pink kangaroosies-roosies.

By the time we got a few verses deeper, Max's arms were flapping like golden wings—*The sun came out and dried the landy-landy; everything was fine and dandy-dandy*—and the kids were clappy and happy. My head couldn't help but bop along. There was a feeling of possibility as the real sun came through the real window.

Max transitioned to the classic "Oseh Shalom," a prayer/song with only twelve words. I started to sing—*Oseh shalom bimromav.* I'd sung the words twelve jillion times on Saturday mornings at our New York synagogue, Dad by my side, loving that I'd taken to Hebrew so easily. I could conjure up his Dad-ness right there—the sweet smell of the oranges he'd squeeze every Saturday for the two of us, fresh juice for the earliest risers—even though there was no citrus in sight at this precise moment.

And just like that, I couldn't get the rest of the Hebrew out of my mouth. The words were knotted up in my throat. They were so stuck I started coughing, loud and barky.

Max hit a wrong chord, but he finished the song and then shuffled the kids out ten minutes early. "Was I an ass about the polyester?" he asked. "Is that what's going on? I think I was an ass."

"The opposite—not an ass. It's not you. It's orange juice. It's my father." It was a weird thing to say, I knew, but I was thinking about the Hebrew lump in my throat.

Max balanced himself on a child-sized desk. "Was it a long time ago?"

"Five months. A hundred and fifty-four days."

"Not long."

I picked up a forgotten pink kangaroo, one of a few— what was a group of kangaroos called? A court? A mob? "It was a Wednesday," I said. "His funeral. And the strangest part was, he wasn't there. Obviously, right? But that's what I remember—that . . . that . . . lack." It was easy to say this thing I hadn't said to anyone to this guy with owlish eyebrows who could be a jerk but also not a jerk.

Max took his glasses off and polished them with that soft shirt. Without a wall of lenses, he looked kind—kinder. "And you're trying not to think of it."

"Yes."

"It's okay, Ruth." He grinned, and it was a smile that lifted up his whole face and made his eyes squish closed. It was a smile that wouldn't look good in a photograph, but it looked good right now. It was a smile that made me not want to be a phony.

"*Is* it okay? *Is* it okay I'm lying to everyone I meet?" A burning in my nose let me know the dreaded tears might not be far behind. "I haven't told any of my friends I come here."

"To temple?"

A Queen Esther mobile, dangling from the ceiling, looked down on us. "That—or that I'm Jewish."

He slid off the desk. "Not lying to me—it's a start."

We walked to the half-empty Social Hall to find the pastry platters picked nearly clean. I poured myself a cup of coffee with too much sugar. Max popped a left-behind cheese danish, misshapen and missing a corner, into his mouth.

"You're disgusting," I said with a grin, handing him a napkin.

His mouth was full, but that didn't stop Max from saying, "You care too much what people think."

I knew he meant the Jewish situation. "Don't all good southern girls?"

"You, a good southern girl? Your hair looks electrified. It looks good."

I put my hand to the floof. "Really? That would save me an hour in the morning."

"Wild is good." He wiped his mouth with the tail of his shirt. "I bet there's a boyfriend."

"A good southern boy."

"The worst kind." He nodded to the clock over the percolator. "Class ended fifteen minutes ago. We can take off. Where'd you park?"

"I'm waiting for my mother to finish her meeting. I don't drive."

"Not ever?"

"No one has a car in New York."

"You're not in New York anymore."

He tossed me his jangly keychain with ten thousand keys.

I tucked a note for Mother under the windshield wiper of the Savoy. Max's car was parked two spots away—a new gray-and-white Bel Air. "My uncle is a Chevy dealer in Chattanooga," he said. The back seat was nearly completely covered with books.

"We'll do a few loops up here, where we won't bump into anyone." Max's glasses slipped down his nose, and part of me wanted to reach over and push them up.

"Are you doing this because you feel sorry for me?"

"Nope." Max helped me inch the seat forward and tilt the side mirror down. "Maybe."

I looked at his profile, at his sharp chin. "I don't want to wreck your car."

"Then don't."

I turned the ignition key, and the engine thrummed to life.

Max showed me how to shift into drive—foot on brake, gearshift on D—and I drove in a straightish line, haltingly, lurchingly. Not so different from Mother or Fontaine, really. When I got to the end of the lot, I braked hard, shifted to R, and reversed.

"Not bad," Max said, after we'd up-and-backed three times. "Want to move on to advanced-beginner lessons, or you want me to chauffeur you someplace?"

I glanced over. "I have to meet a friend for a frosty at the Steakery."

"You can't miss out on that." He rolled down the window and rested his plaid arm half inside, half outside, fingers drumming a mile a minute. "Is this the boyfriend?"

"Yep." I kept my foot on the brake, but I could feel the car alive under us.

"Put it in park, and we'll switch spots."

"I can do it," I said with confidence just out of reach, just out the windshield.

"You don't have a license. And how do you plan on negotiating the turns?"

"Slowly." I shifted back into D and nosed out of the lot, registering how good it felt to punch the accelerator, to leap forward without holding back.

"All right, then. Godspeed."

I headed north on Peachtree, inching away from Midtown toward the too-big front yards and Negro-jockey yard ornaments of Buckhead.

"Did you hear what happened last night?" I said. "My grandfather told me about a cross burning on the front lawn of a Negro doctor." I didn't add: This very morning, I skipped across Fontaine's grass, forgetting that somewhere in town a family woke up to the smell of kerosene.

"Let's hear what terrible thing happened today." Max flicked on the radio. After a weather update—the heat streak was expected to continue—a newsman reported the arrest of thirteen Negro men who sat in the front of a bus in Birmingham.

"That's in Birmingham," I said. "It wouldn't happen here."

"Please. Are you ever going to lose that intellectual naïveté?"

"You're being an ass again."

"Ruth. *Ruth!*"

"What?" I looked at him.

He pressed his hand on my knee. "You ran a stop sign."

Max drove the rest of the way.

After a few miles, he pulled up to the orange-and-white awning of the Steakery. Davis was out front tossing bits of bread to a circle of birds. "The bird feeder—he's the boyfriend?" Max asked.

"He is." I rolled down the window. "Say hey."

Davis waved.

Max leaned—hard—on the horn, and Davis's feathered friends took off, their iridescent chests flashing bright against the afternoon sky.

Davis chucked the rest of his roll into a trash bin and walked over. He stuck his hand in the window and reached across me to Max. "Davis Jefferson," he said, ready with a handshake.

"Max Asher."

"Are you Ruth's driving instructor? I've been telling her—"

"I'm not," Max said.

"So how do y'all know each other?" Davis said.

Max looked at me, and I looked at the floor mat.

"That's up to Ruth Robb," Max said.

"I am so, *so* thirsty," I said to Davis. "Can you get me a frosty?"

" 'Course."

As Davis loped toward the Steakery, where everything inside, even the jukebox, was orange, I surprised myself by holding Max's elbow. Wanting what? For him to unlie my lie for me? His plaid shirt—his hundredth plaid shirt—was soft and perfectly worn in, and I held on to it for a half second too long.

Max passed my hand back to me, but he held on to it for a half second too long, too.

Together, we added up to a single extra second. I got out of the car telling myself a second was nothing, it meant nothing.

Max took off toward Midtown, accelerating effortlessly, his arm raised out the window, a plaid goodbye.

―――――――――

Davis and I shared the frosty in his Rambler. The drink wasn't orange juice, but it was orange—a concoction of ice-cold milk and tangerine syrup that smelled nothing like actual fruit.

"So, how do you know that guy?" Davis asked. "Seems like a weirdo."

"Weird" made me remember my hair was a scare. I scraped it into a ponytail. "Met him with my mother."

"Right—reporters." Davis grinned. "My dad says you can't trust reporters."

"That's not true." I let the not-orange drink freeze on my tongue, wondering if he'd forgotten I wanted to be a reporter. "You may know every tree, every bird in Georgia, but your father doesn't know my mother—or reporters. Reporters, you can trust them as much as you can trust me." I quickly added: "More."

Davis started up the engine. "I like when you're feisty."

Which for some reason compelled me to say, "Max is at Emory working on integration—that's what he's doing." I was testing the waters of the truth.

Davis squeezed my hand. "Let them fight their own fight, Roo." His fingers drifted up under the hem of my skirt, and he kissed me. And those kisses undid me, as always. Those kisses got me focused on Davis and unfocused on anything else.

I pointed to an itty-bitty speck in the middle of his window. "I see a smudge."

"Dirty, dirty." Davis's smile practically ricocheted off the windshield. "Definitely time for the car wash."

We'd been going through the car wash quite a lot since the drive-through opened at the corner of Piedmont and Lenox, the Minit-Man. I'd come to think about car washes and cabins in the same breath, because our trips through the suds started one night the week before, when Davis legitimately needed to wash the Rambler of pine needles and red clay after a day in the North Georgia woods with his brother. Davis couldn't stop talking about taking me up there one of these days to see the Jeff family hunting lodge for myself.

This afternoon, the attendant in white overalls and a white cap asked if we wanted the Supreme or the Extreme. The Extreme was ten cents more and a full minute longer, so that's the one we got. The whole suds situation was six minutes from push-off to towel-off.

Smooth as could be, Davis guided the wheels on to the conveyor tracks and shifted into neutral. The attendant swished a mop through some soap and lathered up the windshield, then pushed a few big buttons on the wall. We were off.

As soon as the front wheels slid into the tunnel, Davis and I slid to the back seat. The first time we drove through, we'd stayed in the front, but there were too many things in our way—steering wheel, gearshift, keys.

We cozied into each other, and I found myself wondering about the novels in Max's back seat. What was he reading? He probably liked Hemingway, whom I loathed.

Davis pulled my knees toward him. "Okay?"

"Very okay."

He cradled the back of my head and—sh-boom—lips, lips, lips. We'd now kissed so many times I knew the curve of his mouth. I knew that one of his incisors was crooked.

The windows frothed up.

I stretched out, and Davis stretched out on top of me, his shoe squished against the door. Our hands were on the move. I knew when to inhale as Davis teased my sweater out from my waistband. He slipped over my bra. I wandered up the back of his shirt.

Water rained down on the hood, like the sky had opened up over us, for us.

I breathed in the smell of soap, of bleach with a hint of sunshine and pine, and let the kisses do the thing they did—flash-flood every part of my mind, not unlike fake rain on a fake-dirty car.

Thwomp. The carpet strips were busy beating the dirt off the not-dirty car. That was our cue—we were near the end and needed to put ourselves back together.

"We need more than six minutes," Davis said, helping me to the front seat.

I tucked my sweater back in.

He kissed a sliver of my stomach that had escaped sweaterdom.

"We could go somewhere else," I whispered, thinking of the two of us in the hunting lodge in the mountains. "Somewhere woodsy."

He nodded. "Night of the Fall Ball."

I nodded back. Six days. I could wait six days.

17

In Love with a Sunbeam

Fontaine was adamant about hosting the picture party late on the afternoon of the Fall Ball. Before everyone came over, I went out to the back porch, where she rocked away, to ask after a cashmere shrug. Surely, she must have a dozen. As a general rule, when one would do, Fontaine had a dozen (black pumps, pink lipsticks, strands of pearls).

"Check the cedar closet, middle shelf to the left," Fontaine said. "But first, sit with me a minute."

I scooched a rocker close to her, so we were side by side in the spongy air, and we rocked peacefully for a minute or more.

"You know, when you're in the middle of the Panama Canal, you can't swing a boat around in an instant," Fontaine said out of the clear blue.

"Should I be following your train of thought?" I kept the rocker going with a push of my toe.

"Your father might have said I'm verboten. No, that's not right. The Jewish word that means too emotional."

"Verklempt?"

"Yes, that. And Ruthie, I want you to know. The business about staying in your social circle is not particular to the Jews. I'd likely say the same thing if you were Catholic. Cynthia Bryant had a Catholic cousin visit from Sacramento, California—an Agnes, I believe. We didn't tell a soul the girl was Catholic or no one would've dated her."

I laughed. "I'm not sure that's better, Fontaine."

"It is," she said, reaching over and sandwiching my hand between hers. "The first ball of your season, it's making me sentimental for balls of the past—your mother's, mine. When I look back—" Fontaine stopped rocking and turned to me. "Now don't interrupt. Let me say my piece. When I look back, I should not have forced your mother. I was the Panama Canal, and she was a ship. And I kept compelling her to turn—compelling her to come to church and compelling her to be a debutante—and what happened? *Pfff.* She turned herself around and went off to college in the North. I don't want to lose you and Nattie."

"We're not lost. We're here." I knew this wasn't about the porch, but I looked around it all the same, taking in the perfect pale blue of the ceiling and the view to the pool. "I want to be here," I said quietly. "I want to go to the flower balls, all of them. I am in love with the South"—and Davis Jefferson—"despite evidence to the contrary."

That made Fontaine laugh and laugh. I loved the way she looked when she was happy—eyes crinkled up, cheeks flushed. "That's my girl. If you're going to go, you might as well win a crown. Not today, of course. Today is out of the cards."

"I'd like a crown." I wasn't sure why this was so very true, but it was. Maybe it was to make Fontaine happy. Or maybe it was to prove I was Davis-worthy or I belonged here. Or maybe I was shallow enough to want the sparkles— that was possible, too.

Fontaine assessed my chances. "You've gone to the requisite T and E's—and you've got the southern lineage. Of course, a few other girls in the city have the same credentials, starting with Gracie Eleet."

"Who doesn't love Gracie? I wouldn't mind losing to her. But I'd hate to lose to Claudia Starling."

"Then don't. And be careful if Claudia offers a hug— that's a sly way to give you a little stab in the backside. The cream always rises!" She threw her arms overhead in victory.

I threw my arms up, too.

"And, win or lose, don't leave me, Ruthie. We've already lost Sara, although I suppose we never quite had her. Oh! By the by, a manila envelope from Sara arrived addressed to you. It's on the demilune in the foyer."

"From Sara?" I tried not to let my voice jump an octave, knowing the envelope must be full of slinkies. "Sara doesn't know what it's really like here—how lovely everything, most everything, is," I said, thinking of Davis and Gracie and flower balls and not thinking of cross burnings and hateful words on brick buildings. "And Nattie, too. Nattie's happy."

"She is—especially when she talks about that dang temple."

Amen. Ah-mein.

———

At the stroke of four, with the sun slanting through the poky pines, the posse arrived, families in tow, for the pre-dance photo-a-thon.

We gathered on the grand lawn. Davis made his way over to Fontaine and Mr. Hank, showing off his good southern manners. Claudia and her parents hadn't been to Fontaine's place before, and they took an extra moment to admire the allée of magnolia trees, not in bloom but still impressive.

"So classical!" Mrs. Starling enthused, her blond hair held back in a tight headband. "Look at those hybrid teas. Is that the one they call the Violet Carson rose?" she asked Mr. Hank.

Mr. Hank shrugged. "Could be."

"Who cares?" Claudia asked, but the way her eyebrows twitched, it seemed she might care a bit.

Oren looked bored out of his gourd, and so did Mr. Jefferson, a giant camera flash hanging around his neck.

We were all slick with sweat in the October heat—eighty-two degrees with heaps of humidity. I couldn't wait to shrug off Fontaine's shrug.

The group fanned out in an arc—boy, girl, boy, girl, boy, girl, girl (Thurston-Ann's Jimmy was l-a-t-e)—and the parents stood across from us, snapping away, asking us to line up just the girls, all of us in rainbow shades of tulle; then the boys, in navy suits, the unofficial uniform; then the boys putting the corsages on the girls; then the girls putting the boutonnieres on the boys.

Just as I was losing hope for Thurston-Ann, Jimmy showed up. And then the bottom fell out of the sky. The rain came fast. "Follow me," I yelled, hiking up my skirt and dashing to the main house. Gracie and T-Ann were at my heels, Claudia, Buck, and Davis right behind them.

The girls and I ducked into Fontaine's powder room, with its pagoda wallpaper, and bouffed up our hair—backcombing and spritzing heavily with the Spray Net that Fontaine kept in a special wicker holder topped with a tassel. By the time we reemerged, the parents were drinking gin and tonics while Birdie passed her cheese straws on a little silver tray, an invisible hand with the canapés.

"These are terrif," Thurston-Ann said, pointing at Birdie with a straw. "Do y'all use paprika?"

"Yes, miss," Birdie answered.

"Birdie's daughter is at Spelman College," I said, wanting T-Ann to appreciate that even though Birdie was a cheese-straw maven, she was so very much more than that.

"Miss Ruth, a word," Birdie said to me.

We ducked into the butler's pantry. "Do not use my children to impress your friends," she said.

"I wasn't—" I said. But then I stopped, because I was. "I apologize, ma'am."

Birdie repositioned her tray and glided back out to the party.

I followed her, feeling several inches smaller. Davis sailed across the room, cheese straw in hand. He took a bite and put the other half in my mouth, like we were sharing a cigarette. I couldn't help thinking: Three-ish hours until we're alone.

"Gracie, are you sure you girls don't want to spend the night here?" Mother asked. I didn't realize she was on our side of the room. "Let me host."

I caught Gracie's eye. After Davis and I'd hatched our spend-the-night idea at the car wash, Gracie helped me figure out the switcheroo details.

We'd sat knee-to-knee on her four-poster bed, and she'd asked me if Davis and I had done the deed. The frankness of the question surprised me. It was a sisterly question, a best-friend question. I told her we'd fooled around. And she said, "The girls here"—Gracie was apparently a speaker for the whole third-year class, which felt about right—"aren't as laced up as you think. We drink early. We marry early. Some of us even mess around early."

"Are you a messer-around-er?" I asked.

"To a point," Gracie said. "I've considered the deed, and Buck has definitely considered it—weekly," she said without a trace of blush. "But it's not for me, not yet. I'm in the no camp."

Was I really ready to be in the yes camp? Advice on these matters wasn't in the pink booklet, that was for sure. But, as Mother herself had said on more than one occasion, not everything worth knowing was sandwiched within a pink cover.

Anyway, the yes-camp plan for the Fall Ball night was this: Gracie was spending the night at my house, and I was spending the night at her house . . . except I was spending the night with Davis, and she was spending the night with T-Ann. I made sure the Eleets had eased over to the bar cart with Mr. Hank before I said, "They have more room."

"Next time," Gracie added, and Mother smiled.

The gymnasium was decorated with bales of hay and a bumper crop of pumpkins. T-Ann and the 'ettes had spent the afternoon twisting orange crepe paper into swoops. Mrs. Drummond patrolled the punch bowl, and a couple class officers manned the record player and speaker setup.

The dance part—with the Everly Brothers and the Coasters sh-booming over the loudspeaker—was not so different from a New York school dance. The wallflower-y couples wallflowered around the snack table. Claudia and Oren, who looked cooler than cool, held punch glasses in one hand (already spiked, no doubt) and each other in the other. And Buck and Gracie, in the role of big man on campus and his princess, were the sun around which the rest of us spun. What was different was me. I was in the circle. I was one of the close-in rays. I was in love with my fellow sunbeam, smiling, dimpled Davis. And, it would seem, vice versa.

My tulle skirt, not tutu full, kept Davis at arm's length, the way Mrs. Drummond of Home Heck told us to dance— with room for the Lord between us.

The music blared and people looked like they were having a grand time, but maybe they weren't; I couldn't always tell when people were pretending here. I was having a blast. We danced slow; we danced fast. Davis held my hand, twirling me until the room went tipsy.

At one point, we ducked outside and he smoke-ringed it up. He delicately put his cigarette in my mouth for me to puff, but I took it out and kissed him instead all over his beautiful face, both of us laughing like fools. Right after the crowning, we'd agreed, we'd take off for his parents' hunting lodge.

We heard the music stop and reentered the gym to see Principal Chalmers clomp up the stage stairs. "Welcome to the Fall Ball and the crowning of our first court of the 1958–1959 season. The first of our seven queens of the year. Can I have a drumroll, please?"

Thurston-Ann and a few of her majorette pals made drumming sound effects. There was no chance it would be me, since this was not a pre-deb event, where family history was a factor. Here the votes were cast by fourth-years, who knew me hardly at all. Fontaine had said as much. Still, it gave me a thrill to know it could be me next time. Or next, next time.

"The secret ballots were counted by Mrs. D.," Principal Chalmers announced. Mrs. Drummond flapped an envelope around.

Claudia squared her shoulders and stood tall, as if pulled skyward by an invisible string. Gracie, closer to me, looked cool as a cuke.

"The first runner-up for Miss Chrysanthemum leads us with her *cheer*-ful disposition," Principal Chalmers announced. "Congratulations, Miss Thurston-Ann Vickery."

"Go, go, go, T-Ann," I yelled, a kind of football chant, which I hoped she'd appreciate.

T-Ann took the stage, and her stomach wasn't pulled in a bit. Good thing Mrs. Vickery wasn't here to poke her.

Principal Chalmers tapped the microphone. "Now, for the Miss Chrysanthemum crown. I'm pleased to say it goes to . . . Miss Gracie Eleet, who happens to have gathered more votes than any other third-year on record."

"Woooooo-hooo," I hooted while Davis gave a two-fingered whistle. Claudia clapped politely, her shoulders fairly slumped.

First-years distributed the prizes. An acorn crown for T-Ann and a goldish tiara for Gracie, who, of course, glowed.

That was our cue. It was time to vamoose.

I didn't even wait for Davis, always a gentleman, to open my door.

18

Spinning Around with
Saxophone Colossus

My dress and I settled into the Rambler. The tulle sprung up around me, unable to contain its happiness.

The drive to Davis's parents' hunting lodge didn't take long—ten-ish minutes—but we bumped from a four-lane road to a two-lane road to a dirt road. I'd always imagined my first time would be in a la-di-dah apartment overlooking Central Park, not that I knew anyone who had an apartment overlooking the park. Instead, I was here with Davis, scooched up next to him, so close I could steer the car if I wanted to. It was crazy to think I hadn't even known him two months ago.

We hit a pothole. I suddenly loved that we were on a rutted road, that we would leave evidence we were here, as if we had the power to shift and rearrange layers of dirt.

Davis turned and kissed me, eyes closed, just a finger or two on the wheel. I swatted him. "Don't get us killed!"

"No one is ever, ever on this stretch." He slapped the dash. "Look at that! The Rambler hit forty thousand miles."

I leaned into him, staring at zeroes on the odometer. They were so festive all lined up in a row. It seemed like an omen. Even the car knew this was a milestone night.

We pulled up to a small log cabin alone on a hill. Davis opened my door, and I took out my overnighter and followed him up the pine needle path.

He unlatched the front door, and a wall of mustiness floated right up my nose.

"Hunting doesn't start for a few weeks," he said, tapping out a slow rhythm on my arm with his fingertips. "My dad hasn't opened the lodge for the season yet."

The place wasn't as big as the word "lodge" had led me to believe—just a small living room and bedroom with bunk beds. "Cabin" was a better fit. "Shack" was a better fit. My heart tanked at the sight of those beat-up bunks. I sure hoped they would not be the scene of the deed.

I kicked off my heels. Dust coated the floor, and motes wafted through the air. I coughed.

Davis smiled his smile, and I suddenly didn't care a whit about motes, whatever motes actually were. "I have something for you," he said. "Check the closet."

237

There in the closet, front and center, was Davis's letter jacket, his name embroidered in loopy script where his heart/ my heart would be. A red ribbon hung loose around the hanger.

"It's a present," he said, filling the doorframe behind me.

A declaration was what it was. A declaration we were an item—the next gift would likely be a pin. Or a ring. My whole body thrummed. "How'd it get here?"

"I drove out earlier in the day. Brought a few things up."

I traced the stitching of his name with my finger.

Davis put the jacket over my shoulders and kicked the door closed. He turned off the lights.

It took my eyes until the count of seven, eight, nine to adjust. I stopped counting pretty quickly, because we started kissing—first, standing; then on the nubbly plaid sofa, where a few leaves had drifted in who-knew-when; then on the floor, where the jacket was the first thing to go.

He unbuttoned the top button of my cashmere shrug, which, of course, was Fontaine's cashmere shrug. He unbuttoned the back of my dress. I wanted him to keep unbuttoning me. I looked right at Davis, but it was too shadowy to see his eyes.

I had on very few clothes—my gunders, bra, slip, and stockings—when I stood up and fumbled my way over to the lamp. I switched it back on. The shade was made of cowhide or something, whipstitched together like puzzle pieces.

If I was going to take the plunge, I didn't want to be in

the dark, even the half dark. I snapped open my pocketbook and removed the slinky Sara had sent me. A peach wrapper with blue lettering: DUREX OPAQUE—GUARANTEED TO BE ABSOLUTELY PERFECT.

"Holy smokes! I'm impressed, Babe Ruth. Just so you know, I had that covered." I didn't want to think who else he'd covered this particular topic with, and so I willed myself not to ask. This night wasn't about anybody but the two of us.

He put an album on the turntable—the B side of *Saxophone Colossus* by Sonny Rollins.

I rested my cheek on his heart, and we were sort of dancing.

"It's not only that I like you," he said.

We were now rib to rib.

"Yes, it is," I said. I felt emboldened by the kisses and the letterman jacket and the light, and even the pieced-together lamp. I was worthy of his like.

"I like you so much I think it turned the corner into—"

I knew he was going to say it. My fluttery stomach knew he was going to say it.

"Love."

"I'm ready." I pressed up against him: my cheek, his chest. Davis put his arms around me—one, then the other. He felt solid in a way I wanted people to feel solid.

"Hold on," he said, untangling himself for a minute. He pulled a basket out from under the coffee table: a hunk of cheese, a sleeve of crackers, a couple apples, a bottle of luke-warm champagne with two paper cups.

"How long has this been here? How long has this cheese been out of the fridge?"

He laughed. "You're worried about the cheese? I brought the basket up with the jacket."

"I guess it's cool enough," I said, but I didn't eat the cheddar.

Davis took a bone-handled knife out of the pocket of his pants, which was the only piece of actual clothing either of us was wearing at the moment, and sliced the apple into perfect arcs.

He popped the champagne. A little bit sprayed my way, and I licked it off my hand. A towel of unknown origin was folded up under the sofa. He shook it open with a flourish and put it on the rug. We centered ourselves on it, an impro-vised bed. I didn't want to be a city mouse at this moment, worrying about the cleanliness of the towel or the fustiness of the leaves, or the age of the cheddar. I wanted to be here, here, here, with this boy in this place.

And then I was, because Davis lowered himself onto me and gave me the kind of kiss I bet people wrote songs—symphonies, colossus or not—about.

The air shifted a few degrees, and the sharp smell of pine needles drifted inside.

My slip was off. His pants—off.

"You, Ruth Robb, are spectacular."

His hand skated over the swoop of my hip. We were pieced together, like that lamp. And he was the one who was sort of spectacular.

What do you wish for?" he asked me after. He got up and picked the needle off the album. It had been *bump-bump-bump*ing at the end of the record.

"I wish for—" I'd had my wish. I had wished for this night with this boy. "I'll be right back." I dashed into the bathroom and wadded up some TP, prepared, as Sara had cautioned, for pain and blood. I had spots of both, but so what.

"Lucky we put in a bathroom this year," he yelled from the other side of the door.

"Oh, come on!" I grinned so stupidly I looked like a completely different person in the smudgy mirror over the sink.

"You would've had to use an outhouse. But I'd have given you a flashlight."

I was back out with my stupid grin and my wish. "I wish," I said to a still-unshirted Davis. "I wish to see Cassiopeia."

Davis put his arms around me like a pair of parentheses. "All right."

I slid his varsity jacket over my gunders and we went outside.

The back porch was small, with a row of rockers facing the woods. I rocked, drawing my knees to my chest and swaddling myself in his jacket, thankful it covered my rear. I was so happy to see my breath was visible—slightly visible anyway. The night, my breath—it was all so decidedly alive.

"Cassiopeia is easy to find because it's shaped like a W," he said. An owl hooted from far off. Davis took my finger and pointed to the sky. "Find the Big Dipper and draw a line through the last star of the Little Dipper, and you'll swipe through Cassiopeia."

I stared. "I don't see it."

"It's there." He twirled his fingers around my insane hair. "The moon is awfully bright tonight, so it's hard to see."

"I hadn't even heard of Cassiopeia until you told me I would love it."

"It's there, whether we see it or not." He pulled me on his lap, facing him, our new optimal kissing position, honed during all those car washes we didn't need. I snaked my legs around him.

A leaf-crunching sound stopped the revelry.

"Is that a chipmunk? Or, God, a deer."

Davis stood up, and I sort of fell out of his lap. We went inside. He pulled on the rest of his clothes and grabbed a walking stick in one fluid motion. "Wait here for me."

I put my tulle back on.

I probably should have been afraid of whatever was out in the woods, but part of me was stuck on the dumb idea that I was sitting here alone—alone after *the* night.

Two minutes went by. Five. Ten. Sixteen.

I poured myself a glass of warm, now-flat champagne. I looked out the not-exactly-clean window and saw nothing—just the faint outline of trees against a sky with constellations I couldn't find.

I debated putting on my shoes and going out after Davis, but surely that was a terrible idea. I debated calling Mother or Mr. Hank (to say what, I wasn't sure), but there was no telephone in sight. I considered various terrible scenarios. Davis had fallen down a ravine. He'd tangled with a bear. Or: He was on the run from me. Or: He was on the run because I was an inept towel partner. Or: He was on the run because, despite my devotion to the pink booklet, Davis somehow knew the real me and took off for the hills.

I knew from chasing away Dad-sadness that the best way to clear the mind (the best way aside from bump-bumping with a boy) was to let in the light. I opened the closet, the bathroom door, the refrigerator, hoping to add little slivers of brightness to the room. I opened cupboards, halfheartedly looking for ingredients to make Fontaine's southern brownies, even though she'd really taught me how *not* to make southern brownies.

Finally, I opened the front door, and from well within the confines of the log walls, I looked outside. I heard a snap of a twig or quite possibly my heart.

Davis came in through the back while I was looking out the front.

"Surprise visitor," he said.

Next to him stood Oren, in jeans and a smudged gray T-shirt. Even so, he was great-looking. In that second, I saw Davis and Oren as they must have looked through countless Kodachrome moments—the photogenic duo on the tennis court, the football field, the country-club green.

"Son of a bitch ran out of gas in Midtown and hotfooted it here." Davis exhaled like he'd been holding his breath for a year.

"Here?" I closed the refrigerator.

Oren threw his two-dimpled smile my way. "Sorry, Ruth. Didn't have any idea y'all were here. Davis'll make it up to you." He dropped a duffel at his feet.

"You *ran* here? With a duffel?" I asked. "Why do you smell like bananas?"

"Yeah," Oren said, then went into the bunk room.

Davis whispered, "I'm sorry. I am sorry the night ended this way."

We settled, hip to hip, fully clothed, on the nubbly sofa for what was left of the night.

"It's all right," I said, thinking I wouldn't remember how the night ended. I would remember how it started and how it middled.

———

Early the next morning, I woke to find Davis erasing evidence of us, packing up the basket and slipping the album back in its sleeve. I changed into my next-day clothes and slung Davis's letterman jacket—a kind of popularity cape—over my shoulders.

Oren's door was closed.

"How will he get home?"

Davis kissed my neck. "His problem."

The road down was twistier than I remembered, and in the light of day it seemed especially bats that Oren would run all the way to the cabin at three or four or five in the morning. I hoped he'd had a flashlight.

Davis pushed the turns, skirting up against the trees at the side of the road, kicking up dust.

"At least we have an excuse to get another car wash," I said, turning on the radio. All static. It matched the noise in my mind—the oooo of last night mixed with oddness of Oren. O's interruption didn't make sense. The whole gas situation didn't make sense. Even the odometer didn't make sense. The numbers didn't add up with those lined-up zeroes from last night, like the miles had rocketed forward knowing Davis and I had made the deed-leap.

Davis flicked the static off and veered to the shoulder.

I clutched the door handle. "What are you *doing*?"

He put the Rambler in park. "I love you, Ruth Tarbell Robb," he said. "I wanted to look at you when I said it."

"I love you—I love you, too."

Somewhere a bird warbled. Davis likely knew the genus and species.

"Let's meet up at the Steakery for lunch, all right?" he said. "After church."

"Lunch? Not lunch—" For some reason it was hard to commit the words to the air. "At lunch—" At lunch, I'd be leaving the temple; I'd already promised to help Max run choir practice. "I'll be singing," I said, happy to have landed on something rooted in truth.

"Singing what?" he said, but then he moved on. He moved on to my thigh, climbing his fingers up under my skirt. "After lunch?"

"You want to come to the main house for one last jump into the pool before it gets covered up for the season?" I suggested.

He nodded, and off we zoomed, ticking past the pines, holding hands until we hit the dip in the road on Peachtree that floated us right out of our seats.

19

Ten Bells

Mother wasn't even home when Davis dropped me off, which was odd but also okay, since it meant I wouldn't need to lie out loud about last night. I hopped in the shower and rubbed Noxzema all over my face, letting needles of water rain down on me, letting thoughts of Davis— and his hands and his saxophone-y music—wash over me, too. I got dressed for Sunday school in a Peter Pan blouse and flared skirt. Everything I put on, I imagined him taking off.

Even though it was woefully early, I called the pay phone on Sara's dorm floor to fill her in on last night's developments. No answer.

It wasn't until I went to make coffee that I saw a note taped to the percolator in Mother's no-vowels shorthand: *SKP TMPL*. In capital letters for emphasis.

But just because Nattie was having a spend-the-night at Leah's didn't mean I needed to skip temple. I'd come to like it there—being adored by the small people and amused/annoyed by the tall person.

I drank my coffee avec sugar, then walked to the main house and looked in the garage. The Savoy was gone. If Mother or Mr. Hank or Fontaine weren't back with the car in twenty minutes—and wherever could they be?—then I'd have to take the bus.

I took the bus.

There weren't many people on the number 23 Peachtree on a Sunday morning. I walked toward the back. It had been a few years since Mrs. Rosa Parks sat in the middle of the bus in Alabama. People seemed to think she sat in the white section, but Dad made sure we knew she was arrested for not moving from middle rows that Negroes were definitely allowed to sit in—at least until those seats were needed by whites.

I slid into a seat across from a lady in a yellow house-keeper's uniform. She wore her hair short, shiny, and curled under. In the reflection of the window, I assessed my own wild-as-air hair: Better down or up? Up, I decided. I wound it into a bun and clipped it in place with a tortoiseshell barrette. I couldn't tell from the bus-blurry glass whether I looked different—older if not maybe wiser—now that I had spent a night with Davis, been skin-to-skin with a boy who had no idea the previously almost-naked girl under his letterman jacket was now on her way to synagogue.

"You missed a piece," the woman across from me said. I turned around. She pointed. "By the ear."

"Thanks," I said. "Should I wear it down? Does it look messy this way?"

She smiled. "It's very becoming."

"Which way?"

"It suits you any which way," she said.

I took my hair down again. Then put it up again.

A siren wailed. One police car passed, then another.

I wondered whether the woman was going to or from work. Then I wondered why she didn't have Sundays off for church, like Birdie and Norma. Then I wondered what difference it made. I was suddenly a wondering machine.

We passed the Steakery and my stomach lifted into my throat, and I knew the bus had hit the dip in the road. A third police car passed by, and a fourth.

The sirens weren't somewhere out there. They weren't the background sounds of New York avenues. They were here, in front of me—a lineup of revolving red lights slicing right across the entrance to the temple.

"Oh, Lord, now it's the Hebrews," the woman said.

"Here! My stop!" I called to the driver and rushed to the front of the bus. "Stop! Stop!"

The bus veered to the curb, and the doors sighed open.

"God bless," the woman called after me.

From the bottom of the hill, the temple looked nearly normal, just a faint trail of smoke wending up its left side. Maybe there'd been a fire in the kitchen, or maybe someone had left a lit cigarette in the Social Hall.

Still, something made me sprint across the street and up the center of the lawn.

Squad cars were parked all pell-mell, noses poking into the grass, and a few fire trucks stood guard at the turnaround at the top. There was water everywhere. My suede flats slid in the mud. I didn't care.

A sea of people surged up the driveway, men mainly, in jackets and ties. All these people, but nobody looked familiar.

I headed toward the smoke by the side entrance—but where there should have been a door, there was nothing. Nothing but a hole, as tall and wide as four of me—ugly, gaping, angry.

A woman came toward me, and it took me a long second, longer than you'd believe, to realize it was Mother. "Ruthie!"

My eyes went straight to her notebook: *Bmb.*

"Oh, Ruthie. It's horrible. Shattered columns, broken windows, plaster ripped off the walls, an office wrecked, damage to the Social Hall, the sanctuary."

"What happened? What *happened*?" An hour ago, I was Davis-daydreaming, slathering Noxzema on my face, and now my head was throbbing with *bmb, bmb, bmb.*

"Dynamite low to the ground against this wall. That's why I left you a note."

"How do you know?" As soon as I asked, I felt sick. I kicked at the grass.

"It came across the wire at the main house. The Teletype went crazy. Ten bells." Her stockings were splattered with red.

"God, was anyone here? Max?"

"It was four in the morning. Did you hear it? I thought it was an earthquake."

"I didn't hear." At four in the morning, I was with Davis, turning the turntable—and the timetable—over in my mind. I pointed at Mother's legs. "Is that blood?"

"Red clay. Mud. Water pipes burst." Mother held my hand. Her grip was fierce.

"Where's Nattie?" I said, letting go of Mother and spinning slowly around, looking at all the places Nattie wasn't. She'd spent the night with Leah, but weren't the rabbi and his house vulnerable?

"I phoned the rabbi's house as soon as I heard. Dina told me she sent Leah and Nattie on bikes around the neighborhood to tell people not to come this morning. She called them her 'Paula Reveres,' spreading the news." Mother's laugh was high, uneasy.

And then her legs jellied, and Mother was knee-first in the mud. "Nattie's safe. We're all safe." Her voice cracked. "But what a world. After your father—"

I helped Mother up, my eyes welling.

She stood, her hose laddered down the front. "I'm going to stay here awhile. Let Daddy take you home." It was only the second time she'd called her father Daddy since we'd become sudden southerners.

"Are you reporting this? Is Mr. Hank letting you? Where's the rabbi? And Max?" Asking about Max again made my throat hot.

"The rabbi is inside. I don't know about Max."

We walked closer to the side entrance—to what used to be the side entrance—and stood elbow to elbow, like I had with Fontaine in Mother's tiara on what seemed like a long-ago afternoon, when sunniness swallowed up all the shade. With Mother now, the view was fully shadow. We took in the hole with jagged wooden teeth and chewed-up bricks and shredded bits of choir robes, some blown clear out to the lawn. Ribbons of metal dangled from the ceiling, looking like they had nothing better to do than sever some-one's hand.

My stomach moved up to my chest and displaced my heart.

Mother kissed the top of my head and held me close.

I stepped back, opened my pocketbook, and took out my own EZ-on-the-Eyes notebook. "Let me stay."

She shook her head.

"I'm a good observer."

Mother glanced at her own notebook, and I knew then she'd agree. By being her daughter, I'd learned how to see things and record them.

"Do not—do *not*—go in the building," she said, her back to the opening.

I nodded, tightening the grip on my pen.

"You see that rock?" She pointed to a silver-flecked boulder at the edge of the parking lot where Max had semi-taught me to drive. "Sit on it. Sit there and witness."

Following orders, I sat on the stone, warm from the sun, not caring about crossing my ankles in the pink-booklet S shape. My feet were sore, and my eyes were sore. The smoke stung the back of my throat, and I was glad.

I wrote down what I always noticed first: what people wore. The detectives, at least I thought they were detectives, looked like waiters from the Club, in dark pants, white shirts, black ties. A fireman's shirt was gunmetal gray. He was talking to a man with his back to me in a navy jacket. Older, familiar-looking men, including Mr. Silvermintz, held their cuffed trouser legs up as they sloshed around the mud.

I made myself look back at the building, straight into the damage, and I took notes about something other than clothes. I counted twenty-six—no, twenty-seven—windows blown out on this side, some of them the delicate stained-glass pieces that had turned Nattie's ankles lilac the first day. Already, I couldn't remember what the windows had looked like, all put back together.

The building shuddered for a half second, and bits of black—bomb confetti—rained down, fluttering against the too-beautiful blue sky. I reached out, wanting to push the flakes of prayer books or activity pamphlets or choir music or plaster flowers from the wedding-cake ceiling into my skirt pockets.

But when I grabbed the confetti, it fell apart. My hands were covered in soot.

I rubbed my eyes, rubbed my nose. I must have slashed ash all over my face, but I didn't care.

A long metal ladder clanged against the side of the building, stretching up fifty feet or five hundred. A fireman, his jacket beribboned with epaulets, barked orders. One man climbed the ladder, then another, then another, then a fourth, positioning themselves at different heights.

The first man unfurled a long black drape, which drifted down slowly, billowing over the building, a giant-sized shroud. Each man grabbed the canvas as it came by, banging nails all around the broken windows, covering the pretty arches with black blanks, covering up the hate after all.

A group of mothers and daughters floated up from the street. A girl—Judy—screamed. She was from Nattie's class and had the teal cat-eye glasses. The rabbi was suddenly at her side. Of course, he'd been here all along, I realized. He was the one in the blue blazer talking to the policeman. He kneeled in front of Judy, eye to eye.

I knew—knew in my bones—the stained glass, the robes, the bomb confetti were revenge for the rabbi and his integration sermons.

The water pipes could get fixed, and the windows could get restained or whatever it was you did with stained glass. But I could never look at this place, and Judy could never look at this place, and feel unhated.

"What a damn shame, Ruthie." I looked up to see Mr. Hank in a fedora. I threw myself into him, my sooty hands around his bony shoulders.

He pulled back. "This is your place."

It wasn't a question, but I nodded.

With his cane, Mr. Hank nudged a few shiny splinters into a pile. He stared down at the shards of lilac glass that had bathed the sanctuary in dreamy light. He offered me his handkerchief. "You've got a little something on your nose."

I waved him off. "I want it there."

"Understood. The police are combing ten blocks in each direction, knocking on doors, stopping cars." He reached down and picked up the glass with the handkerchief, wrapping the pieces like they were a most fragile gift. Then he tapped the press pass hanging around his neck. "I'm going to see what I can find out."

Mr. Hank walked into the damaged temple—and I followed, going inside the building I'd sworn to stay out of.

There were men—firemen, policemen, temple men—taking notes and taking pictures, but no one even blinked at me.

The bomb had blown out the vestibule and buried a bronze plaque listing all the temple members who'd been killed in military service. It had destroyed the sisterhood shop; a bunch of hand-knit baby blankets floated in burst-pipe water. It had toppled a glass case filled with menorahs. I waded through it all and into the sanctuary, where there was no beautiful, delicate light, the windows covered in that black canvas nailed into the surrounding bricks from the outside.

I went up the steps to the bima, the pulpit, and stood in front of the spectacular golden ark. A layer of plaster coated the prayer book open on the lectern. With my finger, I cleared away the dust to read the words: *Oh God, may all*

*created in Thine image recognize that they are brethren, so that, one
in spirit and one in fellowship, they may be forever united.*

This perfect passage made me want to tell Max, to
find Max. The stairs up to our classroom were blocked by
a broken-off column, but I squeezed past.

And he was there, in our doorway. Max's hair was damp,
separated into little fingers on his forehead. He grabbed me
around the waist and hugged me hard. He smelled salty and
safe. My tears, his sweat, it all seemed related, part of the
same ocean.

My arms rested against his back. I could feel him
breathing.

Crumpled in his hand was a flash of pink—a construction-
paper animal, one of the kangaroos I'd cut out while Max
led the kids in the Noah's Ark song. "There's a hole right
through the wall," he said. "Shrapnel everywhere."

I traced my finger along the stupid kangaroo. "What if
the—" I didn't want to say the word "bomb." "What if it had
gone off during class?" I knew Max must have been thinking
it too—the gold robes, the guitar, the pink kangaroo, the *kids*.

"Will you pray with me?" Max's eyes were a watery
smear.

"I can't." I was a faker. Faking Covenant, faking cotillion, faking the Lord's Prayer, faking Judaism. I didn't even
know if I believed in God.

"It's okay," he said, his mouth to my ear. "Do it anyway."

Max said words in Hebrew, soft and fast—and they were familiar. They were my father's words, my New York words.

Instead, I said my own words, barely out loud—Natalie Louise Robb, Sara Eleanor Robb, Alice Fontaine Landry Robb, Arthur Abraham Robb. An incantation. A prayer.

20

The Genus of the Pineapple

"So"—Rabbi Selwick smiled—"this is what it takes to get you to come to services."

He started the meeting at three o'clock exactly, eleven hours after the blast, in the bombed-out sanctuary. The pews were full, as full as High Holiday services, and I had a spot in the front row, along with Nattie, Max, and Leah, and Mrs. Selwick, who was wearing a defiantly cheerful floral dress. Here we were. Here we all were, with the exception of Mother, who'd gone to the newsroom.

The rabbi smoothed the hair that had taken flight the night he and Max came over for dinner. "Let me tell you what we know. Early this morning—shortly before four a.m.—fifty cardboard cylinders of dynamite exploded in our sacred building. The cylinders appeared to be homemade and were packed in a suitcase. The blast woke people from their sleep several blocks away. The building has hundreds of thousands of dollars of damage, but that's unimportant. What's important is this: We thank God no one was hurt."

The air had a metallic taste mixed with a whiff of something sweet, something tropical. I sucked my lips in.

"This is our Leo Frank," the rabbi said, his voice free of his usual singsong dramatics. "What his lynching meant to previous generations, this bombing will mean for ours."

Max nodded, his hands balled up in his pockets, a corner of the kangaroo sticking out of his chinos.

I looked up at the dome; a custodian had turned on all the lights, so it glowed down on us. It seemed ridiculous to have been afraid to climb up there with Max. Now there were bigger things to be afraid of. I wanted to remember this moment, to engrave it like one of Fontaine's note cards. It had happened, and it couldn't unhappen.

The sadness I'd been skipping a step ahead of caught up with me again. The tears started as a trickle, slipping down my cheeks and chin. A few plopped on the collar of the Peter Pan blouse. I wasn't usually a crier, not even after Dad died. But today the smoke and the blasted-out bricks and the broken glass and prayer book ash made me cry, cry, cry.

Rabbi Selwick gripped the lectern. "Mr. Hank Landry of the *Gazette* tells us the paper received notification within fifteen minutes of the explosion. The caller said he was with an organization called the Confederate Underground, a known Klan group." The rabbi looked down at his notes, and those note cards made me want to hug Nattie. My hands were so clammy I thought they'd slide right off her, but they didn't.

"The caller said, 'We bombed a temple in Midtown. This is the last empty building we will bomb. Negroes and Jews are hereby declared aliens.' Already, I've heard from our clergy neighbors. Northside Presbyterian and Wesley Methodist have offered their chapels for our services. East Rivers offered us classrooms for Sunday school. This underground group thought they'd blow this city apart, but the opposite is true."

Mrs. Selwick leaned over and patted my insane, probably electrified-looking hair. The waterworks started again, and I saw I was in good company. Max fiddled with his belt, eyes glued to the buckle. Farther down the row, Mrs. Silvermintz took her sunglasses off, then put them back on.

The mayor, in wire spectacles, took the microphone next. "These criminals, these supremacists, must've wanted to pit our city against itself. Let's prove them wrong." He listed other southern temples that had been bombed by white supremacists, not all of them successfully: Charlotte, North Carolina; Gastonia, North Carolina; Nashville, Tennessee;

Birmingham, Alabama. He told us that on a single night in Alabama, four churches were bombed along with the homes of Reverend Martin Luther King Jr. and Reverend Ralph Abernathy. He reminded us that we were a small part of a larger story of hate, that all along, the clock had been ticking. And now the alarm rang for us.

***

Max drove Nattie and me home. Fontaine, who'd been kept apprised of the goings-on via the Teletype, poured Max and me a drink from Mr. Hank's brass bar cart—a cocktail shaker full of whiskey and hope. She had the little television on, a fuzzy image of Douglas Edwards of CBS News showing pictures of our temple. We drained our glasses while Fontaine got Nattie involved in a game of gin rummy on the porch.

I took Max out to the perfectly aligned chaise lounges, where Frooshka greeted him in her crazy poodle way—all four paws off the ground, mouth wide open. He scratched her behind the ears, and she, and we, settled into the shade.

There were no words to say. None. "Should I get the transistor radio?" I asked Max. "We could listen to music."

"Let's listen to nothing," he said.

I closed my eyes. They didn't sting anymore.

"I don't know," Max said, not taking his own advice. His voice was quiet, and I kept my eyes closed. "The caller said,

'Jews are hereby declared aliens.' What do you say to some-one who believes that?"

I elbowed up and he did the same, and then I noticed the flutter of his pulse at his temple, near those crazy eyebrows. It was like he was transparent, like I could see the bruise of the day, the pain of it all, right there.

We both collapsed back into our respective chaises, and I was reminded of lying on the temple roof, unprotected against the wind, the sun turning purple inside my closed eyelids. But then Frooshka curled around my feet, and I let myself nod off.

I was dreamily thinking of Davis, of last night, of hands—his, mine—when I felt a flick of water on my actual face.

My eyes flew open to see a real Davis standing above me. I shot a glance to the other chaise—empty.

"Tired?" Davis's smile was huge. "Long night last night?"

"What?" The sun was over his shoulder, and his body threw a shadow my way.

"You're not dressed for swimming," he said.

"Swimming?" I'd totally forgotten I'd invited him to the pool. I sat up and saw that Max had relocated next to Nattie, his socks and shoes off, pants rolled up, both of them dangling toes in the shallow end and singing something soft and sweet.

Davis followed my look. "Hey, the driving instructor," he said, nodding to Max.

"Hey." Max shook his feet half dry and stuck his socks and shoes back on. "I'm going to go. When's that next driving lesson, Ruth Robb?"

"Tomorrow." I said it deliberately, wanting to imbue the word with hope and belief. "I'll see you tomorrow."

"I'm going to change for a swim," Nattie said.

Max took off one way, and Nattie, the other—and Davis, he dropped into the chaise next to me.

"Did you hear about it—the bomb?" I asked Davis, rubbing my eyes.

"Yeah. You look cute asleep," he said, hair flopping over one eye.

"Not today I don't—nothing's cute today." You would think this would have been the time to tell Davis everything. What day could be better?

I pulled Frooshka into my lap even though she was too big. I wanted a living, breathing mammal that knew me— knew me and loved me anyway. I put my hand over her heart and let the rhythm of its beats calm me.

We sat there in the early evening light—his skin, his sunshine smell, his bermuda shorts, his breath at my neck. After all the ash, it was so nice, so necessary, to feel love and beauty in the world. And it seemed perfect Davis would be here right now, that he would know I was aching, through osmosis or a scientific term I didn't know the name of.

"It's been a really, really hard day," I said. "I was there."

He jerked his head up. "Where?"

"At the temple."

"On Peachtree?"

I nodded and considered what to say next. "My mother was covering the story."

"Oh, makes sense." Davis walked his fingers inside my shirt to pluck a bra strap. "You want to run my car through the car wash?"

I shook my head. A car wash was more fun when you didn't need one.

"Hi, Davis," Nattie said. She was back in her good old navy bathing suit. *Un, deux, trois*—into the pool she went. Frooshka flopped in after her, a big splash of floof.

"Isn't it freezing?" I yelled over.

"I'll get used to it," Nattie said.

The light was glimmery, the magic hour when everything, from the bushes to the swoop of Davis's hair, was outlined in bursts of gold. Gold like the temple.

Nattie paddled over, hanging off the side, her face covered in pearls of water. "Ruthie, can you bring me the pineapple towel?" It was Dad's favorite—he pined for pineapple, he'd said—and I'd last seen it folded under the sink in the bathroom.

I went inside to grab the towel and to change, but I did

the former and not the latter. When I came back, I found Davis (on land) and Nattie (in water) deep in a conversation about the genus of the pineapple. "'Ananas' is the original name, and it means 'excellent fruit,'" Davis was saying. And it made me love Davis a whole new layer of love. He didn't just know me; he knew what to say to fact-loving Nattie on this dark, dark day.

Nattie held the towel to her face, letting the tail of it dip into the twenty-two thousand gallons of chilly, chlorinated blue.

"Nattie, count for me," I said.

"*Un, deux*—but you're not changed," she said. "*Trois*—"

I dropped down, straight down, soldier-style, and gasped.

My swirly skirt billowed out like a parachute before plastering itself against my goose bumps. I rubbed my arms, oddly happy to feel the prickles.

Then, boom, Davis was in, too—shirt, shorts, tennis shoes.

Nattie fluttered around us, her kicks wobbling the water's surface.

Davis and I sank, together, to the bottom, where it was even more Siberian.

The thin ribbon that separated the air and the water here—gone. The ribbon that separated my heart from Davis's—gone. Davis grabbed me around the waist and spun me, my skirt catching a tiny swell in the shallow end. The pool felt smaller with our clothes on. I blew a long trail of bubbles, saying our family names like a prayer, saying even part of the Shehecheyanu, an actual prayer, until the water between Davis and me was cloudy with air. And yet we could still see each other through the frosty, fading light.

21

In Search of Hickories

I woke to an oppressive rainstorm, which seemed the right weather for a day after a bombing. Mother had fallen asleep in our room, and she was still sacked out next to Nattie. I dressed fast—a vivid grass-green jumper—and walked outside, right through a bunch of puddles, the ground smelling earthy and deep.

The lights were off in the main house, so I parked myself on the porch, kicked off my soaked flats, and rocked. I picked at the hem of the jumper, which suddenly looked an inhuman color against the gray of the day.

From over my shoulder, I heard an authoritative knock and turned to see Mr. Hank tapping on the window of his office with his cane. I went to him, rain-squishy shoes and all.

He was behind his desk, dressed for work. A coffee per-colator perked away on the credenza. Birdie entered the room holding the same silver tray she used to serve Nattie and me those perfect Coke floats our first weekend here. She centered the tray—with an octagonal breakfast plate of a fried egg over grits and a glass of juice—on the desk. "I didn't know you'd be joining in, Ruth. What can I get you?"

"Did you hear, Birdie?" From the side table I grabbed today's paper with its all-capitals headline: JEWISH TEMPLE ON PEACHTREE WRECKED BY DYNAMITE BLAST. "Are you shocked?"

Birdie looked to the window where the rain pelted down and gave a good long sigh. "I am not shocked, I'm sorry to say. Not one bit." She started to leave, her shoes shushing on the Oriental rug. But then she turned around. "Usually, I would find a reason to be busy in the kitchen, but my heart is heavy for you, Ruth. It's a stone."

"Thanks, Birdie," Mr. Hank said.

Her eyes flicked from him to me. "But my heart is a stone more days than I'd care to acknowledge."

Then she exited quick as a match, and I was left with a stone—a boulder, a whole quarry—of worry for us all.

Mr. Hank took the paper from me and unfurled it. "We haven't run a banner in a long time—a headline that stretches across the whole front page."

269

"I couldn't sleep." I rubbed crusties out of my eyes and paced, thinking I likely wasn't the first Landry to carve a pattern on this Oriental rug. My exhaustion was fanning the room's gloomy mood.

Mr. Hank poured me a coffee, black. "Me either. A bomb in Atlanta—can't imagine who would stoop to that."

"Can't imagine," I said, but the reason I couldn't sleep was that I could imagine. I couldn't sleep because of the paper kangaroo and the broken glass—and because of Oren. "Mr. Hank, can I ask you something?"

"What's on your mind?" I noticed then he hadn't shaved. His stubble was salt-and-pepper, and he looked ten years older than he had yesterday.

"Davis's brother, Oren," I started.

"The Georgia Tech starter?"

The rain hit the window in bursts.

"I think—" I studied one of the intricate paisleys on the rug. "I—I happened to be at Davis's family hunting cabin the other night." I glugged the not-sweet coffee, thinking of the heavy warm weight of Davis on me before we heard Oren crashing through the woods.

Mr. Hank said not a word. He'd once told me that the way to get a source to keep talking was to be quiet, that good reporters were good listeners.

"Oren showed up really early that morning. And"—the

thought was so unlikely I had a hard time pushing it out of my mouth—"his story made no sense. Something's off. I can feel it."

Mr. Hank reached to his desk and flipped open his notebook: same as Mother's, same as mine. "Reporters don't go on feelings, but you know that."

"Oren said he was out of gas. It must be ten miles from Atlanta to the cabin."

"What are your questions?"

I looked at him blankly.

"You say Oren showed up in the middle of the night and your reporter instincts went off," he said. "Go through the who, what, when, where, why, and how—which is the most important?"

"The how? The why? The who? It's all important." I put the coffee down, not able to swallow all the bitterness. I wanted to be the kind of girl who could drink coffee black, but I wasn't. "Why did he come to the cabin? If you're out of gas, you buy gas. You don't run to the woods—you don't run to the woods the same night a temple is bombed."

Mr. Hank tapped his cane on the rug to the beat of an unheard tune. "I spent a long year on the crime beat when I was younger. I'll call the detective desk and ask if Oren Jefferson is on their list of suspects. But I don't have much to tell them—a boy took a run on the night of the bombing."

"And another why—why did he smell so odd?" I said. "Not like smoke, but like bananas, of all things to smell like."

"Bananas?"

"Bananas."

"Huh. Some people say the sweet-sour smell of dynamite is like bananas, but there could be a simpler explanation."

Some part of me smashed into a brick wall—a brick temple—because it struck me I'd smelled bananas yesterday, the too-sweet tropical smell that had wafted amid the ash. I wished I knew if Oren had a lifelong love for bananas or something, but of course I barely knew him. I only knew it made no sense that Davis's brother would be involved in something hateful, ugly, vicious, criminal.

Mr. Hank shifted in his chair. "Atlanta has a well-deserved reputation for civility, and many are convinced the bomb was set from outside, that native Atlantans respect and love the city too much to have done such an act. And it's true that the Klan has, of late, been considered up-country rabble-rousers, a bunch of bigoted lunatics. I'd be surprised if a student from Covenant or Tech had reason to be involved. But—"

"But?" The undrinkable coffee was making a move back up my throat.

"But bigots can live anywhere. You take any thousand men around and outside the city, and at least one is going

272

to have a skeleton in his closet that looks an awful lot like a Klansman hood."

From the corner table, the Teletype rang its heart-clutching clang. Five dings. "Go on." Mr. Hank waved toward the machine. "See what we've got."

I tore the bulletin from the lug of a machine and read the first paragraph, the "lede"—intentionally misspelled, Mr. Hank had taught me—out loud. " 'President Eisenhower calls upon FBI Director J. Edgar Hoover to investigate the bombing of the Atlanta temple.' "

"Story's getting bigger, not smaller," Mr. Hank said.

The bulletin had a raggedy edge where I'd ripped it unevenly, and I folded the top over, trying to make a straight line.

But while my hands were on the bulletin, my mind drifted to bigger questions, like how fate had brought me to Atlanta and to Davis and to the temple. "I wouldn't even be here if Dad hadn't died," I said. "Isn't it insane?" The truth of it was so unmissable, I didn't know how I'd missed it. "All the happiness—moonlight and magnolias, Davis, Gracie. It all comes from sadness." I forgot about straightening the bulletin and started tearing little fingers along the paper's side.

"Nothing is all happiness, not even in New York," Mr. Hank said, which seemed the perfect thing to say.

I put the bulletin on top of Mr. Hank's stack. My fingers were jumpy. I flipped up the underside of my jumper and considered the hem. It had a perfect line of sewing-machine stitches, but I worked my nail under one and tugged. The stitches came out in a satisfying rip. In no time, I'd yanked out half the hem, tearing away the hurt—the missing Dad, the bombed-out temple, the mystery brother, the lies I'd told and almost told.

Keeping my eyes on the threads, I said, "Jews tear things—some Jews tear some things—when someone dies."

"I didn't know that," Mr. Hank said.

"I think only more religious Jews do it. I think tearing your clothes is a visible way to show you are torn apart. Or maybe that's too literal."

Mother honked from the motor court. I looked out to see her changed and lipsticked and behind the wheel, Nattie snuggled in tight, enough room for me in the front.

"Go on, Ruthie," Mr. Hank said.

When I stood up, an impressive pile of threads rained down on the Oriental rug.

———

The wipers divided the windshield into two arcs, sweeping from the center to the side, then back, a rainbow without the hues or the happiness. We pulled up to Covenant, where both flags—the US flag and the Georgia flag, with the state seal on one side and the Confederate bars and stars on the rest—drooped wet and sad from the metal pole. No one was waiting at the bench under the tree. No one was waiting anywhere.

By the time I slipped into my chair in Mr. Sawyer's room, the Lord's Prayer was half over. I knew it inside out by now, like I'd been saying the words all my life.

And by the time Davis and I met up after school, it had stopped raining. I hugged him right away, needing to feel his solidness. We leaned against the door of the Rambler, still shimmery with drizzle. "Twenty hours since I've done this," he said, walking his fingers up the bottom of his now-mine jacket, under the hem of my unhemmed jumper.

"Whoa-etta." Five fingers on my thigh and suddenly I was back in the cabin with the thumping turntable. I stayed against him, my cheek on his shirt.

Davis opened the passenger door, and I climbed in, remembering the zeroes on his dash Saturday night, remembering the zero clothes between us, and feeling fiercely sad those firsts were now braided together with the awfulness of yesterday and the worseness of Oren (maybe) and my pile of lies (definitely). I held the empty cuff of Davis's jacket like a hand.

"I keep thinking about what it would be like to wake up with you like we did that morning—to do that all the time," Davis said. We rocketed past the big houses of West Paces

Ferry, and I took in the infinite lawns, the squeaky-clean windows squeegeed by Birdies and Normas between ironing the
pillowcases and serving up the lemon squares. I imagined the
gardeners measuring the distance between the lined-up chaises
by the backyard pools. "I've been thinking that nonstop,"
Davis went on. "To spend all night and wake up in the morning, you still there." At the red light, he touched my lower lip.

"That would be"—I tried to find the right word—
"impossible."

"Nah." Davis drove right past Fontaine and Mr. Hank's
place. The sun slanted through the window sideways, and
his face lit up. "I've got something to tell you, but we need a
hickory tree to sit under," he said.

"Why hickory?" I asked instead of: Are you going to tell
me you know something about me? Or us? Or Oren?

"The leaves are kind of a miracle."

We pulled up in front of the stables of Chastain Park, and
for a panicked second, I thought he was going to ask me to
saddle up one of those horses I didn't know how to ride.

We walked on a curved path alongside trees with heaps
of foliage—clusters of five and seven leaves, grouped together
like a bouquet.

"Hickories," Davis said, slowly backing me up against
the shaggy bark of a huge tree. "I am so in love with you,
Ruth Tarbell Robb."

I loved that he didn't hesitate—that he came right out with the declaration in the light of day, fully clothed, as witnessed by the hickories of the natural world.

"Davis Jeff—wait, what's your middle name?"

"Edwin."

"Okay, good. Davis Edwin Jefferson, I love you."

Heat shot up my neck. How had I not known what I'd so wanted him to know about me?

Davis Edwin took my hand, and we settled into a park bench. He pulled a small velvet box from the front pocket of his khakis. "This has been in the family." He and his floppy hair swooped in for a quick, confident kiss.

A breeze ruffled the hickories, and a five-leaf cluster wandered down from the sky, still damp from the day's rain. Slowly, slowly, I opened the box. Nestled inside was a milky opal ring. "It's so, so pretty," I whispered.

"It was my grandmother's. I asked Momma if I could give it to you. A promise ring. An engaged-to-be-engaged ring. We can make it official the second you turn twenty-one."

"I love it," I said, closing my hands around the ring. "I *love* it." My heart zinged to thinking of our lives at twenty-one. Would I still go to Sarah Lawrence, like Mother, like Sara? Would Davis come north? Maybe Columbia? How many nights could we spend together before I turned twenty-one? A thousand, give or take?

He slid the ring on my hand. "Left hand, third finger—
that's what Momma says about a promise ring. I love everything about you," he said into my rain-crazed hair.

I looked right at Davis, wanting to see myself as he saw
me. But I just saw those freckles, and my eyes welled up.
Would he ever have given me this ring if he knew I was
Jewish? Or knew I had pieces of stained glass from the temple in the top drawer of my dresser? Or knew I worried his
brother had a skeleton in his closet that looked an awful lot
like a hood? All those questions were there, whether I said
them or not—like the constellations Davis said were in the
sky, with or without my noticing.

We stood up, and Davis hugged me, tight and true. I tied
his jacket around my waist, the leather arms like his arms.
"I'm going to sleep with this, the ring and the jacket—don't
laugh." Or do, I thought. I loved his laugh.

He rubbed a spot on the jacket. "My heart is right here—
on my sleeve."

"That's the cuff." I kissed him.

"Still," he said. "I gave you my heart—be careful with it."

22

Perfect Smoke Rings

"You are a *vision*, Ruth," Fontaine said as she zipped me into the Magnolia gown she'd bought me that day at Lumet's.

We'd just come home from the hairdresser, where Frederic did up my hair, plastering the whole pouf into a chignon. Fontaine was tying and retying the sash on the gown when Mother knocked and walked into my room, a move right out of Fontaine's playbook.

"I thought you might rather wear a relic," Mother said. She held her Magnolia dress. The dress I'd tried on at Fontaine's urging on the first day of school. The dress Mother had forbidden me to wear because it represented the pinnacle of shallowness. "I had it pressed—dusted the fust right out of it."

"Alice." Fontaine petted the dress like it was the poodle. "You found your heart."

"Or lost my mind," Mother said, but she was smiling.

Fontaine swiped at her eyes. "After all that's happened this last week, it's even more important to remember the beauty in this city."

"I'd rather we concede the ugliness, Mother, or as you might say, the unpleasantness. But it doesn't mean Ruth can't wear a dress with a story." She held it out, an offering.

Nattie turned on the transistor radio, and Elvis himself, king of more than the casserole, serenaded us. He loved us tender.

I slipped out of the Lumet's dress and into Mother's. It was the perfect blue with hints of gray. Sort of French and sort of southern and sort of sophisticated. My heart hammered against my ribs. I jumped up to see bits of myself in the mirror over the dressing table, thinking I'd last tried this dress on in the pre-Davis era, in a different season, as a different person.

At six o'clock sharp, Davis pulled up in a very clean Rambler. I answered the door, a step ahead of the other women in the house. Davis held a pinkish-coral orchid for me. With his other hand, he wove his fingers in mine, and it was crazy how a little bit of skin-to-skin-ness launched a riot in my chest.

He spun the ring around my not-ring finger. When Mother had seen the opal, she'd said, "Wear it on your right hand—there are no left-hand promises until you're twenty-one." And then she said, "And twenty-one is a lifetime away. You'll have a college degree by then." I moved the ring, but it didn't change the dream.

Davis plucked Mother's dress away from my chest and threaded a stickpin in and out of the silk—right over the right bosom (Mrs. Drummond would be so pleased). The corsage, I realized, was the perfect color for the dress I was no longer wearing.

"Sorry," I whispered into his neck. "I changed my mind at the last minute—family over fashion."

"'S okay," he muttered, but something looked wrong with his smile.

"You forgot the cummerbund," Nattie pointed out. "Boys wear them with tuxedos."

Davis rubbed his chin with the back of his hand. I bet he was thinking, as I was thinking, it wouldn't make a fig's difference later, because the later-plan was to be alone in a borrowed cabana at Davis's club.

As we waltzed out the door, me and my mismatched corsage, he and his missing cummerbund, Fontaine said, "Davis, you make sure that jacket is buttoned up for the photo. The professional will have a setup in the lobby."

"Yes, ma'am," he said.

Fontaine's capital-C Club was decked out with glitter-dusted garlands of the namesake magnolia. One hundred girls from around the city were gathering with their dates on a black-and-white marble dance floor. The band—the Reed Tucker Orchestra, according to the name stenciled on the drum—was already in the swing, playing my very favorite song, "You Send Me" by Sam Cooke. And Davis did send me. Honest, he did.

Claudia, in her stolen charmeuse, was cheek-to-cheek with Oren, showing off a clavicle so sharp it could slice salami. Where had she changed out of her original prim dress? I'd have to ask Gracie. Nearby, T-Ann and her sequins held hands with a dapper-looking Jimmy.

The music was loud, the air sweet, and Davis took my hand as we slow-danced. I closed my eyes and tipped into him, loving that the glitter from the swags drifted onto our shoulders and dusted our fingers, loving this boy, loving Mother, loving Fontaine, loving the temple, loving how the city came together to condemn the bombing, loving that in this one, *one* moment all the pieces were part of a great sparkly whole.

All around us were beautiful couples—so many of whom I didn't know—and it was a reminder Atlanta was a bigger place than the rolling lawns of Buckhead would suggest. I wondered if there were any fellow Jews hiding here. Probably not. Most self-respecting Jews wouldn't be caught dead (or alive) at a club (or Club) that didn't want them.

Someone jostled my elbow, and I moved out of the path of a silver tray.

I turned to see none other than Max in a tuxedo.

"What are you *doing* here?" I said.

"Working." But it wasn't Max—it was just another skinny boy in Buddy Holly glasses offering a canapé. Jewish people probably couldn't even work at the Club.

A part of me was oddly proud—defiantly proud—to be in a club that wouldn't allow me to join. Here I was standing amid the loveliness. My feet on the marble, my lips on the glasses. They didn't want me, yet I was here. But the other half—the getting-louder-in-my-chest half—called bunk. If no one knew who I was, if no one knew I wasn't welcome, then I wasn't standing up for a single thing. I was back to being invisible, and what good came from that?

I looked up to catch Davis's eye. "There's something you don't know about me." There was no air between us, only his tuxedo shirt, my magnolia leaves.

He whispered into my hair. "I know every inch of you."

Before I could get the truth out of my mouth, out of my pores, Claudia and Oren spun into our orbit.

Oren's boozy breath hit me before his words. "Pretty, pretty dress." Oren pinched Mother's skirt with his football fingers.

"Take it easy, O," Davis said.

Oren held Claudia's hips. "I've been thinking of your

dress, too, Claud. Tell me, what color would you call that?" He'd used that very line on Claudia at the swim party.

"I call it Gilded Lily." Claudia's voice teetered along with her heels.

"Or Lumet's Gold," I said.

Claudia's smile soured. "You want to talk about Lumet's? Because then you—"

"Or Choir Robe Gold." I wasn't thinking about Claudia or the dress. And I wasn't thinking about the waiter who wasn't Max. I was thinking about the real Max, who knew the real me. I was thinking about the real temple and the real suitcase with fifty sticks of real dynamite.

Claudia laughed, loud. "Choir robes aren't gold. At our church, they're black."

Oren said, "They're gold at the temp—"

"Shut up, O," Davis said. "Just shut up."

Oren was definitely sloshy. His oxford wing tip was untied, and he stumbled as he left Claudia on the dance floor. Claudia threw up her hands and traipsed after him.

The band segued to Sinatra. I spun Davis around, switching our lead-and-follow. My mind was a needle that kept jumping the groove. Oren knew the color of the choir robes.

Before the song finished, I led Davis by the hand off the dance floor.

On the terrace, Davis leaned in for a kiss.

"That's not why we're out here," I said, backing away from him.

"No?" Davis lit a cigarette and blew a perfect smoke ring, the kind I seemed incapable of learning. "We better not stay long. They're about to crown the court." He slipped one hand into his trouser pocket.

"Oren was there." I hadn't wanted to think it, but now I couldn't unthink it. I rubbed my arms. Finally, there was a chill in the air. Finally, the air felt familiar.

"What? Where?" Davis exhaled. Another perfecto smoke ring.

"At the temple the night of the bombing. Otherwise, how'd he know about the robes—that they're gold?"

Davis paused the briefest moment, and my heart clamped shut. "Must've read it somewhere."

"Davis—"

"Maybe that's not exactly true, but it's in the neighborhood of true," he said, dimple deployed to full effect.

A vein throbbed over my eye. What did that even mean, "in the neighborhood of true"? Did truth have a border, a boundary, a precise pinprick on a map? I said my words quietly, carefully. "Those robes were brand new. Special-ordered from a place in Boston."

"Huh, how would you know that?" He scratched his cheek. "From your mother?"

Right away, I thought of Mr. Hank's reporting tip and didn't say anything so Davis would keep talking.

Davis gave a funny, strangled laugh. "Okay, you got me, but it's not what you think. Let me tell you what happened after O ran out of gas."

I stepped back and right into a sticky patch of leaves. I lifted Mother's dress up and out of the muck and steadied myself on the railing.

"Oren was completely boozed up—he was in no position to drive. So I took him back to the temple. To get the stupid Georgia Tech hat he'd left behind. Thousands of guys in Atlanta have that hat, but O didn't know about fingerprints or what have you."

That explained the miles on the car.

"I had no choice, Ruth." Davis dropped what was left of the cigarette, a smoldering firefly, and went after it with his loafer, grinding it around and around until everything was reduced to ash. "I sped him back, and he got his hat. And those robes—a couple of them—they were out on the lawn. Pieces of them."

Inside my head, I yelled: Davis was there, there, there. But outside my head, I nodded and waited for him to go on.

He swallowed.

I swallowed.

Davis rubbed his fingers along a nonexistent crease in his tuxedo pants. "Oren got mixed up in something with the Jews—one of Cranford's buddies planned it. They stuffed dynamite in a suitcase, but everybody knows that by now. It was a prank that got out of hand, Ruth. That's all."

"It wasn't a prank, Davis. It was a bomb."

"Thank God no one was hurt." On "hurt," Davis's voice quivered. He ironed himself into me—like that night—both of us up against the perfect painted brick of the perfect Club. But unlike all those other times when the feeling of Davis against my hip made my mind go blank, my thoughts stayed clear and certain.

I ran my fingers over the embroidered leaves of Mother's dress and borrowed her nerve. I was trembly. My hands, but also my heart, my eyelids, a spot at the center of my throat. My body was ahead of my mind—it knew I was going to speak up before I knew what would actually tumble, tremble, out of my mouth. "He's your brother, but it's my temple. My father is Jewish. And me, too. I've been going there with my mother and sister for months. I've lied to you—I've lied to everyone."

"What?" Davis snapped, and it came out almost like a laugh. "You're telling me you're Jewish? And you never thought to tell me this before?"

"I didn't tell you, and then I didn't know how to tell you I hadn't told you."

"You spring it on me now? Here? Give me a second." He blew out two short, sharp breaths and tapped his long-toed loafer very, very fast.

I did spring it on him. I gave him a second, two, ten, twenty, while I thought of the mystery miles on the odometer and the phantom hood and the smell of bananas. Finally, I said, "I didn't think you'd want me to be Jewish, or maybe I didn't want me to be Jewish." It was cold enough to see my breath—cold enough to feel like home. "But it's what I am."

The truth of it hung there between us.

A few notes of "That'll Be the Day" drifted out the window.

Davis fisted his hands into his pockets. "He's my brother, Ruth."

Gracie busted through the door. "*There* you are, Roo. C'mon, the crowning is about to start." She handed me her lipstick, but I didn't give a fig.

The night was inside out. I was inside out.

I walked back into the ballroom, and Davis followed me.

Gracie and I joined the other ninety-eight girls in a semi-circle around the edge of the dance floor, our dates standing a respectful distance behind us.

A very petite, very poised woman, who introduced herself as Mrs. Hanshaw, took the stage, standing off-center in front of a microphone stand. She tipped the mike down so it was the right height, and her voice was shockingly deep and syrupy. "As you are aware, the Magnolia Queen and her ladies-in-waiting are the epitome of Atlanta grace. For the last one hundred years, though we skipped a year or two during the unpleasantness of the War Between the States, girls have been presented to society amid magnolia blooms. So, without further ado, I announce this year's Magnolia Court."

The spotlight whooshed around the room.

"Our third runner-up is a girl of great grace," Mrs. Hanshaw said, her mouth curling into a smile. "Miss Grace Eleet, please join me on the dais."

Gracie glided up with Buck on her arm. She smiled left, then right, her every powdered pore exuding charm, and positioned herself across the stage from Mrs. Hanshaw, leaving plenty of room for the remaining runners-up.

Davis plucked a petal off my corsage and rubbed it between his fingers. "I hate that this happened, especially since you're—"

It was suddenly too warm in the ballroom. I felt dizzy and quasi-nauseated, from the spiked punch or the now-obvious truth that no one could live two lives at once.

"Our next lady-in-waiting, second runner-up, is Carol Helen Pepper, whose Magnolia history dates back to the last century," Mrs. Hanshaw announced. A girl I didn't know took the stage, her auburn hair arranged in dreamy waves, a guy with a trim beard by her side.

"I wish I hadn't gone there," Davis said—that simple.

Mrs. Hanshaw continued on. "Our first runner-up, ceremonial of duty but ready to step in at a moment's notice, is the darling Miss Starling. Claudia, please join us."

Claudia and her shiny-as-sable hair and her shoplifted dress made her way up the stairs. Oren locked his arm in hers, smiling wide as a football field.

"Now," Mrs. Hanshaw said, "it is my abiding pleasure to declare this year's winner."

"Got to be you, Babe Ruth." Davis threaded his hand through mine. I could feel a callus on his palm. Had it always been there and I never noticed?

"Our 1958 Magnolia Queen is from royalty indeed. Her mother was queen. Her grandmother was queen. Her great-grand was queen. Ruth Landry—excuse me, Ruth Robb—please take your place in Atlanta history."

The girls closest to me started to clap, and soon the rest of the circle joined in until the room was filled with a round of polite applause. A few girls stepped back to give me a wide, gracious walkway to the stage. I gathered up Mother's gown—darkened by the muck on the terrace—and heel-toed my way up the stairs, not wanting to wobble in Fontaine's heels, not wanting to wobble for any reason whatsoever.

I stood in the center of the stage, the other girls to my right and Mrs. Hanshaw to my left, and my mouth lifted into a pink-booklet smile. I was still holding Davis's callused hand, feeling the strength of his fingers in mine.

Gracie gave me a quick hug and whispered "Congrats" in my ear.

The view was different here—from the stage, looking down, as opposed to from the dance floor, looking up. It was broader, more cinematic, not unlike the View-Master view from the temple's rotunda. From here, I could see all the girls who weren't Jewish and weren't New Yorkers and weren't, probably, fatherless. And weren't queens either.

From a small table, Mrs. Hanshaw lifted a crown made from magnolia leaves, glossy green on top and burnished brown beneath.

I glanced to leaf lover Davis, and he beamed back.

Mrs. Hanshaw settled the crown in my hair, securing it with a pair of bobby pins she slid from her sleeve. "Fontaine's granddaughter," she said with a smile. She wasn't anywhere near the microphone; the smile and the sentiment seemed real, just for me. "How wonderful."

So, this was what it felt like to have a crown on my head.

The leaves bit into my scalp. I reached up to touch them and was struck by how sad it was that these leaves had been alive until someone had come along and clipped them off.

The band played "'S Wonderful," and Claudia, Gracie, and Carol Helen Pepper waved s'marvelously, swiveling their wrists around as if they were a bunch of Queen Elizabeths.

I fished the bobby pins out of my hair and turned them over and over in my fingers.

"Are you all right?" Davis whispered.

I lifted the crown off my head and held it with both hands, like one of Fontaine's silver platters.

Claudia was the first to drop her wave.

Gracie sidestepped over to me. "I've pinned plenty of these—let me help you." She tried to lift the crown out of my hand.

"No—don't." I held the crown tight and closed my eyes. Everyone I loved floated into view. Knock-and-walk Fontaine. Write-fast-with-no-vowels Mother. Set-your-watch-back-thirty-years Dad. Mr. Hank. Nattie. Sara. And Davis. I saw myself, as *my* self, right there in Mother's dress. "I don't want it."

"They chose you," Davis said, hand to my elbow. "It's yours."

"Not anymore," I said, and my voice sounded so strong.

The band played on—*'S awful nice, 's paradise, 's what I want to see*—and everyone in the room kept spinning, oblivious.

Mrs. Hanshaw headed our way with small, quick steps. "Ruth Landry, it stays on your head, dear."

"I'm the wrong girl," I told her. "I'm a Robb, and my father was a Robb."

Mrs. Hanshaw pinched her brows together. "Yes, I know."

I sighed a Mother sigh, because this thing I had to say had needed to be said ever since we'd motored south. "I mean, my father was Jewish," I said to Mrs. Hanshaw, and to Davis and Gracie and Claudia and whoever else was inclined to listen.

Davis was at my ear: "You don't have to say a word more."

Oren, who was on Claudia's far side, snapped his head around.

The band went on to "Tutti Frutti," and the splendidly dressed couples whop-bam-booed.

"But"—Gracie scrunched her nose—"your mother went to church with my mother."

"But"—T-Ann cocked her head to the side—"you said you belong to Wesley Methodist."

"My grandparents, they belong there," I said. "Not me. Not my mother, not my sister, not me. We're Jewish. We're Jewish at the temple on Peachtree." The words came out in short bursts like my lungs might never feel normal again. "I'm sorry." I looked from T-Ann to Gracie—and, of course, to Davis. "I'm sorry about the lying."

Claudia tossed her still-perfect hair. "I knew it—I knew it, and I kept it secret."

I handed the beauty of a crown, in its burnished magnolia glory, to Mrs. Hanshaw, who hoofed it back to the microphone and signaled the bandleader to stop playing. "Well, this is a Magnolia for the memory books," she said, so close to the mike her voice was distorted. Couples gave her their attention. "Miss Robb has decided to pass—to abdicate, let's say, her crown. And so . . . And so the honor goes, quite naturally, to the first runner-up."

Claudia stepped into the spotlight. Of course Claudia looked positively radiant. Of course she looked like royalty.

"Introducing our newest Magnolia Queen, the darling Miss Starling." Mrs. Hanshaw anchored the crown on Claudia's head to a smattering of applause.

"You keep surprising me," Davis said, the words sliding down my ear to the vicinity of my heart. "Forget the club, forget my parents. Forget it. We want to be together, we'll be together." He spun me around, Mother's dress swanning behind me.

And the band was back, the dancing was back, and Davis and I were back, whirling to a swoozy Nat King Cole song. Where my crown would have been, Davis ran his fingers, sharp with the smell of smoke, through my hair. I tangled my fingers with his.

Our dreamy duet came to a grinding halt when someone flipped on the way-too-bright overhead lights. Two men in dark suits with big shoulders pushed in amid the tulle and tuxes.

"Looking for Oren Jefferson," one man said, a holstered gun visible under his jacket.

"Who wants to know?" Oren said, dual dimples in evidence. A few dancers laughed.

"Oren Jefferson, you are under arrest for the bombing of Temple Shir Shalom."

Prickles of sweat bloomed all over my face and neck.

Oren yelled to Davis, "Call Dad."

Claudia put her hand to her crown. In the light, her lipstick was too harsh and her drawn-on eyebrows had half rubbed off.

Davis turned to me, his voice hushed. "Remember, I was with you that night. I was with you all night, our night."

The other man stood eye to eye with Davis. Smooth as butter, Davis said, "Sir, my father will straighten this out." He extended his hand for a shake.

The officer took Davis's hand and didn't let go. "Davis Jefferson, you are also under arrest for aiding and abetting the bombing of Temple Shir Shalom."

"He was with me," I blurted out. "He was with me the whole time."

The men in the suits paid me no mind. They marched the Jefferson brothers out of the ballroom—two sets of handcuffs, one heartbreaking night.

23

North Stars

After swearing to tell the whole truth, I sat very straight in the wooden witness chair. I willed Davis to look my way. And he did, just long enough to give me his single-dimpled grin.

His parents, pale and worn out, sat directly behind him in the courtroom. Next to Davis was his attorney, Mr. Ewell, with silver hair so shiny it looked greased down with baby oil.

The attorney walked over to me, standing so close I could see a gobbet of something between his very white teeth. "Good morning."

I spun my pearls in nervous circles against my collarbone. Fontaine had given me my own strand for "the holidays" (she

296

wasn't ready to acknowledge Hanukkah yet, she'd said). My eyes landed on Sara, who'd ridden the Greyhound all day yesterday. She was snugged in next to Nattie, both of them in Fontaine-gifted pearls, with Fontaine and Mr. Hank on either side. The foursome had gotten here before Mother and me, and I felt better seeing them lined up, my North Stars, even though I knew there was only one North Star.

Beyond my family, I scanned the rows—rows that looked like pews. I started at the back and raced forward, past Rabbi and Mrs. Selwick, Mr. and Mrs. Silvermintz, Gracie and Thurston-Ann and the rest of the pastel posse, Buck and Jimmy, and Claudia, who'd positioned herself next to Mrs. Jefferson and behind Davis. Oren wasn't in the courtroom. He and Cranford and the hunting friends were still awaiting trial. Mr. Hank said Davis's lawyer must have worked real hard to unyoke Davis's case from the others.

I glanced up to the balcony, and sitting alone, front and center, was Max. I hadn't seen him when I'd first walked in because I'd forgotten the simplest thing—to look up.

Mr. Ewell stepped toward the jury of twelve men, all white, all in white shirts, one with a white mustache. "Miss Robb. Please tell us where you were the evening of October eleventh of last year."

I had gone over these questions and answers with Davis's lawyer at his fancy downtown office. "At the Fall

Ball, otherwise known as the Chrysanthemum," I said. I'd already told my family everything about the night (except for Nattie, to whom I white-lied), but my eyes slid away from them all the same.

He nodded. "And after the ball? If Davis Jefferson was with you, he was surely not at the temple. Mr. Jefferson could not be in both places at the same time, isn't that right?"

"Objection." The other attorney, a Mr. Haupt, with mile-long legs and a guarded smile, shot to his feet.

My fingers found their way to the underside of my dress and tugged at the hem, rending it like I did my jumper the day after the bombing, like a mourner, like the Jew I was, even when I pretended otherwise.

"I'll restate," Davis's lawyer said. "I'm sorry to put you on the spot—a lovely young lady." His tongue worked over that bit of food. "Were you with Mr. Jefferson until morning?" There was a wheeze, or maybe it was a gasp from somewhere in the back. "You are still under oath," he reminded me.

I looked at Davis for two seconds, ten, twenty. Davis, who'd been straightening his tie, probably gearing himself up for that trademark smile, dropped his hands to his lap.

"The witness will answer," the judge said.

"I was with him." I answered what I'd been asked.

"Thank you, Miss Robb." Davis's attorney sat down next to his client and gave a good broad grin.

The other attorney stood up. "Miss Robb, were you and Mr. Jefferson together every minute—every minute—of the night in question?"

I took a breath. I'd practiced what I would say in front of the mirror over the bureau, watching how my lips looked as they formed the right words. Simple words—words that didn't have to be clever or charming. "Yes" looked almost like a smile, but "no" forced your mouth into a startled O. Now I could hear the blood thrumming in my ears, like the unearthly sound of the long-distance phone line, except everyone I loved was right here in this courtroom. Everyone except Dad, but I felt him here, too.

I let out the breath and answered. "Not every minute. About five a.m., Davis disappeared." I wound the thread from my hem around my finger.

Mr. Haupt straightened up, looking even lankier. "For how long did he disappear?"

"Until he came back with Oren." I uncrossed my ankles from their S position and I looked to Gracie, but she was suddenly engrossed with a speck of something on her skirt. I tried to catch Davis's uncatchable eye. I remembered the mixer, the ivy that was a yew, the car wash that was more than a car wash. I remembered turns around the turntable. It was love, and it was fast, and it was true. Davis—of course Davis—but all of it, all of them. The just-for-iced-tea glasses delicate enough to break your heart. The nickname-bestowing best friend. I'd fallen in love with the whole she-bang. I kept spinning the thread, spinning it tighter, until the tip of my finger turned the color of a bruise.

"Is it possible Davis Jefferson went to the temple that night?" Mr. Haupt asked.

"Yes," I said. And then I said yes to the rest, just as I'd rehearsed, telling the truth quickly and with confidence. The mystery miles, missing hat, moonlit robes, smell of bananas, club-terrace confession. Yes to it all.

I glanced at Davis, who was folding and refolding a piece of paper, eyes drilled to the defendant's table.

"You may step down," said the judge.

I got up, wrinkled sheath, torn-up hem, and all, glad the dress looked like it had gone through something. The sunlight streamed through the courthouse windows, and I walked across stripes of light back to our row. Sara gave me a sideways hug, and Mother handed me my pocketbook. I couldn't keep my hands still, clicking the latch open and closed, until Mother put her hand over mine and we listened to the lawyers' closing arguments.

The prosecutor went first, summarizing the evidence against Davis, circumstantial though it was, along with my non-alibi. "There may be no smoking gun, no smoking bomb, but he withheld information critical to the authorities.

300

Remember, a good young man can be capable of unconscionable acts."

Davis shifted a bit, enough for me to see the sun hit his impossibly handsome face.

I sighed a Mother sigh, and she leaned over and swept a piece of my hair from my face.

Davis's attorney stood up. "Mr. Jefferson did not aid and abet this bombing. Do not be swayed by the version of events put forth by the witness. Her testimony is not fact—it's simply her interpretation. It's not a crime to be loyal to one's brother. It's not even a crime to be opposed to the Jewish race, not that I'm saying that's Davis Jefferson's point of view. This is a law-abiding Christian, an athlete with a Southeastern Conference future. Let him fulfill his destiny."

With that, the case went to the jury.

———

Eighty-four minutes later, after we'd swilled cup after cup of awful coffee, we got word: The jury was back. The Landry/Robbs sat as a family—shoulder to shoulder to shoulder to shoulder to shoulder to shoulder. I imagined Dad sitting next to me, in our usual order.

Max slid into the row behind me.

The talk in the room hushed as the clerk stood in front of the judge's desk and announced, "All rise."

Mr. Hank, his cane crooked in his elbow, was the first to his feet. Fontaine twirled the middle strand of her triple-rope pearls. Nattie held one of my hands, and Mother took the other.

Davis stood up, squared his shoulders, and buttoned his blazer.

To the jury, the judge said, "On the charge of aiding and abetting the bombing, in the case of the People versus Davis Jefferson, what be your verdict?"

Davis turned to look at me. When he wasn't smiling, he was dimple-less. When he wasn't smiling, he was just a boy.

The mustached man said, "We the jury, duly sworn to try the issues in the above entitled case, find the defendant, Davis Edwin Jefferson, not guilty."

Tears burned the corners of my eyes—tears of relief that Davis wasn't found guilty and tears of grief that I found him guilty, at least in the neighborhood of guilty.

I'd had that very conversation on the telephone with Sara just after the Magnolia. I'd stayed up most of the night, while Davis's father arranged bail for his boys, spinning Davis's grandmother's ring along with the idea of what he had and hadn't done. The next morning, I snuck the keys for the Savoy, drove without running any stop signs to the Jeffersons' place on the other side of Nancy Creek, and dropped a breakup note in his mailbox.

Now, Mr. Jefferson clapped Davis on the back. "Justice was served, my boy!"

"The state will appeal," Mother said. Her hand stroked the back of my head.

"State can't appeal, Alice," Mr. Hank said. "Can't undo a not-guilty verdict."

"You did the right thing," Sara said to me. Nattie nodded fiercely.

I sat with a thud. "But it made no difference," I said.

"Oh, a difference was made," Fontaine said, her perfume filling the air. "I told you when y'all arrived: It's a gift knowing what to do." I squinted, not following her Fontaine-ism. She went on. "At the time, I was talking about the rules of the pink booklet. And I was right—but I was also wrong. Etiquette-ly speaking, a lady should keep her opinions to herself."

"But—" I said.

"But"—Fontaine nodded—"when hatred shows its face, you need to make a little ruckus. And you, dear Ruthie, you made a very important little ruckus."

I gave Fontaine a kiss on the cheek.

Gracie headed my way, T-Ann at her side, both of them in short kidskin gloves and cashmere twinsets; no doubt they'd consulted with each other about how to dress for a trial.

Just as the girls were close enough to say hey, T-Ann peeled off with a curt wave. Gracie stopped, her smile just a step behind.

"Well, Ruth, maybe I'll see you around. The Valentine's Gala is open to everyone in the city, even public school girls."

I was still shallow enough to miss it—the dresses, the club (and the Club), the sweet tea, the Cokes—now that Nattie and I had transferred to public school.

"Thanks, but I'm helping out over at the newspaper on weekends," I said. "Just a copy girl—running bulletins from one section desk to another."

Gracie tilted her head. "How nice for you," she said before drifting away.

Mr. Hank took off for the newsroom while the rest of the family went to lurch the Savoy around.

Max stepped into my row. "Ruth Robb."

"Max Asher," I said.

"Turns out you're righteous."

That made me smile. "Sometimes."

"You can use that, you know—that righteousness."

"What? You have a picket line for me?"

He shrugged. "Always. There's a boycott Saturday—downtown stores."

I hoped it wouldn't be the lovely Lumet's.

The Jefferson family and friends made their way up the center aisle of the courtroom to resume their well-mannered, well-manicured lives—Mr. and Mrs. Jefferson, followed a few seconds later by Claudia, then Davis.

Davis, ever the gentleman, stopped and let the others pass before speaking to me. "You took me by surprise up there, Ruth." His foot tapped a jillion miles a minute, a frantic metronome. "But I know you said what you thought you had to say. At least it's behind us now."

"That's my cue to move on," Max said.

Davis's hand hovered inches from my waist. "Maybe I'll see you at the Valentine's Gala?"

"I'll help," I called over my shoulder to Max. "With the stores. I'll be there." I turned back to Davis. "We can't. I can't."

"I know." Davis's jaw twitched. "But it would be nice, right? It was nice."

I clicked my pocketbook open and took out a handkerchief, pale blue with Mr. Hank's monogram in the corner. I unwrapped it and pressed the opal ring into his palm.

"Don't," Davis said, the ring wobbling in the center of his hand. "You *know* me. I'm not one of them. I'm on my brother's side, and I'm on your side, but I'm no cross burner. I'm no Jew hater."

A long quiet hung between us. A trace of fragrance lingered, and at first I thought of Fontaine, but then I realized it was Davis—his signature mix of sunshine and soap and pine and possibility. "You can't be on two sides," I said finally. He couldn't defend Oren and be somebody I love.

"Ah, c'mon, Babe Ruth." Davis slipped the ring into his pocket and opened his arms, ready for me to step inside them.

I could imagine how it would feel, his fingers pulsing against my back. I flinched, even though we weren't touching. A tremble worked up my body—toes, knees, stomach, heart. The tremble shoved its way right up to my throat. "Bye, Davis."

Then Claudia was at his elbow. "Let's get a move—we're celebrating at the club." She whipped her hair around in her ever-Claudia way and guided him up the aisle.

I thought of all those nights, at the club and not at the club, and how I'd still somehow never seen a constellation. And I thought, constellations weren't the point. Constellations were just a bunch of separate stars. They didn't become constellations until you connected them, one to another. Like families, like sisters, like friendships, like prayers.

And, anyway, it turned out Nattie was memorizing all eighty-eight constellations. I didn't need Davis in order to fall in love with the night sky.

Out front, Mother and the others were waiting in the Savoy, all of them bathed in late-day brilliance. Nattie flung open the passenger-side door, and I jumped in.

Author's Note

The people in this book, along with their sweet teas and misdeeds, trials and betrayals, are fictional. Ruth, Davis, Fontaine, Covenant, Temple Shir Shalom, Rabbi Selwick, the Magnolia Ball, the whole premise—inventions, all.

The seed of the story, though, is inspired by a real-life event—the bombing of Atlanta's oldest synagogue, the Hebrew Benevolent Congregation, better known simply as "the Temple." In the 1950s and '60s, the Temple was a center for early civil-rights advocacy, led by the outspoken and charismatic Rabbi Jacob Rothschild, who urged his (sometimes reluctant) congregants to join the fight for racial justice.

The bomb—fifty sticks of dynamite detonated early on October 12, 1958—caused extensive damage, though, fortunately, didn't hurt anyone. Still, the blast was front-page news at the *Atlanta Journal* (a paper with the tagline "Covers Dixie Like the Dew") and at newspapers around the country. President Eisenhower condemned the bombing while detectives and FBI agents fanned across the city. Soon five suspects, known for their anti-Jewish beliefs and membership in the National States' Rights Party and other white supremacist groups, were arrested. The high-profile trial of the alleged ringleader of the bombing ended in a mistrial, and his second trial ended in acquittal. Eventually, charges against the other men were dropped.

And yet the bomb had a lasting impact on the city; many leaders thought it brought Atlantans together, black and white, Jew and Christian. The mayor at the time, William Hartsfield, took a strong stand: "Whether they like it or not, every political rabble-rouser is the godfather of these cross burners and dynamiters who sneak about in the dark and give a bad name to the South. It is high time the decent people of the South rise and take charge." Rabbi Rothschild's widow, Janice Rothschild Blumberg, titled her own memoir of the blast "The Bomb That Healed."

Years later, in the early 2000s, my family moved to Atlanta, where we became members of the Temple and were welcomed with a hearty "Shabbat shalom, y'all." But the memories of what had happened there still reverberated. Our younger daughter attended Sunday school in one of the classrooms that had been bombed decades before.

And the hate has continued to echo. In Charlottesville, Virginia, where our older daughter lives, in the summer of

2017, white nationalists brandished torches in front of Thomas Jefferson's rotunda, yelling, "Jews will not replace us." And then in Pittsburgh in the fall of 2018, eleven congregants were shot during Saturday morning services at the Tree of Life synagogue. I watched the unfolding horror of the Pittsburgh shooting on TV news with my eighty-eight-year-old father, remembering the bat mitzvah the whole family had once attended at a different synagogue nearby. As the names of the dead were read, I kept thinking that my dad could have been one of them. And then I thought, it could have been *any* of us—over and over, across decades and state lines.

Almost sixty years to the day after the 1958 Atlanta bombing, I found myself pulling up a copy of the sermon Rabbi Rothschild delivered to his congregants after the blast: "Out of the gaping hole that laid bare the havoc wrought within, out of the majestic columns that now lay crumbled and broken, out of the tiny bits of brilliantly colored glass that had once graced with beauty the sanctuary itself—indeed, out of the twisted and evil hearts of bestial men has come a new courage and a new hope." The sermon was titled "And None Shall Make Them Afraid." All these years later, I want to believe these words are both a challenge and a stand taken by all people of good faith, no matter what faith that is.

I'm indebted to a variety of books and other resources for helping me capture the mood of Atlanta in the 1950s—

fashion, manners, news reporting, school segregation, anti-Semitism, and so on. An incomplete list: *As But a Day* by Janice Rothschild Blumberg; "Counterblast: How the Temple Bombing Strengthened the Civil Rights Cause" by Clive Webb; *The Race Beat* by Gene Roberts and Hank Klibanoff; *Rich's: A Southern Institution* by Jeff Clemmons; *Screening a Lynching* by Matthew Bernstein; *The South and the Southerner* by Ralph McGill; *Vogue's Book of Etiquette* (circa 1948) by Millicent Fenwick; *Where Peachtree Meets Sweet Auburn* by Gary Pomerantz; and especially *The Temple Bombing* by Melissa Fay Greene, which I read and reread. On a much lighter note, I obsessed over vintage issues of *Mademoiselle*.

While researching in Atlanta, I poked around various archives—as much as I'd read about the events, there was no substitute for seeing the primary documents: the yellowed newspaper columns of Ralph McGill, the editor and publisher of the *Atlanta Constitution,* who won a Pulitzer Prize for his editorials following the bombing; typewritten sermons from Rabbi Rothschild; and fat scrapbooks stuffed with debutante invitations and photographs.

Grateful thanks to the following people and places for granting access and providing context: Gabrielle Dudley and Kathy Shoemaker at the Stuart A. Rose Manuscript, Archives, and Rare Book Library at Emory University; Jeremy Katz, director of the Cuba Family Archives at the William Breman

AUTHOR'S NOTE

Jewish Heritage Museum in Atlanta; Sue VerHoef, director of oral history and genealogy at the Atlanta History Center. Thanks, too, to Bette Thomas, docent at the Center for Civil and Human Rights museum, who, in a serendipitous conversation, shared her memories of movie nights at the segregated Fox Theatre. And a heartfelt thanks to Mark Jacobson, executive director of the Temple in Atlanta—when I asked if I could take another look from the building's rotunda, which I'd done years ago as part of a leadership class, he said, "You're always welcome to come home."

Any mistakes—of fact or of tone—are mine alone.

Acknowledgments

I'm wildly lucky to have my own (decidedly not pastel) posse to sustain me.

Rosemary Stimola, a wonder of an agent, believed in this book early and often, and it's a glorious feeling to have her in my corner.

Elise Howard, editor extraordinaire, made this book better, smarter, and deeper with her incisive questions on simply everything, plot infelicities to emotional payoffs. From our first conversation, I knew the book was in excellent hands. Everyone at Algonquin has been epically wonderful—especially Sarah Alpert and Ashley Mason, and Brittani Hilles and Caitlin Rubinstein.

Nova Ren Suma said one June afternoon at the Djerassi Artist Foundation: "I think my editor might like this"—Nova, you have been so wise, and I have much to learn from you about being curious and daring on the page.

ACKNOWLEDGMENTS

Janice Rothschild Blumberg, whose late husband, Jacob Rothschild, was the rabbi at the time of the bombing, graciously shared her memories and gently challenged some of my assumptions, encouraging me to dig deeper into the idea of belonging, for which I am deeply grateful.

A group of über-smart and observant women read for representation, bias, and accuracy (though any missteps are one thousand percent on me). Namely: Claire Hartfield, author of the superb book *A Few Drops of Red: The Chicago Race Riot of 1919*; Marilyn Kaye, author, who grew up in Atlanta a few years after the bombing took place; Ebony Wilkins, author and educator; Reverend Toni Belin Ingram, a dear friend and senior pastor at Greater Turner Chapel AME Church in Atlanta; Ellen Rafshoon, a US history professor at Georgia Gwinnett College; and Martha Neubert, a one-in-a-jillion friend and confidante who is dean of equity and social justice at Northfield Mount Hermon in Massachusetts.

A trio of brilliant, badass friends—Atlantans, attorneys, or both—read carefully, pens in hand: Sharon (Shag) Silvermintz, an Atlanta native who grew up going to the Temple and knows her way around synagogue shenanigans; Barb Riegelhaupt, a career law clerk, who gives stellar advice on any number of things, including courtroom logistics; and Carol Eisenberg, a former Atlantan, current attorney, and all-around mensch.

Marjan Kamali, an excellent writer and equally excellent friend, read multiple drafts over multiple years—her faith in the book has been a boon (shout-out, too, to her daughter Mona Tavangar and her ad hoc focus group); Lee Hoffman and Charity Tremblay gave extraordinary critiques and from-the-heart camaraderie; Kate Burak, director of the writing program at Boston University's College of Communication, has been a most inspiring boss; and Lara Wilson, specifically, and GrubStreet, more broadly—Lara read a draft at just the right moment and told me to make everything worse.

The writing ecosystem of the Upper Valley has been so very welcoming—especially Cindy Faughnan, with whom I've spent many Monday mornings in parallel writing play at King Arthur Flour; the Norwich Writers' Group, with its insightful and thoughtful discussions; and farther up the road, the VCFA community, where the seeds of this novel really took root at a writing retreat a few years back.

I'm thankful to my parents for creating a childhood home that embraced inclusion, social justice, creativity, and perseverance.

Finally, to my family: to Annie and Jane, my two very, very favorite people, who have taught me, as we've moved hither and yon, the grace of both fitting in and standing out. And to Ralph, the truest true person I know.